A Haunting

in the

Hammocks

D. S. Rever

A Haunting in the Hammocks

This is a work of fiction. Names, characters, places, and incidents are products of the author's imagination or are used fictitiously. Any resemblance to actual events, locales, or persons, living or dead, is entirely coincidental.

Published by Dolly Rever Creative
Raleigh, North Carolina

ISBN (Paperback): [979-8-234-00817-6]
ASIN (eBook): [B0GP6J29KT]

Cover design by the author
Interior design and formatting by the author

Printed in the United States of America

www.dollyrever.com

For Matt and Colt—

as constant and true as the light at

Cape Lookout.

"The past is never dead. It's not even past."

— William Faulkner

Prologue

August, 1717

Captain James Thorne pulled out his spyglass, his steady gaze fixed on the horizon, where he could barely see the moonraker sails of merchant ships making their way in and out of the inlet. The coast of North Carolina rose like a whisper through the morning mist, low and wild, with barrier islands stretching like fingers between the Atlantic and the sleepy harbors beyond. Invictus, her sleek hull gliding silently through the early light, slowed its approach as the mouth of Topsail Inlet came into view. Her sails were drawn in a quiet ballet, and her anchor dropped with the soft splash of iron, waiting for the incoming tide to rise. Captain Thorne stood tall; his hands clenched behind his back, his sharp eyes fixed on the town nestled just beyond the shore—Beaufort Town, Thatch's rumored sanctuary. But Thorne was not dressed in his admiralty blues; he had traded his regal Royal Navy captain's coat, with its gilded cuffs and polished brass buttons, for a humbler uniform. His frock now bore the more spartan trim of a lieutenant, the familiar epaulets removed, and his hat exchanged for one worn and battered from the air. Even his signet ring had been slipped into a pouch and tucked in the back drawer of his desk in the great cabin. It was a calculated deception. If he were to step foot in Beaufort openly as Captain James Thorne, the Crown's appointed hunter of pirates, he would be marked, watched, or worse—dead before sundown, but as a mere naval officer on leave, he could walk the town as an observer, like a stranger or a shadow. He could listen, collecting intelligence, and if fortune favored him, confirm that Captain Edward Thatch, the man the Crown knew as Blackbeard, had taken root in the hammocks.

Once a privateer, Thatch had risen to become the most dreaded pirate captain on either side of the Atlantic. They called him Blackbeard, but sailors whispered other names too—the Devil of the Carolinas, the Ghost of the Sea, the King of Rogues. He was known for his towering frame and his black beard, which he braided and laced with slow-burning hemp fuses that he would light before battle. As smoke curled around his face, he looked more like a demon than a man, eyes blazing beneath a tangle of smoke and shadow. When Thatch bore down upon a merchant ship, most surrendered without a fight; they heard what happened to those who didn't. Now, he was holed up somewhere on the Carolina coast, disappearing into marshes, creeks, and barrier islands where most Navy vessels couldn't follow.

But Captain Thorne intended to find him.

Chapter 1

As HMS Invictus cut northward, bound for the colonies, Captain James Thorne ran his hand along the polished wood of the quarterdeck's rail. He loved this vessel; he had stood upon her decks in countless battles; he felt the surge of adrenaline as her sails caught the wind and carried her faster than any other ship on the sea, knowing that soon, he would be sailing into enemy territory—a territory of the most feared pirate ever to sail the oceans.

Invictus glided across the deep cerulean blue water of the Atlantic Ocean, her sails full with the humid southern wind, her deck alive with the energy of men on the hunt. Invictus was more than just a ship; she was a masterpiece of naval engineering, built to be one of the fastest vessels to sail the oceans. She was designed for outmaneuvering enemy ships, chasing down pirates, and carrying the pride of the British Royal Navy across the sea.

As Captain Thorne stood upon her deck, the vast expanse of open water stretching wide before him, he knew that Invictus was unlike any other vessel he had ever commanded. She was a fifth-rate frigate, sleek and swift, with a cutting hull that sliced through the water like a blade. She was crafted for speed and agility, with a narrow beam that reduced resistance and allowed her to glide over the waves, making her faster than heavier warships. She had a sharp, raked bow that parted the sea effortlessly, giving her an advantage over broader-built merchant ships and galleons. Her stern was reinforced, built to withstand cannon fire, ensuring she could hold her own in battle, and her triple-masted rigging allowed her to harness every bit of wind, with over 30 sails, including topsails, staysails, and studding sails, to maximize her velocity. With a favorable wind, she could reach a speed of 14 knots or more, making her one of the fastest ships in the Royal Navy's fleet.

Despite her speed, Invictus was not built for flight; she was built to hunt. She carried 26 broadside cannons, lining her deck like iron teeth, each capable of firing deadly rounds into enemy hulls; she boasted eight swivel guns mounted along the railings, used for cutting down boarding parties and enemy sailors, and a reinforced hull, capable of withstanding heavy bombardment in naval combat. With her lethal combination of speed and firepower, Invictus had been sent on countless missions to track down pirate fleets, escort valuable cargo, and enforce the Crown's rule upon the seas. She was, in every way, a predator.

Her deck was a world of constant motion, where sailors moved in perfect synchronization and were trained to handle her power and speed with precision. The quarterdeck was where her captain stood as he gave navigational orders to his skilled helmsman, a man who would wield the great wooden wheel beneath his hands, giving him command of the ship's course. The main deck was lined with cannons, their iron barrels gleaming under the sun, always ready for battle, and her ratlines were a web of rope ladders stretching high into the towering masts, where agile topmen climbed to adjust the sails, their lives depending on their grip and balance. The gun deck below was a dark, echoing place where powder and shot were stored, and sailors moved in a deadly dance to load and fire in the heat of battle. She carried a crew of 200 men, hardened sailors who had braved tempests, war, and treachery. They were loyal to the King, faithful to the ship, and most loyal to their commander, Captain James Thorne.

Captain Thorne was a man who commanded both ships and attention. He was tall, standing well over six feet, with broad shoulders that made him appear every bit the seasoned naval officer he was. His posture was always straight and disciplined, reflecting his years in the Royal Navy's elite ranks. Despite being only 25 years old, he carried himself with the authority of a man twice his age, his presence on deck enough to silence the rowdiest of crews and make even the most experienced sailors stand at attention. His face was as sharp as the cut of a blade. Thorne was handsome but not in the polished way of courtly gentlemen. His features were chiseled and sharp, a face sculpted by wind and as if the sea had carved him from stone and storm. His high cheekbones cast subtle shadows beneath his piercing blue-gray eyes, the color of a hurricane-tossed ocean, reflecting the depths of his cunning and unyielding will. His firm, square jaw was always clean-shaven, a mark of naval discipline, but by day's end, a shadow of stubble often framed his face, making him look more like a rogue privateer than a royal officer. He had a faint scar that ran just across his left eyebrow—a reminder of a past battle, a skirmish at sea where he had nearly lost an eye. His hair was the color of sunlit sand and sea oats, bleached from years at sea, and it fell like windswept waves just past his shoulders, often tied loosely at the nape of his neck with a strip of leather. Unlike many Royal Navy elitists who powdered their hair, he wore his tied back by the Admiralty's standards. Seldom, when left free, it would fall just below his shoulders, catching the light of the sun during the day and appearing almost bronze beneath the moonlight. It was the kind of hair that gave him an air of nobility and rebellion, making him look just as much a pirate as a naval captain.

He wore his Royal Navy uniform with a distinct air of authority—not because he needed to prove himself, but because the men under his command revered him for it. His dark navy-blue frock coat was tailored to perfection, the gold epaulets on his shoulders gleaming in the sunlight, marking him as an officer of high rank and regard. Polished brass buttons that ran down the length of his coat were engraved with the insignia of the Crown, a reminder of the power he served, and beneath the coat, he wore a crisp white waistcoat, meticulously fastened, with a high-collared cravat, tied with precision. His knee-high black leather boots were polished yet bore the scuffs and wear of a man who did not merely command from the quarterdeck—but fought alongside his men. On most days, his sword, a finely crafted cutlass with an ornate hilt of silver and brass, was strapped to his side. It was a weapon as much a part of him as his ship, but beneath the immaculate uniform, beneath the titles and decorum, there was a man who had lived and breathed every facet of his life serving the King. Thorne had become a legend among the fleet—one of the youngest captains in British naval history, rising through the ranks before the age of thirty. He was called "The King's Wolf," known for his ability to hunt down enemies with precision, to outmaneuver larger and slower warships, and to lead his men into victorious battles on the high seas. Despite Thorne's age, his name carried weight in the Admiralty halls and across the lower decks alike. He had earned his title not through family fortune or political favor but by relentless skill, brutal efficiency, and a mind for the sea that few could match.

The Invictus was one of the fastest in the fleet, and Captain Thorne had hunted down more pirates than any other officer in His Majesty's service. But Thatch would be different; he was a ghost in the water, and if the reports were accurate, he wasn't alone—he would be accompanied by his notorious second in command, Israel Hands. There were whispers of a network of pirates who moved between the islands and coastal towns. Some believed he had even purchased a property—a West Indies-style white house built in a hammock of gnarled live oaks and Spanish moss near a quiet port called Beaufort Town.

Thorne's mission was simple: find Thatch and lead the charge, but Thorne did not expect Beaufort's disarming charm—or the eyes of a young woman watching from the shore. He saw her through his glass as Invictus drew closer, her figure lit gently by the morning sun. She stood in front of a three-story house on a grassy rise, half-shaded by live oaks and draped in silvery Spanish moss. The house itself was plain by the standards of Charleston or London, but it stood with the quiet authority of something older than time.

And so did she.

The golden glow of the late morning sun casting halos around her was a woman unlike any he had ever seen. Her hair was as dark as the depths of the sea, spilling over her shoulders in wild curls. She held herself with grace but not fragility, confidence shining in her spellbinding gray eyes. She wasn't dressed in silks or powdered like the daughters of courtly families; her gown was modest, the linen fluttering in the breeze, but her eyes met his, even from a distance, and his heart arrested, unmoored from duty in an instant. He felt his breath leave him. In a split second of his eyes falling on her, he understood how the singular face of a woman with the beauty and essence of a goddess could launch a thousand ships and lead nations into war. At that moment, Captain James Thorne became a man walking two lines: one between truth and duty and the other between deception and desire. He stepped onto the Beaufort Town dock as Lieutenant Thorne, a man on assignment, but he soon learned that fate had already chosen a different course.

Chapter 2

Sarah.

He didn't know her name. He didn't know she was Captain Edward Thatch's daughter or that her lineage would soon force him to make an impossible choice. But he knew one thing: he was lost from the moment he saw her. Thorne had not stepped onto enemy soil expecting to be undone by a woman's smile. He had spent the past seven years chasing pirates, watching ships burn, and hauling criminals before the gallows. He had seen men beg for their lives and had ordered cannons to sink vessels beneath the waves without hesitation, but Sarah Thatch had stormed into his world like an unexpected squall, her presence upending everything he thought was steady and sure. She was not timid. She did not shy away from the uniform he wore and didn't tremble at the sight of a naval officer in her father's town. Instead, she met his piercing gaze with an amused smirk as if she already knew she had completely besotted him. "Looking for something, Lieutenant?" Her voice was warm, edged with curiosity and laced with a hint of a challenge.

Thorne, caught between duty and temptation, forced a smirk of his own. "That depends," he murmured, stepping closer. "Would you be willing to help me find it?"

He remained in Beaufort Town, pretending to be nothing more than an officer on shore leave, gaining the town's trust, especially that of the men who operated in the shadows, and in doing so, he lost himself in Sarah. Every stolen glance, every whispered conversation under the cloak of night, every moment their hands brushed in the quiet corners of the town sealed his fate. He should have been focused on his mission, but how could he when Sarah Thatch had already claimed him, mind, heart, and soul?

It was in her laughter that warmed him like sunlight, in the way her fingers traced over the scars on his hands, the way she spoke of the sea as if it was something living and breathing, something to be loved rather than conquered. He had never known love like this. For weeks, he had remained under the Crown's orders, an officer walking among thieves and traitors, gathering information on Blackbeard's fleet, his men, and his movements. Yet, the more time he spent in Beaufort, the less he cared about his duty because there was Sarah; she had entangled herself in his heart like the tide upon the shore—constant and inescapable. Thorne would steal any moment he could with her, and they often walked the winding paths of the marshes, their boots leaving imprints in the wet sand. He listened as she spoke about the creatures of the sea, about the ships she had sailed on since childhood, the freedom that came with the wind at one's back and nothing but the horizon ahead. They sat beneath the shade of ancient oaks, her head resting against his shoulder, their voices hushed conspiracies of love and longing. At first, she called him Lieutenant Thorne, teasing and formal, but eventually, she only called him James; each time she did, it chipped away at his loyalty to the Crown, carving out something new and reckless inside him. During one of these stolen moments, beneath a sliver of a moon, Sarah turned to him with a quiet seriousness in her gaze.

"I know who you are," she said softly.

James stiffened. "And who is that?"

She didn't look away. "A man at war with himself." He exhaled sharply, looking out toward Taylor Creek, where the water lapped at the pilings of the docks, reflecting the glow of lanterns from the ships moored nearby. Sarah shifted closer, lowering her voice. "You were sent here to hunt my father, weren't you, Captain?"

James stilled, every instinct in his body urging him to deny it, to lie, to protect his cover, but this was Sarah, and damn him, he could not lie to her. "Yes," he admitted, his voice rough. "That was why I came."

She studied him for a long moment. Then, she reached for his hand, threading her fingers through his. "But it is not why you are still here."

James closed his eyes briefly, letting the truth settle in his chest. “No,” he murmured. “It is not.” And in that moment, he knew—he wanted to spend eternity with her, whatever the cost.

Chapter 3

The tavern at the edge of town was thick with the scent of pipe smoke, brine, and spilled rum, its creaky floors warped from air and years of storms. Candlelight flickered in iron sconces along the walls, casting wavering shadows over the faces of sailors, merchants, and townsfolk pressed into crowded wooden booths. Thorne sat alone at a corner table, the amber glow of his drink reflecting in his eyes as he stared down into the depths of his glass. He wore no uniform tonight, just a plain linen shirt, open at the throat, the sleeves rolled to his elbows. The sword at his hip still rested in its scabbard, but his hand stayed near it. He always knew when he was being watched, and tonight, he felt eyes upon him. The murmur of conversation dropped off sharply as loud laughter from across the room, and the sharp notes of a drunken fiddler faded into sudden silence.

That's when the door creaked open.

A gust of night air spilled inside, thick with the scent of the sea and danger. A figure stepped into the doorway—broad-shouldered and towering, silhouetted by the lanterns behind him. The candlelight danced across his great black beard, braided into sections and tied with ribbons of crimson and bone. Wisps of smoke curled from the ends of slow-burning fuses laced within it, casting a ghostly halo around his head. He wore a long midnight-colored coat, open over a waistcoat stitched with Venetian gold thread, and his boots thudded heavily on the floor as he stepped fully into the light. There was no mistaking him. The room went still; even the drunkest sailor held his breath. His gaze swept across the tavern slowly, taking his time, letting the weight of his presence settle over the room like a storm cloud. Then, with a crooked smile, he turned his gaze on Thorne.

Thorne had escaped death a dozen times in his years at sea. He had faced cannon fire in the chaos of battle, survived the tempest of the open ocean, and even escaped a mutiny when he was just a midshipman, but standing in the dimly lit tavern, the air thick with smoke, rum, and tension, he found himself staring down the one man who made his blood run cold.

Blackbeard.

The notorious Captain Thatch sat down at the scarred wooden table, leaning back in his chair, his coal-black eyes locked onto Thorne, studying him with predatory interest. The legendary pirate was larger than life, his beard smoldering, tiny embers glowing like the eyes of demons in the low light. Behind him, his most trusted men stood silent, their hands resting on their cutlasses, waiting for the command to strike. Thorne's spine remained straight, but his hand twitched near his sword hilt. He could take one, maybe two men, before they cut him down. Thatch exhaled a cloud of smoke, his lips curling into a dangerous grin. "How pleased I am to make the acquaintance of the storied Captain Thorne, or shall I call you The King's Curr?" he said at last, his voice gravelly and measured in a thick Bristol dialect, like the sound of iron grinding against rock. "How long did you think you could dance in my town without me noticing?"

Thorne held his gaze. "If you know what I am, you know why I have not acted."

"Aye," Thatch said, tipping his head. "Because you've been distracted," he sneered. Thorne didn't move, but his pulse hammered in his ears. Thatch leaned forward, his grin widening. "By my Sarah." The entire room seemed to still.

Thorne's grip on his sword tightened, his breath a slow, measured inhale. Thatch chuckled darkly. "Oh, don't look so surprised, lad. Think I haven't noticed how you look at her? I know a man besotted in defeat when I see one." Thorne said nothing but didn't deny it—that would have been insulting. A dangerous gleam flickered in Edward Thatch's eyes. "Now, tell me, Captain Thorne—what exactly am I supposed to do with you?"

Thorne could feel the weight of every man in the room watching him, waiting for the order to gut him where he stood. He was seconds away from meeting his death at the hands of the most feared pirate on the seas, but Thatch had not drawn steel. Instead, he pulled a gold coin from a pocket hidden within the chest of his waistcoat, flipping it with calculated ease back and forth between his fingers. "I want to marry Sarah," Thorne said evenly.

Thatch arched a brow, intrigued. "Do you, now? Well, I would be findin' it hard to see how a dead man would make a befittin' husband, as it were." A long, considering silence fell between the two rivals. Then, Thatch leaned back in his chair, rubbing a thumb along his jaw. "The King has launched a full naval blockade across the Atlantic to protect the East India Company's cargo fleet, and I want to know every ship, every port, every trade route they've secured." Thorne took a careful breath. Captain Thatch studied him, eyes dark and unreadable, and then his grin returned, but this time, it was sharper. "And I want something even more important than intelligence."

"And what would that be?" James asked without a flinch, his expression confident and steady.

"You will return to Kingston. You will report to the governor of my false whereabouts, leading the Navy to believe I've moved my fleet to the far West Indies. Upon delivering this insight, you will await further orders from me. If you truly mean to marry my Sarah, you will cut ties with the Crown, and you'll have to do more than feed the King lies. After all, you are far more useful to me alive than you are dead."

Thorne swallowed hard, hoping it went unnoticed. Thatch took a slow sip of his rum, his eyes never leaving James'. "What say you, Captain Thorne?"

Thorne inhaled. "I shall acquiesce. When I return to Kingston, I will await your command. Upon my return to Beaufort Town, I *will* marry your daughter."

Thatch tilted his head, studying him. Then, slowly, he grinned. "Now that," he said, "is what I hoped you would say."

The deal was struck that night. Captain Thorne would sail back to Jamaica with his fleet, reporting that Blackbeard's operations had moved south to the western Caribbean. The Crown would send its warships on a fool's chase, leaving the Atlantic unguarded. In the meantime, Thorne would gather intelligence—maps, ship manifests, military secrets—and bring them back to Thatch. When he returned to Beaufort, he would command a new ship in Captain Thatch's fleet and commit his life to Sarah. It would be the only way to have her. And so, Thorne would set sail for Jamaica, knowing that when he returned, he would finally claim the life he wanted.

But fate had other plans.

Chapter 4

Sarah Thatch had always known that love and freedom demanded sacrifice. She had grown up among sailors and rogues, watching men live and die by the sea, understanding from a young age that the ocean gave everything and took everything away just as swiftly. But when she had met James Thorne, something had shifted inside her. He had been different from the others—not just because he was a naval officer, a man of discipline and duty, but because he had looked at her like she was the horizon itself. And now, he had gambled his entire future for her.

She stood behind a pillar toward the back of the tavern, the scent of sweat, rum, and pipe smoke thick in the air as the men around her whispered about the Royal Navy captain who had made a bargain with the devil himself. Her father had told her not to interfere, but she couldn't stay away. She listened from the shadows, watching as James stood before her father, unflinching, unwavering, as he struck a deal that would change the course of his life forever. She knew exactly what he was giving up; James Thorne was a captain in the Royal Navy, a man with a future set before him—honor, status, and command, and he had just cast it all aside for the chance to marry her. She should have been afraid for him; she should have begged him to reconsider, to leave Beaufort before it was too late, before he was deeply entangled in her father's world. But she didn't. Deep down, she knew the truth: James wasn't running from the Navy—he was running toward something greater, and he was meant to be so much more than just a knight under the King's command.

A pirate's life was a dangerous one. The gallows loomed for any man who crossed the King's laws, and the sea was filled with betrayal, mutiny, and war. But James was not just any man; he was the most revered captain in the Royal Navy. He sailed many a storm without flinching; he'd been outmatched by three men in a sword fight before breaking a sweat; he was one of the best seamen on the ocean, and she knew it. He had a mind for strategy, a body built for endurance, and a relentless heart in pursuit of what he wanted. He would become one of the most powerful men in maritime history if he were willing to play this game to outmaneuver the British and trade false intelligence in exchange for power, freedom, and *her*.

Her father saw it, too. Captain Edward Thatch was not easy to impress, yet he was intrigued by Thorne—he knew he would make a powerful ally if the wind blew the sails the right way. Sarah's heart pounded in her chest as she watched her father extend his massive, calloused hand, sealing the deal that would make James one of them. For a moment, as he shook her father's hand, his gaze flickered toward her, and that was when she knew. He hadn't done this just for her; he had done it because he wanted more than a life under the Crown's rule—he had done it because the sea had already claimed him long ago.

Later that night, Sarah found James standing at the end of the docks, staring at the dark water, the lantern light casting golden flickers over his sharp profile. She approached quietly, the breeze lifting her hair, carrying the scent of the marsh and something unspoken between them. "You don't have to do this," she said softly, though they both knew that was a lie.

James turned, his blue eyes burning with certainty. "I want to."

Sarah studied him for a long moment, searching for doubt, for hesitation. There was none. "You're going to make a dangerous enemy," she murmured. "The Crown doesn't take kindly to traitors."

James let out a slow, humorless chuckle. "Then it's good that I will no longer belong to them."

She stepped closer, placing a hand on his chest, feeling his heart's steady, unshaken beat beneath her palm. "Do you regret it?" she whispered.

His hand covered hers, pressing her fingers against his chest as if he wanted to brand the moment into his skin. "I regret nothing," he said, his voice steady as the tide. "So long as I have you."

Sarah closed the space between them, pressing her lips to his, sealing a promise far stronger than words. She had never belonged to any man before, but she belonged to James, and together, they would carve out a future of salt and fire, storm-wild seas and untamed hearts. A future that the Royal Navy could never provide nor take from them.

The eve of his departure had arrived; as the tide pulled low and the sky turned to shades of ink and fire, James found Sarah waiting for him at the edge of the dock, her bare feet brushing against the worn planks. "You're late," she teased, glancing up at the darkening sky. Her voice was light, but her eyes were shadowed by something heavier.

James smirked, stepping behind her. "Would you have waited for me all night?"

Sarah tilted her chin, her lips curving. "I suppose that depends."

"On what?" He said.

She turned to face him. "On whether you'll finally teach me what you promised."

James arched a brow. "Navigation?"

She nodded. "If I am to sail with you one day, I must know how to find my way home."

A warmth coiled in his chest at the certainty in her voice. He took her hand, leading her toward his waiting skiff, the small wooden boat bobbing in the gentle current. They pushed off from the dock, rowing out into the still waters of Taylor Creek, where the glow of town faded behind them. The air was cool and thick with humidity; the only sound was the soft lapping of the tide against the hull. James leaned back, gazing up at the vast sky above, where the first stars had begun to shimmer. "See that one?" he said, pointing toward a bright star above the horizon. Sarah nodded. "That's Polaris. The North Star." His voice softened. "No matter where you are, no matter how lost you may feel, that star will always lead you home."

Sarah watched him, her expression unreadable. "Why is it that you love the sea?"

James hesitated, then said, "Because the sea has no walls."

She smiled at that, resting her chin on her knees. "It calls you back every time, doesn't it?"

His gaze drifted back to the stars. "This time, I do not want to answer." Sarah's breath caught, but she said nothing because they both knew the truth: the sea was not so quickly abandoned. And neither was fate. The wind filled the sail, carrying them away from the harbor, past the distant silhouette of Carrot Island. The water glowed silver beneath the starlit sky, and the world felt limitless—as if they were the only two souls on earth. Sarah sat on the transom, her hands steady on the tiller as James leaned against the mast, watching her. "You look as though you were born for it," he murmured.

She grinned, eyes glinting in the darkness. "Perhaps I was."

He slid down the gunwale, placing his hands over hers, adjusting her grip on the halyard. "Here," he whispered. "Feel the wind. Let the boat guide you, not the other way around." Sarah closed her eyes, inhaling deeply as the sail snapped above them, the wood creaking beneath. For a moment, there was only silence, only the rhythm of the sea and their breaths entwined.

Then, softly, James spoke. "When I return, I will never sail away without you, and with me, I will bring the riches of the world and lay them at your feet."

Sarah didn't answer right away. Instead, she reached up, tracing her fingers along his cheek. "I don't care about exotic treasures; I only want you. Promise me you'll come back," she whispered, her touch lingering.

James covered her hand with his own, pressing it against his chest. "I swear it," he murmured. "On the sea, on the stars—on my very soul."

Chapter 5

The morning James would set sail, Sarah met him at Hammock House. The sun had not yet risen, and the world was wrapped in the quiet hush of dawn, but she was already waiting, standing at the threshold of the home they had dreamed of sharing. She had never given her heart to any man before, but James Thorne was not just any man. He was not like the others who had sought her hand, who had whispered empty promises under the cover of night and looked at her as a prize to be won rather than a soul to be understood. James saw *her*, and when he left, she needed him to carry more than just a memory of her—she needed him to carry proof of their love, a promise that she would be waiting when he returned. And so, she gave him the portrait.

The painting had been finished only days before his departure. It was a masterful piece, painted in soft oils, rich with color and warmth, capturing Sarah exactly as James saw her—fierce, beautiful, wild, and untamed. The artist had even captured the fire in her eyes, the way the light caught the deep storm-gray hue, giving her the look of someone who knew the ocean like she knew his soul. Sarah had commissioned it not as an act of vanity but as a vow. It was a way for James to see her face every day, no matter where the sea carried him. A reminder that his heart had a home waiting for him in Beaufort. When she placed it into his hands, she met his gaze steadily, her fingers lingering on the gilded frame. “This way, you won’t forget me,” she murmured.

James let out a quiet chuckle, but something raw in his expression told her he was feeling everything she was feeling, too. “I could never forget you, Sarah,” he said, his voice steady. “Not in a thousand lifetimes.”

She swallowed hard, willing herself not to break or let the weight of their parting settle in too soon. “When you return,” she whispered, “you will bring this back to Hammock House, and we will hang it over the mantel, where it belongs.”

James reached up, brushing a thumb along her jaw, his touch featherlight. “I swear it,” he murmured. “On the sea, on the stars—on everything I am.”

Sarah nodded, unable to say more because if she did, she might beg him to stay, and she would never ask him to give up the ocean, not when it was as much a part of him as she was. When Invictus set sail, James did not turn back. She knew he didn’t need to because he carried her face with him, watching over him from the portrait that he would keep close to his heart in the cabin of his ship. She imagined him looking at it each night, running his fingers along the painted lines of her face, remembering how she held his gaze when she gave it to him. She imagined him whispering, “Soon,” because it was never a question of if he would return… only when.

And so, she waited.

For months, she would row across Taylor Creek to Carrot Island so she could stand on the sandy beach overlooking the sea, searching the horizon for his ship. She whispered his name to the wind, believing that somehow, across the vast expanse of the ocean, he would hear it. The weeks after James's departure had been the longest of Sarah's life. She had never known the world to feel so empty, so vast, so utterly still. Before, Beaufort Town hummed with life, the days filled with the smell of salt and the sound of sails snapping in the wind, the nights spent in whispers of stolen conversations, secret rendezvous at the docks, and the warmth of James's hands against hers. But now, the town felt different—she felt different because she was waiting, and waiting changed everything.

Every morning, Sarah climbed the rocks at the edge of town, where the land met the water, slapping against the sand and shells in a never-ending song of longing. She watched the horizon, her eyes searching for a familiar set of sails, a dark hull cutting through the waves—anything that would tell her he was coming home. Some days, the ocean was kind, and the sunrise painted the sky in hues of gold and rose, whispering promises that he would return soon. Other days, the sky turned grey, the wind cold and unforgiving, and she wondered if she would ever see him again. James had sworn he would return, and Sarah had never once doubted his word, so she waited.

She tried to keep herself occupied. She spent her days helping manage the family affairs, ensuring Hammock House was kept in order, tending to the town's merchants who relied on her father's protection and influence. But in the quiet moments, when the world slowed, she would sit at her writing desk, the candle burning low, and put pen to parchment. She wrote letters meant for James, pouring her thoughts into words she knew he might never see. Some she sent, entrusted to sailors in her father's fleet who promised to pass them along through channels that stretched across the Atlantic. Others she tucked away in a small wooden box, letters that were never meant to be delivered, only written to lessen the weight in her chest. She told him about the tides, about how the seasons were shifting, about how she still waited by the beach at dawn, searching the sea for him. She told him how she missed the way his voice carried in the wind, how she still felt the imprint of his hands against hers, and how she kept the mantle in Hammock House bare, waiting for him to bring the portrait home. She ended every letter with the same words:

"Come back to me."

No letters came back. There was no word, no whisper, no sign that James had received them. Weeks turned to months, and still, nothing. At first, she convinced herself it was simply the way of the sea. The ocean was vast and unpredictable, and James was on a dangerous mission. He could not send letters easily, not when his life depended on secrecy, and then, as winter deepened and still there was no word, the whispers began.

"The British are hunting traitors."

"The Crown is cracking down on pirates."

"The Royal Navy is moving ships into the North Atlantic."

Fear began to coil inside her, slow and suffocating. She had never feared for James before. He was strong and capable, one of the finest seamen to ever sail these waters, but what if his true mission had been discovered? Even the greatest sailors could not fight the weight of a nation's vengeance. Still, she did not allow herself to believe the worst. Not yet, because doubt was a poison, and she would not drink from its cup, at least not until she knew for certain.

By early spring, something changed. Sarah could not explain it, but she felt it—a shift in the wind, an unease settling deep in her bones. She no longer went to the rocks and no longer wrote letters. Something inside her whispered that James was already on his way back to her. And yet, it did not bring her comfort because instead of longing, she now felt fear, and she didn't understand it. She had learned, long ago, to trust the sea when it spoke to her, and the sea was whispering that something was coming—something terrible—something that would change everything.

Chapter 6

Kingston, Jamaica – March 1718

Captain James Thorne had stood before admirals and the governor, and he had spoken falsehoods with the confidence of a man who had never told a lie and walked away unscathed. But none of it mattered now because he was finally going home.

To Sarah.

To the life he had chosen, the future he was ready to claim. As Invictus cut through the waters of the Caribbean, bound for the colonies, Thorne felt something he had not felt in a long time—certainty. For months, he had played the part of the loyal British captain, carefully feeding his superiors just enough information to keep suspicion at bay. When he stood before His Majesty's Council, he had delivered his fabricated report without hesitation. "Captain Edward Thatch and his fleet have been sighted off Hispaniola. They are believed to be using the island as a stronghold and will soon be sailing toward Curacao." It was a carefully crafted lie, but certainly plausible enough to send the Royal Navy in the wrong direction—far enough away that Blackbeard and his men could move undetected. In the meantime, Thorne had done what no naval officer should ever do—He had delivered Blackbeard's fleet the most valuable intelligence possible. The East India Company's cargo ships had been moving in secret under heavily guarded routes, but Thorne had intercepted the naval orders detailing exactly where and when they would pass through. By now, Thatch would already have the upper hand, his fleet waiting like sharks in the dark waters. And Thorne? He had followed Thatch's order, but Blackbeard wasn't finished with him yet—not by any means.

Port Royal, once the jewel of British power in the Caribbean, was now a haven of rotting grandeur, a place where the tides washed away civility. Salt-worn shingles, leaning clapboard taverns, and muddy alleys buzzed with flies and the smell of sewage, sweat, and something far more dangerous—freedom. It was here that Captain Thorne stepped off the small skiff and onto the crumbling wharf, the morning sun veiled in sea mist, his boots landing on the wood with purpose. He wore no uniform now, just a coarse linen shirt, a black sash at his waist, and a tricorn pulled low to shadow his eyes. He'd come alone, but he wasn't unarmed. At a waterfront tavern called the Pearl, in a back room, air reeking of grog and gunpowder, lantern light glinted off the brass hilt of Thorne's sword as he crossed the threshold. Blackbeard's second-in-command waited. He was a tall, hawk-nosed man with a shaved head and sea-worn skin—known only as Hands, his allegiance to

Blackbeard signaled by the silver earring carved like a skull dangling from his ear.

"Yer late," Hands said without looking up. "Tide's been waitin' on ye."

Thorne removed his hat. "I was being followed—lost them in Villa de la Vega."

Israel Hands smirked. "Yer gettin' better at this." He pulled out a tattered chart and laid it across the table, weighting the corners with two iron shot. A black X marked a ship in port. Thorne immediately knew—Invictus. "Thatch wants her." Hands jabbed a finger. "She's fast, nimble. Perfect for slippin' through blockades…Aye," Hands said, grinning… "Swiftest warship in His Majesty's fleet. She's built to outrun anything on the sea—and fitted for war. That's the ship we need for what's to come and a strong captain on her quarterdeck."

Thorne didn't speak at first. Invictus was more than a vessel. She had been his proving ground, his weapon, his command. But now, if he were to truly break from the Crown, she would become his symbol of defiance. "She's secured in Kingston," Thorne said slowly, "with a full complement of loyal men."

"Loyal to you or to the flag they swore under?" Hands raised a brow. "It doesn't matter," he muttered to himself, "We'll be savvy to it soon enough." He pushed a sealed scroll toward James. "Orders, forged in

London. They'll place you in command of a new commission— a patrol of the Windward Passage. The crew won't question it until it's too late."

Thorne didn't reach for the scroll. "You expect me to turn on my own men."

"I expect you to choose the course you already set," Hands said. "The Navy has you shackled as a weapon for the Crown, now Thatch is offering you freedom and riches beyond your wildest dreams." Hands's smile twisted. "And the cost? A little blood, maybe some fire, but you'll still be standing on the right side of the waterline when it's done if you play yer hand right."

When the sun crested the edge of the Caribbean two days later, Captain Thorne walked up the gangplank of the HMS Invictus, uniform crisp, forged orders tucked into his coat, and a handpicked crew of twelve pirates dressed in crisp redcoats, their faces shaved, boots polished, and each armed to the teeth beneath the illusion of civility. The crew saluted their captain's return, unaware they'd just welcomed the beginning of their end. He strode the deck with the familiarity of a man returning home and the resolve of one planning to set it ablaze. "Prepare for departure," he ordered. "We sail within the hour." The crew moved quickly, trusting him without question. They admired him, and they followed him. Hands' men slipped silently below deck, where the powder stores were checked and the anchor raised. Thorne climbed to the quarterdeck and stared out at the sea, his fingers tight around the rail.

He gave the signal at sunset once they were far enough out to sea—a single lantern held high and dropped to the deck. Within moments, the lower decks erupted with shouting, steel clashing, and muskets discharging. Loyalists resisted; some fought back, some begged, and some jumped to their fate into the black waters. Thorne stood above it all, torn in soul but not in action. He would not waver, nor would he look back.

By nightfall, the ship no longer belonged to the Crown; it belonged to Captain James Thorne— the pirate. The bodies of those who resisted were wrapped and buried at sea. The others were brought before him, their wrists bound, faces bloodied, expressions wary. "You've served the King," Thorne said, looking each man in the eye. "Now I offer you a new flag."

Silence.

Then a young midshipman stepped forward, eyes blazing. "You're no better than the men we hunted."

"Aye," Thorne said. "You're right—I am no better…as I am far worse." He turned to the rest. "This is your choice! Fight for a king who hides behind gold and parchment, or swear to no crown but the one you make with your own hands, and sail for freedom and fortune! You will adhere to a simple code of which you all have an equal stake…or…you'll be left behind in the tide." Some refused. Some were silent, but most, hungry for freedom or too afraid to refuse, knelt and swore. The British ensign was struck down from Invictus' mast and replaced with a black flag, its sigil stitched hastily: a white hourglass bleeding from the top, flanked by crossed cutlasses—the mark of a sovereign captain. Thorne rechristened her *Sovereign*, a name that echoed with defiance, and with her, he sailed for Bermuda, where Blackbeard's fleet waited among the limestone bluffs and coral reefs, hidden like wolves among the shoals. The plan was in motion, and James Thorne would never again wear the king's uniform on the deck of his ship.

Chapter 7

Bermuda, shrouded in haze and framed by jagged coral, rose from the turquoise sea like the edge of an old world. Beneath the limestone cliffs, a narrow inlet concealed a small, protected cove—St. George's Bay, quiet to the untrained eye but teeming with hidden menace. There, under moonless skies, Thatch's fleet lay at anchor. A dozen ships rocked gently on their moorings, their sails furled and lanterns covered. Vessels from every corner of the Atlantic—brigs, sloops, and schooners, each armed to the teeth, were anchored in the protected cove, crewed by outlaws who answered to no flag but the one they raised themselves. When Sovereign entered the bay—its hull still bearing the elegant lines of the HMS Invictus but now stripped of royal colors—Blackbeard himself stood on the quarterdeck of the Queen Anne's Revenge, his newly captured frigate, arms folded across his massive chest.

Fires burned low in the iron braziers around the cove, casting long shadows across the sand. Seaspray glistened on Thatch's coat, his beard, beaded with rubies and sapphires, curled with the humidity. His eyes gleamed like twin coals when Captain Thorne walked up the gangplank to the Revenge's deck, flanked by his first mate and a half-dozen of his newly loyal crew. Thatch said nothing at first. He simply looked Thorne over, as if measuring the man who had once hunted him. Then he spoke, his voice low and thunderous. "You've made your choice, Captain Thorne."

Thorne nodded once. "Aye."

A crooked smile tugged at the corner of Thatch's mouth. "Invictus was a gift, lad, the Navy will bleed to lose her." He clapped a heavy hand on Thorne's shoulder. "You've done more than turn your coat. You've claimed your power." Thorne didn't flinch beneath the pirate's praise. He felt the weight of his decision more deeply now—not with regret, but with certainty.

"I've done my part," Thorne said. "Now I ask for yours."

Blackbeard gave a grave nod and gestured toward the line of ships behind him. "Charles Town is next."

Inside the great cabin of the Queen Anne's Revenge, Captain Thatch unfurled a detailed chart of the Carolina coast. Pins and markings covered the harbor entrances, fortifications, and known patrol routes. "Our men in Nassau report that the Crown's fleet is chasing ghosts in Hispaniola. That gives us a window." He traced a line with his finger. "We strike Charles Town hard and fast—seal the mouth of the harbor with three ships across the channel, the others circling like sharks." Charleston bled gold. The city was one of the wealthiest ports in the American colonies, overflowing with merchant ships, silks, and slaves, but what Blackbeard wanted most was not cargo—it was leverage. "Their governor's got the ear of Parliament," he'd said. "Their merchants fund half the trade between here and London. If we cripple Charles Town, we send a message to the Crown: No port is safe." But there was another reason—one that he hadn't voiced until later, when the wine flowed deeper. "My men are dying," Thatch said, quieter now, his eyes hard. "Sickness took six last month. We need medicine—quinine, laudanum, opium, tinctures, and Charles Town's got warehouses full of it, locked behind iron fortifications."

Thorne studied the map, already reading the tides, calculating approach and risk. "Their governor won't expect anything so bold."

"Which is why it will work," Thatch growled. "We'll block all movement—nothing in, nothing out. They'll beg to pay our price. And when we sail away, they'll remember the names Queen Anne's Revenge and Sovereign like the echo of cannon fire."

"And my name?" Thorne asked.

Blackbeard's grin widened. "They'll remember you, Captain. The man who turned the king's blade into a pirate's banner." He raised a crystal goblet of blood-red claret and held it out to Thorne. "To Charles Town."

Thorne poured his own glass of the red wine, clinking his against the Pirate King's. "To Sarah," he said.

Thatch's eyes darkened slightly. "Aye. But not until the job is done. The girl waits—but glory does not." They drank. At sunrise, the fleet weighed anchor, sails unfurling like wings of war. The sea turned silver beneath them, and the wind rose strong and steady from the east. Only Poseidon was watching, and Charleston had no idea history was in the making.

The wind came in heavy over the low swells, thick with the scent of cedar marsh and gunpowder. By dawn, the Carolina coast had emerged from the morning haze like a faded map—flat, sun-blanched, and still. But in the harbor of Charles Town, life bustled unaware. Ships came and went, merchants unloaded crates of cloth and rum, and the city's wealthiest citizens sipped coffee and tea on their shaded verandas—oblivious to the wall of sails descending upon them from the sea. Blackbeard's fleet moved into position like a noose tightening around the throat of the harbor. From the deck of the Sovereign, Captain Thorne watched through his spyglass as their trap began to take shape. Sloops and brigs—each flying false merchant flags—drifted into the outer roads and anchored in calculated intervals. Below deck, their gun ports were closed, their broadsides hidden, their crews still as death. Blackbeard's personal flagship, Queen Anne's Revenge, loomed at the center like a black leviathan. Her sails were reefed but ready. Her cannons were primed. Captain Thatch lowered his glass and looked to the sky; the wind was shifting favorably; it had begun. He had no intention of burning the city; he only meant to squeeze it, slowly and surgically, until the colony's most powerful men begged to be spared. By mid-morning, Thatch raised his own signal flag—a skeletal demon stabbing a bleeding heart—and fired a warning shot across the bow of a merchant ship entering the harbor. It missed wide, but the message was clear.

Aboard The Sovereign, Thorne watched the port boil into chaos. Ships reversed course. Dockhands shouted. Church bells rang from the towers. Then, the true blockade began. Three pirate ships moved forward and formed a wall across the channel, cutting off Charleston's only access to the Atlantic. No ships could pass—no letters, no goods, no escape. Blackbeard's crew seized incoming merchant vessels, confiscating not just cargo but hostages—some of Charleston's most prominent citizens. A dozen men were taken from the decks of captured ships, their hands bound, their names cataloged. "We'll turn them loose," Thatch muttered, "when we have what we came for." Thorne couldn't deny the brilliance of the strategy; this wasn't a battle; it was a siege and a show of strength more psychological than bloody.

And it worked.

Within two days, the city sent out envoys in small boats, waving white handkerchiefs and trembling under flags of truce. They offered money, but Thatch refused. "We want the chests from the apothecaries—the sealed vaults—all of it, and no games." It was delivered within the day. Six casks of medicine, opiates, and tinctures were rowed out to the Queen Anne's Revenge under armed escort. In exchange, the prisoners were released —unharmed but shaken, returned to the docks in silence. As Blackbeard's fleet finally sailed away from Charles Town, wind at their backs and their holds heavier, Captain Thorne stood at the helm of Sovereign, watching the shoreline fade behind them. He had seen battle; he had seen blood, but this—this was a different kind of power. Not brute force, but command. Blackbeard had brought a colony to its knees without firing a single deadly shot.

The men celebrated, rum passed between decks, music and laughter rising with the salt spray. And yet, as night fell, James Thorne's thoughts turned away from victory. He stepped back from the revelry, his gaze fixed on the horizon—toward Beaufort, toward Sarah. He had held up his end of the deal. Now, it was time to claim what he had been promised: Sarah. He could still see her face in his mind, as vivid as the portrait she had given him, as clear as the first day he had laid eyes on her. And when he reached Beaufort, he would finally be free. By the time Sovereign reached the North Carolina coast, he would not step foot onto the Beaufort sand and soil as Captain James Thorne of the Royal Navy. He would be Captain Thorne, a pirate by oath and soon-to-be husband of Blackbeard's daughter. His father, an admiral of the British fleet, would call him a traitor. His fellow officers would call him a disgrace. But James?

He would call himself a man in love, and that was worth more than any crown.

The voyage north was slow, the winds shifting unpredictably as if the ocean itself was warning him to turn back, but James did not waver. He spent his nights below deck, staring at Sarah's portrait, running his fingers along the frame, whispering to himself the future they would have. "I will be with you soon." He had not foreseen the storm gathering ahead of him. He had not anticipated the cruel hand of fate waiting for him upon his return because by the time he set foot in Beaufort again, everything he believed in would shatter. And his love for Sarah, the love that had made him defy a king, betray his country, and surrender everything he had ever known, would be the very thing that led him to his death.

Chapter 8

The ship crested over the rolling swells, its sails catching the golden hues of the setting sun as it glided into the familiar waters of Topsail Inlet. A false British ensign snapped in the evening breeze, its crimson and white stark against the deepening twilight. Captain Thorne stood at the bow of Sovereign, his grip tight on the worn brass of his spyglass. His heart pounded as he raised it to his eye, focusing beyond the harbor, past the bustling docks, toward Hammock House—the stately yet modest home that sat on the rise, overlooking the town like a silent guardian.

He had been away for ten long months, navigating treacherous seas, acting in treason of the British Crown under the guise of a captain working in the King's best interests, and then turning his life to piracy where news of the Siege of Charles Town would spread like wildfire up and down the colonies and across the ocean. The end of the journey was in sight, and it was her, Sarah. The woman he had pledged his future to, the woman he had longed for with every aching moment since he'd last seen her standing on that very porch as his ship sailed out to sea. He had dreamed of this return, imagined the moment he would sweep her into his arms, promising her he would never leave without her again. He adjusted the focus of his glass, his breath catching as he spotted a figure standing at the railing of Hammock House. His pulse quickened. She was there, but she was not alone. Thorne stiffened, his jaw clenching as the shadow of another man stepped forward. Even from this distance, he could see it—the unmistakable intimacy of the embrace, the way she tilted her face toward the man, their closeness undeniable. A sharp, searing pain lanced through his chest.

Betrayal!

His hands trembled as he lowered the glass, his vision narrowing as the waves churned beneath him. Everything inside him twisted violently—a surge of disbelief, heartbreak, and fury rising in his throat. The ship's bell rang, signaling their approach to port, but Captain Thorne was already turning away, his boots pounding the deck, his mind set on one thing alone: he would confront the man who had stolen her from him, and he would challenge him to the death.

Sovereign had barely settled into the harbor before Thorne stormed down the gangplank, his boots striking the wooden dock with purposeful fury. The salty air was thick with the scent of tar, fish, and the ever-present musk of the sea, but he hardly noticed. His mind was fixed on Hammock House, on the betrayal he had just witnessed from the deck of his ship. Sailors bustled around him, unloading cargo and calling to one another, but their voices were a dull hum in the background as

Thorne moved through the familiar streets of Beaufort. He had dreamed of this homecoming, imagined Sarah running to him, imagined the warmth of her touch, the softness of her lips after months of cold nights at sea. Instead, he had seen her held in the arms of another man. The streets blurred past him—rows of timber-framed shops, the hustle of merchants, the clinking of tankards in taverns where men laughed and drank away their worries, but he had no laughter left in him. His sword weighed heavily at his side, and his heartbeat was like a war drum pounding in his ears.

As he reached Hammock House, he barely took in the grandeur of the home that had once felt like a sanctuary; now, it was a house of treachery. The door stood slightly ajar as if welcoming him in, and he strode inside without hesitation, his hands curling into tight fists, his jaw locked in rage. From the parlor, he heard laughter, a man's laughter with a sound that sent a fresh wave of fury crashing through him. He stormed into the room, his presence like a gust of wind before a hurricane, and the moment Sarah saw him, she gasped, her breath caught in her throat.

Her eyes, those same eyes that had once looked at him with devotion and love, were wide with shock. The man beside her turned sharply, and Thorne locked eyes with his enemy—the enemy who had stolen his future. The man straightened, his posture strong and sure, and his stance one of a trained fighter, yet his brow furrowed in confusion rather than guilt. Captain Thorne did not hesitate. He didn't demand an explanation, and he didn't call for satisfaction; he simply drew his sword and lunged. The other man barely had time to react. The whisper of steel slicing through the air was his only warning before he instinctively reached for his own blade, meeting Thorne's attack with a deafening clash of metal. Their duel exploded through the house, the force of each blow shaking the very walls. Thorne fought with reckless fury, his rage blinding and his footwork aggressive. He pushed forward relentlessly, his strikes aimed to wound, to end, to take back what was his. His opponent—the stranger who had stolen Sarah from him—was skilled, and he met Thorne's assault with practiced ease, his defense fluid, his movements controlled. He did not fight out of anger; he fought to survive. Sparks flew as their swords clashed again, a desperate dance of death through the candlelit parlor.

They battled up the narrow staircase, boots thundering against the wooden steps, their silhouettes flashing in the glow of the wall sconces. Thorne drove the stranger back, forcing him toward the third floor, rage fueling his every move. He saw nothing but betrayal, nothing but her in the arms of another man. When they reached the landing, Thorne saw his chance—a brutal downward strike, a final killing blow. He raised his sword high, but the stranger sidestepped at the last second, his blade catching Thorne across the ribs.

The world lurched sideways. Thorne's grip failed. His vision blurred.

Then—

He fell.

The weight of his own momentum carried him backward down the stairs, the pain in his chest sharp and unbearable. His body crashed against the wooden steps, his sword slipping from his fingers, clattering against the floor. He landed in a broken heap, gasping for breath, the ceiling above him spinning. Somewhere in the distance, he heard Sarah's scream. Her footsteps pounded toward him, and a moment later, she was kneeling beside him, her hands cradling his face and her tears warm against his skin. His body felt heavy, the weight of his failing heart dragging him into the abyss. Sarah turned to the stranger, panic in her voice. "James, he's my brother!" The words didn't register before his vision darkened completely. The last thing Captain James Thorne saw before darkness swallowed him whole was Sarah's face, etched in grief and horror, calling his name. And then, he was gone.

Sarah clutched James's lifeless body, her fingers trembling as she pressed her hand against his wound, as if she could will the blood to stop flowing. But it was too late. The warmth of him was fading. His sword, once so steady, lay abandoned beside him, the metal reflecting the flickering candlelight in a cruel mockery of the battle's end. Her brother stood frozen, his chest rising and falling in rapid, shallow breaths, the hilt of his own weapon still clenched in his hands. He looked down at James, at what he had done—at what James had forced him to do—and a strangled sound left his throat. "I—"

Sarah turned to him, her voice raw with agony. "Go." He hesitated, his face pale, eyes wide with disbelief. "Go!" she screamed, and without another word, he turned and disappeared into the night, leaving only the scent of sweat and blood in his wake. Sarah bent over James, her sobs shaking her entire body. Her hands, once meant to welcome him home and to hold him with love, were now stained with his blood. "James," she whispered, brushing damp hair from his forehead, her tears slipping onto his cheek. His expression had softened in death—as if, for just a moment, the anger had gone, and only sorrow remained.

A gust of wind howled through the house, rattling the shutters as if the world itself was grieving with her. The weight of his death settled into the bones of Hammock House, into its walls, its very floor. The halls of the house were steeped in silence; the lingering scent of blood and sweat hung in the air. Moonlight leaked through the tall windows, casting silver bars across the blood-slicked floorboards at the second-floor landing where James Thorne's body lay crumpled, his once-pristine tunic dark with blood and his hand still loosely clutching the blood-stained silk of Sarah's skirt. His head rested in her lap, her trembling fingers tangled in his hair, her cheeks streaked with tears. She didn't speak. She didn't cry out. She simply held him—rocking gently—refusing to believe the life had drained from the man she had waited so long to see again.

The door burst open downstairs, and boots thundered inside. Her father hurried up the stairs, flanked by his fiercest men, but halted when he saw his daughter on the landing, cradling the fallen naval captain. For the first time in memory, the devil of the seas stood in silence. His gaze dropped to James, the man he had come to call an ally, the only one he had allowed to love his only daughter, and the man who had given up power under the Crown of England for the sake of her heart. Thatch slowly knelt beside Sarah, his great hand resting on her shoulder.

She looked up, her voice cracking like shattered glass. "He didn't know… He thought I had betrayed him. He thought—he thought my brother—" Thatch closed his eyes. He knew what must have happened. No duel, no warning, just a sword, drawn in heartbreak. Now, James Thorne was dead—not at sea, not in glory—but in the house he'd risked everything to return to.

Two days later, under a gray morning sky, Captain Thatch stood at the edge of Beaufort's Old Burial Ground, flanked by men who had sailed with him for a decade or more. James's body had been washed, dressed in silks, and topped with an ornate wool frock, his sword polished, and returned to his side. But, there would be no coffin—no standard burial for this man. Thatch refused to let the Royal Navy or the colonists tarnish James's name with slander or vengeance. Instead, he made a decision that would confuse future generations and shield the truth. "He'll be buried standing—facing east," Thatch told the gravediggers.

"Facing east?" one man asked.

"Aye. Toward the sea he loved, and his birthplace in England," but Thatch truly wanted James to face east in the direction of Hammock House—to Sarah. They dug deep, driving the grave far below where others lay, setting the body upright, encased in timbers, sword at his side, and his eyes—forever closed—facing the woman he'd died for. Blackbeard himself carved the wooden marker. It did not bear the name of a pirate nor even a captain. It simply read:

"A British Officer, Laid to Rest, 1718."

No rank and no cause, just a quiet truth veiled by intention so that his grave would not be desecrated. So there, Captain James Thorne would remain undisturbed, standing in eternal vigil until he would one day be reunited with his beloved Sarah.

Captain Thatch was now the most hunted pirate in the ocean. He had already refused the King's pardon and had run his flagship aground in Topsail Inlet, coming into Beaufort Town. As word quickly spread of his blockade of Charles Town harbor, he knew he wasn't safe staying in one place for too long. It was time for him to slip up the coast toward his favorite haunt in the colonies…Ocracoke. The night before Blackbeard sailed north, he paid one last visit to James Thorne's final resting place. He lowered his hand on the carved marker and whispered to himself, "Rest well, lad. Watch over her. I'll see to the rest." And with that, Thatch turned and vanished into the shadows of the wild oaks, never to be seen in Beaufort again—leaving behind a secret only the dead would keep.

And so, Captain Thorne remained.

From that night forward, the people of Beaufort whispered of the tragedy that had taken place in Hammock House. For years, visitors claimed that on moonlit nights, the wooden staircase creaked with unseen footsteps, as if a restless soul still walked the halls, reliving his final moments. Some swore they had seen candlelight flicker in the windows despite the house being long abandoned. But, the most chilling story of all was the one told only in hushed tones—that sometimes, on the night of a full moon, the floorboards in the second-story landing were stained red, as if James Thorne's blood had seeped into the wood itself. And, if one listened closely enough, they could hear the wind whisper through the trees—"Sarah, I have longed for you." He would remain. Waiting. Watching…for Sarah to return to him. For the love he had died believing wasn't his.

Chapter 9

Present Day

Sarah Whitaker had always felt different.

Not in the way that some girls felt when they didn't quite fit in with their classmates or when they had interests that strayed from the norm. Sarah's difference was something she could never quite explain—a presence that lingered just beyond sight, an awareness she had carried her whole life. But the truth was, even if she didn't possess that unexplainable sense of the unseen, people would still take notice of her because Sarah looked like she had stepped out of another time.

Her long, dark hair fell in soft waves down her back, the color rich and deep, as if it had absorbed the midnight sky itself. Sometimes, in the right light, it reflected hints of dark auburn, but mostly, it was black as ink, smooth as silk, cascading over her shoulders like a river. Her eyes were her most striking feature—a stormy shade of gray, flecked with gold, shifting between cool steel and soft twilight, depending on the light. People often told her they were mystifying, hypnotic, the kind of eyes that seemed to see straight through a person. But, it wasn't just their color that made them memorable—it was the way she held her gaze, the way she studied the world with quiet intensity as if she were always looking for something just out of reach. Her features were fine and delicate but strong at the same time, giving her an almost otherworldly beauty—as if she had been sculpted from moonlight and shadow, a figure lost in time. Her pale skin refused to tan, just like her father's, always carrying a hint of porcelain against the sun-kissed golden tones of her mother and brother. She never paid much attention to her own reflection, but others did.

Though she was only seventeen, there was a timelessness about her, a grace that seemed to belong to another century. It wasn't just her appearance; it was the way she moved—quiet, deliberate, as if always listening, always waiting for something no one else could hear. It was the way she would pause in old places, fingertips grazing weathered brick, aged wood, and the cool iron of antique railings as if she could feel the echoes of history beneath her touch. And, it was the way she dreamed. Her dreams had always been vivid, unsettling, filled with things she had never seen, yet somehow remembered. Ships drifting into the harbor beneath a crimson sky. The scent of brine and candle smoke in an old house. A voice—whispering her name on the wind. She never told anyone about the dreams.

Sarah had always known things she shouldn't. Not in the way of a child who overheard secrets whispered behind closed doors or someone who pieced together knowledge through logic and observation. No, Sarah's knowing was something else entirely—something that came from a place she could neither explain nor escape. She had never spoken about it, not even to her parents, because how do you explain to someone that you remember things you've never lived?

Her first memory of the dreams came when she was barely five years old. She had woken up in the middle of the night, her tiny hands clutching the blanket as she stared at the ceiling, her heart pounding as if she had just run through a storm. She had dreamed of a house by the sea—an uninspiring, lonely house perched on a grassy knoll where the wind howled through the rafters like a living thing. The house was dark, its windows empty as if watching her, its heavy wooden door swaying open with a groan. In the dream, she had stepped inside. A candle flickered in a hallway, casting shadows that stretched and twisted along the wooden floor. The air was thick with the scent of salt and aged timber, and the sound of whispered voices echoed from the floor above. She hadn't understood who they belonged to—but one of them was calling her name. She had awoken with a sharp gasp, confused and frightened, but when she told her mother about the dream, she had simply been soothed back to sleep, reassured that little girls dream of many things, and sometimes, those dreams just feel real. But that wasn't the only time she dreamed of the house. It wasn't the last time she heard the whispers. And it wasn't the last time she felt like something—or someone—was waiting for her.

Sarah never questioned her memories of the ocean, even though she had never lived by the sea. She knew the smell of salt air before she had ever been to the coast. She knew the way wooden ship decks creaked beneath heavy boots before she had ever stepped foot on a boat. She knew the weight of thick velvet skirts brushing her legs, the roughness of wool cloaks, the tightness of a corset—yet she had never worn any of those things. And still… she could feel them.

When she was seven years old, she and her family took a trip to the beach for the first time. Sarah had walked along the docks with wide, curious eyes, reaching out to run her hands along the gunwales of old boats as if searching for something she had lost. When they visited a historical reenactment, she stared at the actors in their 18th-century clothing, her expression unreadable. Finally, she turned to her mother and whispered, "They're wearing it wrong." Her mother laughed, thinking it was just a child's imagination running wild. But Sarah knew; she had always known. Through the years, the feeling had never left her. Sometimes, it was as simple as hearing the crash of waves and feeling a pull in her chest, as if something was calling her home. Other times, it was shadows in the corners of her vision, whispers on the wind that no one else could hear. And sometimes, it was the overwhelming certainty that she had walked these streets before, even though she knew she never had. Her mother always told her she had an old soul. Her grandmother had called her fey, a word Sarah had once looked up—it meant strange, otherworldly, touched by something unseen. She had never really thought about actually living in a past life.

Until now. Until she saw him.

Chapter 10

Even when she was small, sitting cross-legged on the hardwood floor of her bedroom in Atlanta, she'd sketch the shadows of tree branches cast across her window as if they held secrets no one else could see. While other kids drew stick figures and animal blobs, Sarah painted faraway places—some she had visited, others only imagined. Now, she was a rising senior with dreams much bigger than the southern city where she'd grown up. New York City called to her like a beacon in a midnight sea, and she'd already pinned a Metropolitan Museum of Art postcard to the vision board above her desk—*Someday*, she had scribbled underneath it in soft pencil. She had big plans to study art and design at Parsons or Pratt and, eventually, earn a place among the curators of the Met. She was the quiet one in her family—observant and pensive. Her art was her voice.

Her mother, Valerie, a polished socialite with a year-round tennis tan and a planner full of charity luncheons, never quite knew what to make of Sarah's stillness, but she always understood it was important to give her daughter the space and quiet she needed, after all, Sarah was an honor student and a talented artist from an early age—she never worried about what the future would hold for her. Her father, Pierce, a commanding trial lawyer with a Harvard Juris Doctor and a presence that filled every room he entered, adored Sarah. Although his days and often many nights were spent in his war room, neck deep in preparations for upcoming trials, he always found time here and there to take her to museums when he could. He told her how talented she was and how much he admired her artistic abilities, even if he wasn't entirely sure she could carve out a living from it when she graduated from college.

When her family rented a coastal cottage in Beaufort, North Carolina, for the summer, Sarah packed her watercolor tin, a set of travel brushes, and her sketchbook before she even thought about sunscreen. She didn't expect the town to stir anything more than light inspiration—certainly not the unraveling of a centuries-old mystery that felt eerily personal. But something about the town felt off-kilter in the most delicate, magnetic way. The light here was different from any place she had seen before. It was softer and older—like the past had never quite let go. The first time she laid eyes on this quaint seaside town, she felt as though she had stepped into a place untouched by time that strangely felt like home—not her home in Atlanta, but something different. The town, nestled along North Carolina's Crystal Coast, wasn't just a beach town—it was a place with a soul, a history woven into every brick alley, every salt-worn dock, and every whisper of wind that carried the scent of the sea and marshes.

Her family's car rolled slowly down Front Street, the town's historic waterfront, where old live oaks draped in Spanish moss lined the sidewalks, their gnarled branches forming a canopy of shade over the boardwalk at the waterfront park. Pastel-colored houses with white picket fences and overflowing flower boxes stood in perfect rows, their wide porches inviting passersby to sit and watch the world drift by. Beyond the houses, Taylor Creek shimmered under the late afternoon sun, the water reflecting the sky like polished glass. Boats rocked gently at their moorings, and Sarah could see people walking along the wooden boardwalk, their voices mingling with the cries of gulls overhead. The sight of Carrot Island in the distance caught her attention. A narrow stretch of land, wild and untamed, it was home to the famous wild horses, descendants of the Spanish mustangs that had roamed the Outer Banks for centuries. Sarah had read about them in travel guides, but seeing them now, their dark silhouettes moving along the dune ridges, their manes catching in the breeze, felt almost like spotting ghosts from the past.

As her father navigated through the narrow streets, Sarah took in the charm of the historic district. There were no towering hotels, no neon-lit boardwalks—only centuries-old homes, quaint storefronts, and the kind of stillness that suggested life moved at a different rhythm here. They passed by the Beaufort Historic Site, where colonial buildings stood proudly, some dating back to before the Revolutionary War. A woman in a long cotton dress and bonnet walked across the lawn, likely a tour guide for the Living History Museum, and just beyond, the Old Burial Ground rested beneath a canopy of ancient oak trees, its worn tombstones leaning at odd angles, a quiet reminder of the lives that had come and gone before them. Her mother, flipping through a visitor's pamphlet, smiled and said, "This place is going to be good for us. It's much slower and more peaceful." Sarah wasn't sure she agreed. Yes, it was beautiful. Yes, it was charming, but there was something else here, too —something she couldn't quite name yet, something that made her feel as though she was meant to be here.

Their rental cottage sat just a few blocks from the water, a weathered white house with blue shutters and a wraparound porch shaded by a magnolia tree in full bloom. The scent of marsh and jasmine filled the air as Sarah stepped out of the car, stretching her legs after the long drive. Inside, the house was cozy and filled with antique furniture, as if it had been frozen in time. Wide-plank wooden floors creaked underfoot, and the windows, slightly warped from age, framed views of the lush backyard, where a brick garden path disappeared into a tangle of wildflowers and ivy-covered trellises.

Sarah's younger brother, Ethan, wasted no time claiming a room, tossing his bags onto the bed before racing outside to check out the porch. Their father, having grown up by the sea, was a lifelong fisherman at heart. He leaned against the kitchen counter, already flipping through a maritime map of the area, likely plotting out the best fishing spots. He had already booked several charters from Beaufort and Morehead City in hot pursuit of catching the tastiest fish in the ocean—not to mention fish that knew how to put up one heck of a fight. After all, this part of the country was known as “Sportsman’s Paradise.” Their mother unpacked groceries, chatting about quaint restaurants they should try, and upcoming farmers’ markets filled with fresh seafood and homemade pastries. Sarah, however, wandered upstairs to her room, setting her bag down by the window.

The house creaked softly in the summer heat, as if it were settling around her. She took a deep breath, inhaling the scent of aged wood and the lingering briny air. It was charming. Old, steeped in history, and something about it hummed beneath the surface. The feeling from before returned—that strange, inexplicable sense that she was stepping into something much bigger than just a summer vacation. After unpacking, and curiosity piqued, she decided to go for a walk. She wanted to see the town, to explore its old cobblestone streets and gardens, and get lost in its quiet corners.

But, she hadn’t meant to wander this far.

At first, the streets had been bright and welcoming, lined with colonial homes and tidy flower beds. But the farther she walked, the more things changed. The road beneath her feet turned to packed dirt, the houses spaced farther apart, their once-manicured lawn giving way to wild, untamed grass. A breeze picked up, rustling the oak trees overhead. Sarah’s skin prickled. She wasn’t sure when, exactly, the atmosphere shifted, but suddenly, the air felt different. And then, at the end of the unassuming dirt road, she saw it.

The house.

It was old—not grand, not towering, just there, weathered and forgotten beneath the swaying branches. Its three-story, double-porch facade was peeling, the shutters slightly askew. A wooden sign, faded from time, barely clung to its post:

Hammock House.

Sarah slowed. The name rang in her mind like a distant bell. Had she read about it somewhere? Seeing it in a book? There was something familiar about it, something lingering. She took a step forward, and that was when she saw him.

Still. Silent. Watching.

Her breath hitched.

The man on the porch was still as stone, his tall frame rigid against the fading afternoon light. His navy coat, though worn with time, still clung to him with an air of authority. The brass buttons gleaming on his long navy frock caught the light in a way that made them seem almost too real—a stark contrast to the rest of him. His face was pale, almost unnaturally so, like parchment left too long in the sun. His tricorn hat, slightly askew, framed a face that might have once been handsome but was now shadowed with something darker. His jaw was set tight, and his lips pressed into a thin, unyielding line. But it was his eyes that made Sarah's stomach drop. They weren't just watching her —they were looking through her, piercing and hollow, filled with something deep and unreadable. Cold… unwelcoming. She was frozen in place.

The air between them felt thick, as though she had stepped into a space where time no longer moved. The weight of his stare pressed against her ribs, rooting her to the spot. Her pulse thundered in her ears, but she couldn't move, couldn't breathe, couldn't even blink. He didn't speak, nor did he shift. He just stared. And then, he was gone. The porch was empty. Sarah staggered back, gasping for air as if she had been underwater. Her legs trembled, and the distant sounds of town—the laughter of tourists, the rustling of leaves—felt disorienting and too far away to reach her. For a long moment, she just stood there, her breath coming in short, uneven bursts. Then, without thinking, she turned and ran.

Chapter 11

Back at the cottage, Sarah sat cross-legged on her bed, staring at the pale blue walls but seeing nothing. Her mind replayed the moment over and over—the specter's face, his rigid stance, the way his eyes had cut straight through her. That hollow, unrelenting stare, the way the air thickened, the way she had felt trapped beneath his gaze as if her body had forgotten how to move. Her heart pounded when she thought about it. It had been so real. More real than any flicker or whisper or strange sensation she had ever felt before. And yet, now that the initial fear had faded, something else had settled in its place. A small, undeniable sense of relief. For years, she had wondered if she had imagined her abilities. If the strange awareness that had awakened in her as a small child had been nothing more than an overactive imagination. But the moment she saw him —the moment their eyes locked—she knew. This wasn't a dream. It wasn't a trick of the light.

She had seen him.

And he had seen her.

That thought sent a fresh wave of unease through her. Because now, she had to ask herself—why her? Why, all of a sudden, was she able to see him instead of only sensing his presence? Had she somehow summoned him just by being near Hammock House? Or had he been waiting for someone like her to come along? She hugged her arms around herself. She had spent years trying to convince herself she was just an ordinary teenager, but she wasn't. She had never been. And whatever happened today—whatever the apparition wanted—it was only the beginning.

A soft knock on her door pulled Sarah out of her thoughts. "Sarah?" Her mother called. "Dinner's ready."

Sarah blinked. She hadn't realized how much time had passed. The room was dim now, the sun dipping low behind the trees outside. She slid off the bed, smoothing out her shirt before stepping into the hallway. The smell of seafood filled the cottage—grilled fish, hushpuppies, something buttery and warm. Normally, the scent would have made her stomach growl, but tonight, she felt…hollow.

The small wooden dining table was already set, and her parents chatted as they dished out plates. Her younger brother, Ethan, shoveled mashed potatoes onto his plate like he hadn't eaten in days. Sarah slid into her chair, trying to act normal.

"Have a good walk around town today?" Her dad asked, taking a sip of iced tea.

Sarah hesitated, her fingers tightening slightly around her fork. What was she supposed to say? *Yeah, I got lost, found a haunted house, and saw a ghost. Pass the butter*? "Yeah," she murmured instead. "It was nice."

Her mom smiled. "See? I told you you'd love it here. It's such a charming town."

Sarah forced a nod. Her dad was already moving on to another topic, talking about some fishing trip he wanted to take that weekend. Sarah barely heard him. She pushed her food around her plate, her appetite gone. Every so often, her eyes flickered toward the window, toward the growing darkness outside. She couldn't stop thinking about him. The way he had looked at her. Like he had been waiting. After a few more minutes of pretending to listen, Sarah finally set her fork down. "I think I'm going to head to bed," she said quietly.

Her mom frowned. "You're not hungry?"

"Just tired," she lied.

Her dad shrugged. "Guess that walk wore you out, huh?"

She nodded, standing from the table. "Yeah. Night."

Her mom gave her a curious glance but didn't push. "Goodnight, sweetheart."

Sarah slipped away, climbing the stairs to her room. She closed the door softly behind her, then stood there in the quiet for a long moment. She should have felt safe here. But as she crawled into bed and pulled the covers up to her chin, all she could think about was him and how different the air had felt that day, as if something had woken up, like she had stirred something. And she wasn't sure she could ignore it.

After what seemed like hours of lying in bed reflecting on the confrontation, she finally drifted off to sleep, dreaming about the house in the hammocks, with long tendrils of Spanish moss hanging from the tree limbs, softly swaying in the summer breeze like curtains framing the path to the house. The windows were dark as if the inside of the house hadn't seen light in a couple of hundred years. In her dream, she walked up to the porch of the long-abandoned building, climbing the old, creaky wooden stairs to the front door. The heavy, solid oak door was gilt with an ancient brass knob. She watched the knob turn on its own, and suddenly, the door opened with a long creak into total darkness. She sat straight up in bed, wide awake, only to find it was the next morning. Sunlight stretched across the foot of Sarah's bed, warming the sheets and casting soft golden patterns against the walls. She blinked, disoriented for a moment, the heavy weight of sleep still clinging to her limbs, and then she remembered. The dream. Hammock House. The way the door had opened on its own. It's ancient brass knob, turning with a deliberate slowness before swallowing her in darkness.

Sarah shivered as she sat up, pushing her tangled hair out of her face. The room was filled with quiet sounds of morning— gulls calling in the distance, the rustling of tree branches outside her window, and the faint clinking of dishes from the kitchen downstairs. She exhaled, rubbing her arms. As eerie as the dream had been, it didn't feel like a warning. It felt like something else entirely.

An invitation?

A nudge to explore deeper?

The weight of that thought settled into her chest, and she swung her legs over the edge of the bed. If her dream had come from her own subconscious, it was clear—her mind wasn't letting this go. And neither was she. Determined now, she grabbed her phone and checked the time. 7:42 AM. The town was already waking up, and so was she. She padded over to the dresser, pulling open the top drawer where she had hurriedly unpacked her suitcase and stuffed her clothes the day before. She grabbed a pair of denim shorts and an oversized t-shirt, slipping them on before running a brush through her hair. The sea air had left it slightly wavy, and she didn't spend too much time bothering to tame it. As she stared at herself in the small mirror hanging over the dresser, she wondered—*Do I look different*? She didn't. But she felt different, like something had shifted. It was as if a thread had been pulled loose, and now there was no tightening it again. She glanced down at her wrist, where a simple braided bracelet—one she had made years ago—rested on her skin. Absentmindedly, she twisted it between her fingers, grounding herself. Finally, she grabbed her small canvas bag from the chair, stuffing her phone and a notebook inside. If she was going to start looking for answers, she might as well take notes. After brushing her teeth, she slipped on her sandals and headed downstairs.

The cottage smelled of coffee and ocean air. Her father was already sitting on the front porch, mug in hand, scrolling through his phone as he enjoyed the early morning stillness. Sarah hesitated in the doorway before stepping outside. The air was thick with the warmth of summer, the humidity already creeping in despite the breeze off the water. Her dad glanced up as she approached, raising an eyebrow. "You're up early."

Sarah shrugged, shoving her hands into her pockets. "Figured I'd go out and explore a little."

He took a slow sip of his coffee, considering her. "Town's nice in the mornings. Less crowded. You going anywhere in particular?"

She hesitated for half a second. "Just wandering."

He didn't press, only reached into his pocket and pulled out a folded $10 bill. "Grab yourself something at the farmers' market. They've got fresh croissants. And get some cocoa—you need something in your stomach before you start running around."

Sarah took the money with a small smile. "Thanks." Her dad leaned back in his chair, lifting his mug in an unspoken *be safe* before turning his attention back to his phone. Sarah stepped down from the porch and onto the worn brick path leading to the street, her thoughts still swirling as the morning sun cast long golden light through the trees. Today, she was going to find answers. And something told her she wouldn't have to look far.

Chapter 12

The morning air in Beaufort was thick with the scent of the sea, warmed by the sun and laced with the faintest trace of something sweet—maybe vanilla, maybe cinnamon—drifting from the direction of the farmers market. Sarah walked at an easy pace, the events of the night before still humming at the back of her mind, but the town's quiet energy kept her grounded. Shops along the main street were just starting to open, their doors propped with antique brass stops or weathered wooden signs welcoming in the early crowd. The boardwalk, which would be buzzing with tourists by midday, was still calm, save for a few locals enjoying the morning breeze and the sight of sailboats bobbing lazily in the harbor.

It was the kind of place that felt old in the best way—like history wasn't just something in books but something that lived in the worn wooden planks of the docks, in the brick paths that lined the waterfront, in the faded paint of the colonial-era buildings that had stood for centuries. It was the kind of place that whispered stories. And today, Sarah was ready to listen.

The farmers' market was nestled in a shady square near the waterfront, where oak trees stretched their limbs over booths selling fresh produce, handmade crafts, and baked goods. The air smelled of warm bread, honey, and fresh herbs, mingling with the salt of the nearby sea. She made her way toward the bakery stand, where rows of golden croissants sat neatly stacked behind the glass display case. Their flaky layers shimmered in the morning light, crisp and buttery, just waiting to be pulled apart.

She was just about to step forward when she noticed someone else already at the stand. A girl about her age stood at the counter, carefully selecting croissants from the basket. Her long, windblown, curly brown hair was pulled into a loose ponytail, and she wore a faded T-shirt tucked into cutoff shorts, looking completely at ease in the lively market setting.

"Are these from this morning?" the girl asked the vendor, pointing to the croissants.

The elderly woman behind the counter beamed. "Fresh out of the oven at five a.m. Real butter, just like the ones in France."

The girl grinned. "I'll take three."

Sarah watched as she handed over a few crumpled bills and took the small paper bag, which quickly showed grease spots from the still-warm croissants. The girl turned, and for a split second, their eyes met. Sarah hesitated, unsure whether to look away, but the girl smiled. "You've gotta try one. They're insanely good."

Sarah smiled back, stepping forward as the vendor turned to her. "What can I get you, sweetheart?"

"Just one croissant and a cocoa, please," Sarah said, handing over the $10 bill.

As the woman moved to prepare her order, the girl lingered near the stand, opening her bag and tearing off a piece of croissant. The layers separated in crisp, golden sheets, revealing a soft, buttery center.

"You're new here," she said, glancing at Sarah as she popped a bite into her mouth. "I would've remembered seeing you before."

Sarah gave a small nod. "Yeah, my family's renting a cottage for the summer."

The girl smiled. "Welcome to Beaufort, then." She dusted a few crumbs from her fingers before holding out her hand. "I'm Abigail. But everyone calls me Tilley."

Abigail Tillman was the kind of girl who made an impression before you even had a chance to say hello. With her thick-rimmed glasses always slightly askew and her untamed curls pulled into a ponytail that never seemed to stay in place, she had a sort of adorable chaos about her—like Velma from Scooby-Doo if Velma were a rising senior at Beaufort High School with a closet full of museum T-shirts and a shell necklace she'd worn since fifth grade.

Sarah shook her hand, feeling an instant sense of familiarity as if she had met Tilley somewhere before. "Sarah."

"Nice to meet you, Sarah," Tilley said, tucking her bag of croissants under her arm. "So, what do you think of Beaufort so far?"

Sarah hesitated, wondering how much she should say. She could just talk about the town's charm, the boardwalk, the cute shops.

Or she could tell the truth.

That she had wandered too far the day before. That she had stumbled upon Hammock House. That she had seen something—someone—standing on the porch, staring at her with dark, hollow eyes.

Tilley watched her expectantly, tilting her head slightly as if she could already tell there was more to Sarah's answer.

Sarah took her croissant and cocoa from the vendor, hesitating for just a moment before deciding—Maybe she had found exactly the right person to talk to. Sarah hesitated, wondering how much she should say. She could tell Tilley the safe answer—that she liked the town, that it was charming and different from anywhere she'd spent time before. But the truth sat heavily on her tongue that she had wandered too far. She had seen something she couldn't explain. That part of her was still shaken, but another part—the part she wasn't ready to talk about—felt drawn back to Hammock House in a way she didn't understand.

Instead, she simply said, "It's… interesting."

Tilley smirked, tearing off another bite of croissant. "That's one way to put it."

Sarah took a sip of her cocoa, glancing toward the boats moored along the waterfront. "So, you live here year-round?"

"Born and raised," Tilley said proudly. "My dad's the curator of the Maritime Museum, so I've spent my whole life surrounded by ship models, artifacts, and old maps." She grinned. "And more than a few ghost stories."

Sarah's grip tightened slightly around her cup, but she kept her expression neutral. "Ghost stories?"

Tilley nodded, her eyes glinting with amusement. "Beaufort's full of them. This town is old, and old towns don't let go of their past so easily."

Sarah forced a small smile, but her heart was suddenly racing. She wanted to ask—Have you ever heard of Hammock House? But she didn't.

Instead, Tilley shifted, tucking her bag of croissants under her arm. "If you're interested in learning about the town, the best place to start is the Maritime Museum."

Sarah blinked. "Oh?"

Tilley nodded. "It doesn't open for another hour, but I'm opening up today. You should come with me—hang out in the museum library for breakfast before we unlock the doors for tourists."

Sarah hesitated. She had been planning to look for answers. She just hadn't been sure where to start. Now, the answer had fallen right into her lap. And if Tilley knew even half as much about Beaufort's history as she claimed to, then maybe Sarah could get some of the information she was looking for. Finally, she nodded. "Yeah. That sounds great."

Tilley grinned. "Perfect. Come on, I'll give you a proper introduction to Beaufort."

Sarah followed her down the sunlit street, the weight of her dream, her encounter, and the ghost of Hammock House still pressing against her mind. She had come looking for answers; now, it seemed, the answers were finding her.

The Maritime Museum stood quiet and unlit, its large windows reflecting the golden morning light as Sarah and Tilley stepped up to the entrance. The heavy wooden door creaked slightly as Tilley fished out a key and unlocked it, pushing it open to reveal a dim interior. Sarah hesitated just inside the doorway, blinking as her eyes adjusted to the darkness. The air smelled of aged wood and iron—like the scent of an old ship that had been at sea for centuries. Though the museum was empty, something about it felt alive, as if the walls were brimming with stories waiting to be told.

Tilley didn't seem to notice the eerie stillness. She strode confidently inside, her footsteps muffled by the creaking floorboards. "Come on. The light switches are in the main hall, but I usually wait until I've had my morning coffee before turning everything on."

Sarah followed her deeper into the museum, the dim glow from the front windows fading as they stepped into a long, shadowed corridor. The walls were lined with artifacts—wooden ship wheels, antique compasses, and faded nautical charts pinned behind glass. A few mannequins stood in the hallway, dressed in old sailor uniforms, their lifeless eyes just barely visible in the darkness. Sarah forced herself not to shudder. "Not creepy at all," she muttered under her breath.

Tilley chuckled. "Wait until you see the mannequins in the pirate exhibit. Their eyes follow you."

Sarah shot her a look. "Great. Something to look forward to."

Tilley was gregarious in a way Sarah wasn't used to —someone who didn't just talk, but delighted in conversation. She had a sharp wit, a louder-than-expected laugh, and the uncanny ability to carry an entire discussion while also reorganizing a drawer of maritime ephemera or handing out scavenger hunt maps to a group of excited third graders. She was, as Sarah would quickly come to learn, very into her job at the North Carolina Maritime Museum. But "job" might have been the wrong word—it was her kingdom.

Tilley had grown up in the belly of the museum like it was a second home. Her mother, Margaret Tillman, was the current Director of Operations for the Queen

Anne's Revenge Conservation Project, and Tilley had spent more hours cataloging artifacts, cleaning glass display cases, and attending lectures about 18th-century piracy than most museum interns twice her age. Unlike most kids in Beaufort, who spent their weekends on boats or at beach bonfires, Tilley would gladly trade a day on the water for a behind-the-scenes tour of recovered shipwreck artifacts or a new shipment of pirate memorabilia for the museum gift shop. And she had big plans.

One day, she would take over the Queen Anne's Revenge project. She would lead expeditions. Manage restoration labs. Deliver TED Talks. Maybe even publish a book called What Pirates Leave Behind. "I've already written the first chapter," she told Sarah with a grin as they traversed the dark museum corridor.. She had a way of talking about the past like it was alive—like if you listened closely enough, you could hear the whispers of long-dead sailors echoing up from the floorboards. For Sarah, who had always lived quietly on the edge of things, Tilley was a whirlwind of energy and enthusiasm. And strangely, exactly the kind of person she needed.

Tilley led her through a doorway at the end of the hall, pushing it open to reveal a cozy, windowless room lined with shelves of old books and artifacts. A fireplace took up one wall, its mantel cluttered with small model ships, and in the center of the room sat a large wooden table, its surface covered with open books and scattered notes. The library. It felt different from the rest of the museum—warmer, more lived-in. The kind of place where time didn't feel so distant. Tilley tossed her bag of croissants onto the table and flicked on a small lamp, casting a pool of golden light across the wood. "This is where I spend most of my time when I'm here. It's way better than the front desk."

Sarah ran her fingers along the spines of the books on the nearest shelf. Some were thick, bound in leather, their titles barely legible from years of wear. Others were modern, full of crisp photographs and printed maps. "You're really into this stuff, huh?" Sarah asked, sliding into one of the worn chairs.

Tilley grinned, pulling two croissants from the bag and handing one to Sarah. "You have no idea."

The croissants were still warm, their golden layers flaking apart at the slightest touch. Sarah tore off a piece, letting the buttery pastry melt on her tongue as she listened to the quiet crackle of the fireplace.

"So," Tilley said, taking a sip from her thermos, "since you're new here, I assume you don't know much about Beaufort's history?"

Sarah hesitated before nodding. "Not really."

"Well, consider this your first lesson," Tilley said, sitting back in her chair. "This town was built on the backs of sailors, merchants, and, of course, pirates. Lots of them."

Sarah raised an eyebrow. "Pirates?"

Tilley grinned. "The pirate. Blackbeard himself. He ran his ship, the Queen Anne's Revenge, aground just a mile out in the inlet. Some people think he did it on purpose to get rid of his crew."

Sarah's interest was piqued despite herself. "And they found it?"

"Oh yeah. Not just the shipwreck—artifacts, too. My mom is the director of operations for the project." Tilley leaned forward, her excitement obvious. "We have the ship's bell right here in the museum."

That caught Sarah off guard. "Seriously?"

Tilley smirked. "You'll see. As soon as we finish eating, I'll give you a tour while I turn on the lights."

Sarah nodded, but her mind was only half on the conversation. Because as fascinating as Blackbeard's history was, she wasn't here for pirates. She was here for something else. Something just as old and just as significant. Something told her that somewhere in this museum—between the maps and ship logs and glass cases of artifacts—there was a piece of the past that would lead her closer to the truth about Hammock House. She just had to find it.

After finishing their breakfast, Tilley dusted the croissant crumbs from her hands and stood. "Alright, time for the grand tour."

Sarah followed her out of the library, back into the dim corridors of the museum. The space still carried the weight of the past, but now, with Tilley leading the way, it felt less eerie and more alive—like each display was a portal to another time. As they passed through the main hall, Tilley flipped on the overhead lights, one section at a time. The museum slowly awakened, revealing its vast collection of maritime artifacts—weathered wooden figureheads, rusted ship tools, and antique maps with curling edges. The scent of aged paper and polished wood filled the air. "Okay," Tilley said, motioning Sarah toward a large exhibit space, "now for the good stuff."

Sarah stepped into a room dominated by a massive glass display case. Inside, relics from Queen Anne's Revenge gleamed under soft lighting—iron shackles, cannonballs, and fragments of the ship's rigging. And at the center of it all, resting on a raised platform, was the ship's bell. She stared at it, taking in the way its bronze surface was pitted and worn by the sea, yet still proud, its engraved letters barely visible beneath the oxidation. “Impressive, huh?” Tilley said, watching Sarah’s reaction.

Sarah nodded. “It’s hard to believe it’s real.”

“Oh, it’s real,” Tilley assured her. “Dated back to the early 1700s. When they pulled it up from the wreck, it was buried under layers of sand and coral, but the engraving was still there.”

Sarah peered closer. Faintly visible in the metal were the words:

IHS MARIA—ANO DE 1705.

“The inscription is Latin,” Tilley continued. “It translates to ‘Jesus and Mary.’ They think it was a prayer for protection, but obviously, that didn't work out too well for Blackbeard.”

Sarah smirked but barely heard the last part of Tilley’s sentence because something else had caught her attention. A photograph. It hung on the wall just beyond the exhibit—a black-and-white image, slightly grainy, depicting a familiar three-story house with a double-porch facade. Hammock House. Sarah’s breath hitched. She stepped closer, her fingers tingling as she read the caption beneath it:

Hammock House, Beaufort, NC. Believed to have ties to Blackbeard.

Her pulse quickened. "Why is this here?" she asked, glancing at Tilley.

Tilley followed her gaze, then shrugged. "Oh, Hammock House? It's rumored that Blackbeard might have owned it at one time."

Sarah's stomach flipped. "Owned it?"

Tilley nodded. "Or at least stayed there for a while. There's no solid proof, but a lot of people believe he used it as a hideout between raids. And some even say his daughter lived there."

Sarah's skin prickled. "Blackbeard had a daughter?"

Tilley smirked. "Supposedly. It's just a legend, but people say she lived in Hammock House long after he was gone. The weirdest part?" She gave Sarah a sideways glance. "Her name was Sarah."

Sarah's blood ran cold. She stared at the photograph, her mind spinning. The house. The ghost. The name. This couldn't be a coincidence. Could it? Sarah tore her eyes away from the photograph, turning to Tilley with a mixture of excitement and unease. "Wait

—Blackbeard's daughter lived there? *And* her name was Sarah?"

Tilley smirked, crossing her arms. "That's what they say. But it's all rumors—no official records prove she even existed."

Sarah's heart pounded. "But why would people think she did?"

Tilley shrugged. "Stories get passed down, especially in a town like this. Some say she was born here, hidden away so no one would connect her to him. Others say she came to Beaufort after his death and lived in Hammock House until she disappeared."

Sarah's skin prickled. "Disappeared?"

Tilley leaned against the wall, her expression amused at Sarah's growing intrigue. "Vanished without a trace. Some say she ran away, others say she was murdered. And—" she paused for effect, lowering her voice slightly, "—some say she still haunts the house."

Sarah's throat went dry.

Tilley grinned. "I could give you the whole wild history of Hammock House, but I have a better idea."

Sarah blinked. "What?"

Tilley pushed off the wall. "You should go on a ghost tour."

Sarah furrowed her brows. "A ghost tour?"

"Yup." Tilley grinned. "My friend Peter runs one. He dresses up like a pirate and gives the best ghost tours in town. He knows every story, every haunted building, every weird legend Beaufort has to offer."

Sarah hesitated. A ghost tour. The idea made her stomach twist—not because she was afraid of ghost stories, but because she had already seen something, and she wasn't sure she wanted to hear other people's versions of the truth when she was still trying to figure out her own. But at the same time… If Peter really knew everything, maybe he had information she wouldn't be able to find anywhere else. "When's the tour?" Sarah asked, keeping her voice casual.

Tilley grinned. "Tonight. 8 PM. It starts near the boardwalk, just past the general store."

Sarah exhaled slowly. "Alright. I'll go."

Tilley gave her an approving nod. "Good choice. Who knows? Maybe you'll even get to meet a ghost up close."

Sarah forced a small laugh, but deep down, she already had. And she had a feeling tonight's tour was going to bring her even closer. Tilley glanced at the clock mounted on the museum wall and sighed. “Alright, I'd better get everything squared away before we open. Can't let my dad think I'm slacking.”

Sarah smirked. “Wouldn't want that.”

“But,” Tilley added, “I'm totally in for the ghost tour tonight. It's been a while since I've gone on one, and honestly, Peter gets way too into character. It's fun to watch.”

Sarah felt a flicker of relief. The idea of going on a ghost tour alone wasn't exactly appealing, but having Tilley there made it feel… easier. “Sounds good,” she said. “I'll meet you at the boardwalk at eight.”

Tilley gave her an approving nod. “See you then.”

Sarah hesitated for half a second before adding, “And… thanks.”

Tilley raised an eyebrow. “For what?”

Sarah shifted her bag on her shoulder. “Just… being cool. I mean, I’ve only been here a day, and I already feel like I have a friend.”

A grin spread across Tilley’s face. “You *do* have a friend. And trust me, you’re gonna need one in this town.”

Sarah chuckled. “Noted.” With that, she turned toward the exit, stepping back into the warmth of the summer morning. Instead of heading straight back to the cottage, Sarah took her time, wandering through the quiet side streets and hidden gardens that wove between the historic homes.

The town was alive in its own way—bougainvillea spilled over wooden fences, bees hovered lazily over patches of lavender, and the scent of salt and flowers mixed in the air. As she walked, she let her fingers skim the tops of the iron gates that lined the narrow alleyways, the cool metal warming under the late morning sun. She had come to Beaufort expecting nothing more than a slow, sleepy summer. Instead, she had found something else— a house with a haunted past. A name that tied her to it in ways she couldn’t explain. A ghost with dark, piercing eyes who had seen her just as clearly as she had seen him. And now, a friend who might be able to help her understand it all. As she stepped up the porch steps of the cottage, Sarah took one last glance back toward town. Tonight, she would hear the stories Beaufort had to tell, but something told her she was already living one of them.

Chapter 13

Back at the cottage, Sarah set her bag down and exhaled, rolling the tension out of her shoulders. She needed to clear her mind. The morning had been… a lot. Between the dream, the photograph, and the eerie coincidence of her name being tied to Hammock House, her brain felt tangled with too many questions, too many connections she wasn't ready to face just yet.

She glanced at the small wooden desk in the corner of her room, where her watercolor supplies sat neatly packed in her travel bag. Yes. That was what she needed. Something normal. Something familiar. She grabbed her supplies—a well-loved travel tin of watercolor pans, a pad of thick cold-pressed paper, and a pencil—before making her way to the front porch.

The air was warm but comfortable, the soft breeze carrying the scent of briny marsh and honeysuckle. Seagulls called in the distance, and the creak of a passing bicycle echoed down the street. She settled onto the wooden steps, resting her supplies on her lap.

Just paint something simple, she told herself. Something easy. Her mind wandered back to the morning—how the sun had caught on the petals of deep pink bougainvillea, how lavender had swayed in the breeze near the market.

Flowers.

Yes, she'd paint those.

She took a deep breath and pressed the tip of her pencil to the paper, but instead of soft petals and twisting vines, her hand moved with a mind of its own. Lines curved into wooden slats. A wide front porch emerged. A set of gnarled trees stretched their limbs, draped with Spanish moss. A shadowed doorway, heavy with time.

Sarah's chest tightened as she lifted the pencil. Hammock House stared back at her from the page. It was exactly as she had seen it in her dream—the darkened windows, the porch stretching like an invitation she wasn't sure she wanted to accept. Her fingers tightened around the pencil. She hadn't meant to draw this. She had barely even thought about it. And yet, somehow, it had found its way onto the paper, as if her hands knew a truth her mind wasn't ready to face. She swallowed, forcing herself to breathe. This wasn't the first time her art had surprised her. Ever since she was little, painting had been more than just a hobby—it had been a way to understand the world, a way to put down feelings she didn't always have words for. And now, her hands had spoken before she could.

She glanced down at the half-finished sketch. Maybe this wasn't just a house. Maybe this was a message. Sarah stared down at the sketch, her pencil still hovering over the page. She should set it aside. She had meant to paint flowers, something light and simple to clear her mind. But now that Hammock House had appeared beneath her hand, unbidden yet deliberate, she felt a pull deep in her chest. She had to see it through. Slowly, she set down her pencil and reached for her travel tin of watercolor pans, flipping it open to reveal rows of soft, well-worn colors. The tin was smudged with old pigment, proof of the hours she had spent lost in her art. Dipping her brush into a small cup of water, she let the bristles soak before pressing them to the pan of Payne's gray—a deep, stormy blue, perfect for shadows. With careful strokes, she pulled the first wash of color across the paper, letting it seep into the grain. The shape of the house darkened beneath her touch, its empty windows deepening into hollow voids. She worked instinctively, as if her hands already knew the path forward. Muted browns and ochres for the aged wood of the porch. Faint strokes of mossy green, capturing the Spanish moss draping from the trees. A soft, eerie glow of pale yellow—just the faintest hint of light—brushing the edges of the sky, as though dawn or dusk lingered on the horizon, uncertain of which way to fall. As she painted, she lost herself in the movement, in the rhythm of color bleeding into water, shaping something that had once only existed in the depths of her mind.

This wasn't just a painting; it was real. It was the house she accidentally wandered to; the one she had dreamed. The house where she had seen him. A shiver traced her spine, but she didn't stop—she couldn't. The brush moved of its own accord now, shaping each shadow, each whisper of wind curling through the trees. The creak of the old wooden porch seemed to echo in her ears, as if the memory of the place had seeped into her fingertips. The final strokes came slower, more deliberate. She deepened the shadows beneath the eaves, darkened the doorway just enough to feel endless, an invitation—or a warning. Finally, she stopped. She exhaled, staring down at the finished painting. Hammock House, exactly as she had seen it in her dream; exactly as she had seen it yesterday.

A heavy silence settled around her. The town's distant sounds—the gulls, the breeze, the occasional passing car—faded, leaving only the quiet pulse of her own heartbeat. Sarah set the brush down beside her. She didn't know what it meant. But she knew one thing for sure: she wasn't done with this house, and it wasn't done with her. She sat back, studying the painting as the last bit of dampness faded from the paper. The colors had settled into the page, the shadows deepened, and the moss swayed with an eerie stillness. It was just a painting—just paper and pigment—yet something about it felt alive as if the house was watching her…like it knew she had seen it.

A cold chill crept up her arms, but she shook it off. She hadn't meant to paint Hammock House, but now that she had, she couldn't bring herself to stop looking at it. She carefully lifted the page, stepping inside and up to her room. The cottage was quiet, her family out on their own morning routines. Sunlight streamed through her window, golden and warm, but it did little to chase away the lingering sensation from the painting. She found a bare spot on the wall beside her bed and grabbed a roll of tape from her desk. Pressing the painting to the wall, she stepped back. Now, whenever she lay down, she would see it. Hammock House.

Maybe it was foolish, but something inside her told her she needed to keep looking at it. To remind herself that what she had seen was real, that it wasn't a dream and that something was waiting for her. She sat on the edge of her bed, staring at the darkened windows she had painted. Tonight, she would go on the ghost tour, and maybe she would finally start getting some answers.

Chapter 14

The cottage was quiet, save for the occasional creak of the old wooden floors and the rhythmic ticking of the kitchen clock. Sarah stood at the counter, slicing a tomato for her sandwich, the knife making soft, deliberate taps against the cutting board. The late afternoon light poured through the window above the sink, casting golden stripes across the counter and warming the tiled floor beneath her bare feet. Her mother had called earlier, her voice cheerful as she invited Sarah to join them for lunch at the beach club.

"Come on, honey, you should get out in the sun! A little vitamin D will do you good."

Sarah had thanked her but declined, offering a half-hearted excuse about wanting to rest. Her mom had sighed but didn't push, saying they'd be back before dinner. Now, as she sat alone at the kitchen table, biting into her simple turkey and tomato sandwich, she let her mind wander. Tonight. The ghost tour. Actively seeking out things that go bump in the night, or stand there in broad daylight, as it were. She still wasn't sure how she felt about it. On one hand, it was a normal thing—tourists took ghost tours all the time, and the stories were just that—stories.

But on the other hand…

Her gaze flicked toward the stairs, where her bedroom door stood slightly ajar at the top of the landing. She didn't have to look to know what was inside. The painting. Hammock House, its image seared into her mind.. A house she had never been to before yesterday. A house she couldn't stop thinking about. A house where she had seen something—someone—that no legend or ghost tour could fully explain. She took another bite of her sandwich, chewing slowly. Did she really want to hear what Peter had to say about it? Or was she afraid that whatever he said might confirm what she already knew deep down? That she hadn't imagined any of it. That the apparition was real, and that he had seen her, too. Sarah exhaled, resting her elbows on the table and rubbing her temples. There was no avoiding it. Something had changed the moment she set foot in this town, and she was no longer sure if she had found the mystery—Or if the mystery had found her. With her head in her hands, she closed her eyes taking in the vision of the house in the hammocks. The sun hung lower in the sky, casting long golden light through the windows as Sarah heard the front door swing open.

"We're back!" her mother called.

Sarah stretched in her chair, closing a book she had been half-heartedly flipping through, and wandered toward the living room. Her mother was setting her tennis bag down near the door, her face flushed from exertion but glowing with post-match satisfaction. Ethan, on the other hand, looked less enthused, kicking off his sneakers before collapsing onto the couch with an exaggerated sigh.

Sarah smirked. "Rough game?"

Ethan groaned. "Mom made me play doubles with some old people. They took it way too seriously."

Her mother rolled her eyes. "They were perfectly nice, and if you'd put in half as much effort as you do in video games, you might have won."

Ethan just grumbled something unintelligible into a couch pillow.

Sarah chuckled before turning to her mom. "I made a friend today."

Her mother perked up. "Oh? That was quick."

Sarah nodded. "Her name's Tilley. Her dad's the curator of the Maritime Museum, and she gave me a little behind-the-scenes tour before they opened. It was pretty cool—tons of old artifacts, shipwreck stuff, even the bell from Blackbeard's ship."

Her mother smiled as she peeled off her tennis visor. "See? I told you this summer wouldn't be so bad."

Sarah hesitated for a beat before adding, "She also invited me to go on a ghost tour tonight."

Her mother raised an eyebrow. "A ghost tour?"

Sarah nodded. "Yeah, her friend Peter runs it. Apparently, he's really into pirate history and knows all the old stories about town. Can I go?"

Her mother hummed in thought, then shrugged. "I don't see why not, as long as you're careful and stick with your friend."

Sarah let out a breath of relief—this was easier than she expected. "Thanks, Mom."

"But—"

Sarah stiffened. There it is.

“You have to bring Ethan with you,” her mother finished.

Sarah’s stomach dropped. “Wait, what?”

Ethan immediately sat up. “No way.”

Their mother gave them both a look that meant the decision had already been made. “It’s a family-friendly tour, isn’t it?”

Sarah opened her mouth, then closed it. Technically… yes.

“You can both use some fresh air, and it’ll be fun,” her mother continued, brushing past Sarah toward the kitchen. “Besides, I think it’s a great way for Ethan to learn more about the town, too.”

Ethan scowled. “Why do I have to go?”

“Because your sister’s not going alone at night,” their mother said simply, rinsing her water bottle in the sink.

Sarah sighed, pressing her fingers to her temples. This was not part of the plan.

Ethan groaned dramatically. “Fine. But I’m bringing my earbuds, and I’m going to listen to Metallica.”

Sarah exhaled in defeat. At least he’d probably tune out most of it.

Her mother turned back to her with a small smile. “You’ll have fun. Just be back by ten, alright?”

Sarah nodded, though her stomach was already knotting with frustration. This was supposed to be her thing, but now, she’d have to spend the evening dragging her younger brother along for the ride. Still, she couldn’t shake the feeling that the night was going to be important. She just hoped Ethan didn’t ruin it. She sighed, but her frustration eased as she glanced at her younger brother. Ethan may have been an unexpected addition to the night’s plans, but the truth was, they got along well—most of the time. Sure, he could be annoying, but he wasn’t that bad. And even though he was younger, his height made him look like he could be the older sibling. He liked to use that to his advantage, standing just a little too close or smirking down at her when he wanted to get under her skin. She rolled her eyes. “Fine. But don’t embarrass me.”

Ethan stretched out on the couch dramatically. “I would never.”

Sarah smirked. “Uh-huh.”

Despite herself, she felt a little better knowing he was coming along. Even if he wasn't particularly interested in the ghost tour, it was nice to have someone familiar by her side. Besides, if anything weird happened, Ethan was the type to brush it off like it was nothing. Maybe that would help keep her grounded. She glanced at the clock—7:30 PM. *Time to get ready*. She had no idea what the night had in store for her, but one thing was certain: this ghost tour was going to be far more than just a tourist attraction.

Chapter 15

The boardwalk was alive with energy. The scent of the sea and Beaufort's culinary delights drifted through the air, mingling with the distant laughter of tourists and the hum of boats rocking in the harbor. As Sarah and Ethan wove through the evening crowd, the sound of excited chatter grew louder. When they rounded the corner near the meeting spot for the ghost tour, Sarah immediately understood why.

A large crowd had gathered, forming a loose semicircle around someone standing in the center. Tilley, who was scanning the area, spotted Sarah and waved at her hurriedly. "Come on!"

Sarah and Ethan made their way toward her, but Sarah's attention was drawn to something else—a single long feather, sticking up from the middle of the crowd like a flag in the wind. It tipped backward slightly, revealing a leather tricorn hat perched atop the head of a very tall, very confident young man.

And beneath that hat—a handsome face, about nineteen or twenty, tanned from the sun, with a roguish kind of charm and a mischievous twinkle in his eyes. He was dressed in early 18th-century clothing, and not in the cheap, costume-y way that most reenactors did. His tunic, once white, was now slightly worn and dingy beneath a gray silk waistcoat finished with brass buttons. His blousy red-and-ivory-striped breeches were tied neatly just below the knee, and he wore white silk stockings tucked into leather boots that looked straight out of a history book. His entire ensemble was so convincingly old-fashioned that for a moment, Sarah wondered if he really had stepped out of another time. His sun-bleached hair fell in loose waves just above his shoulders, framing his strong jawline. But what stood out most wasn't just his appearance—it was the crowd's reaction to him. People were wild for him, laughing and posing for pictures as he struck dramatic pirate-like stances. He looked like a real pirate, and judging by the way he held himself, he loved playing the part.

He had a commanding presence, but not in an intimidating way—more like someone who knew how to hold attention without asking for it. His smile, when he greeted the group, was crooked and warm, and when he caught sight of her, he hesitated—just for a moment. And that was when Sarah felt it, a tug somewhere low in her chest. It was as if a thread had been yanked tight between them, invisible but undeniable. She wasn't used to feeling that around anyone—least of all boys around her age, but Peter was different. He had that same magnetic energy that seemed to pulse through the old streets of Beaufort, something woven from history and sea mist and the weight of unspoken things. She swallowed and looked away, suddenly too warm in the summer air. Tilley grinned beside her and nudged her arm. "That's Peter," she whispered. "He's kind of a local legend." Sarah nodded, but her eyes had already drifted back to him. He moved through the crowd with the ease of someone used to being watched, tipping his hat, offering cheeky comments to a few eager tourists, but every so often, his gaze flicked back to her—measured, curious, maybe even a little startled. And Sarah found herself wondering if he felt it too. That strange familiarity—that pull.

Peter had already spotted her just beyond the edge of the crowd before she saw him—a girl he'd never seen before, yet something about her presence struck him like a sudden shift in the wind. She was standing beside Tilley, her posture slightly reserved, but her eyes sharp and watchful as they scanned the group. Her dark hair fell in soft waves past her shoulders, and the warm light of the streetlamp above cast a soft glow on her skin, making her seem almost ethereal. But it was her eyes that held him—storm-gray, steady, and far older than seventeen.

Time stopped.

For a moment, Peter felt like he wasn't standing in modern-day Beaufort at all, but in another century entirely, staring across a courtyard or ballroom at a girl who had once stolen his heart under candlelight. He blinked, and the moment passed, but the sensation remained. She didn't look like a tourist. She looked like she belonged to the town—or maybe the town belonged to her. It wasn't just her beauty, though that was undeniable. It was something else, something deeper and older. A feeling he couldn't name curled low in his chest, like his heart was recognizing a story it hadn't finished living. He didn't believe in soulmates, not really, and yet, he couldn't shake the sense that he'd seen her before. Or dreamed of her, or possibly waited for her.

Sarah watched him, curious but calm, her expression unreadable. She barely had time to process her first impression before Tilley grabbed her wrist and pulled her closer. "Sarah, Ethan—meet Peter the Pirate."

Peter walked toward them, flashing a broad, self-assured grin. He placed a hand over his heart dramatically. "My dear, I know every face in this town. And yours, I do not." "Alas! You must be the newcomers."

Sarah smirked. "That obvious?" Ethan, who had originally planned to spend the tour drowning out ghost stories with his music, was now standing a little taller, eyes wide with curiosity. Sarah nudged him. "This is my brother, Ethan."

Peter studied him for a moment, then nodded approvingly. "A fine young sailor, I presume?"

Ethan grinned. "I mean, I could be a pirate if I wanted to."

Peter laughed, clapping him on the back. "That's the spirit! Stick with me tonight, lad, and I'll tell you all the secrets of this town." Peter smiled holding Sarah's gaze for a moment as he stepped back to address the crowd "Welcome, brave souls, to the haunted streets of Beaufort! Tonight, we walk the same ground as pirates, lovers, traitors, and the lost…" But as he spoke, his gaze kept drifting back to her.

He cleared his throat and moved into the tour, turning toward an old brick building on Front Street and beginning the first tale of the night. He kept his voice steady, his posture confident—but beneath the surface, something ancient stirred, whispering a truth he didn't know he needed to hear. She wasn't just anyone, and this night wasn't just another one of his tours. Ethan's earbuds—once his escape plan—remained untouched in his pocket. For the first time that evening, Sarah felt her initial reluctance about Ethan tagging along start to fade. This was going to be an interesting night.

The lanterns cast flickering light against the cobblestone streets as the ghost tour officially began. The group, a mix of tourists and locals, huddled together, hanging on to Peter's every word as he wove tales of Beaufort's haunted past. Their first stop was Clawson's Restaurant, a historic building that had once served as a general store in the late 1800s. Peter leaned on his walking stick—a carved wooden piece that looked suspiciously like a repurposed pirate cutlass—and lowered his voice for dramatic effect. "This building has seen many lives—first a general store, then a boarding house, and now a restaurant. But some say… some know… that not everyone who walked through its doors ever left." Sarah glanced at Ethan, who had crossed his arms but was clearly hooked.

Peter smirked at the reaction from the group before continuing. "It started as whispers in the kitchen—pots clanging when no one was there, the sound of footsteps on the second floor, long after closing time. Then came the sightings—a woman in old-fashioned clothing appearing in the upstairs windows."

He paused, his voice dipping lower. "The most famous story? A dishwasher working late one night heard a loud crash from the dining room. He went out to investigate—found nothing out of place—until he turned around." Peter let the silence stretch, his gaze moving across the crowd. "There, standing in the middle of the room, was the figure of a woman—dressed in white, her face hidden by a bonnet. And before he could say a word, before he could even breathe—she vanished."

A ripple of unease went through the group, and someone near Sarah whispered, "creepy".

Peter grinned, satisfied, before tipping his tricorn hat. "That, my friends, is just the beginning."

As the tour wound through the narrow streets of the historic district, the night deepened, and the air grew cooler. The group eventually reached the Old Burial Ground, the final resting place of centuries' worth of Beaufort's past. Tall, weathered headstones jutted from the ground at odd angles, their inscriptions softened by time. A low stone wall surrounded the cemetery, vines creeping up its edges like fingers reaching for the past. Peter led the group down a narrow path, stopping at a particular grave marked by a simple, worn stone. "This," he said, his voice steady but solemn, "is the final resting place of one of Beaufort's most famous spirits." Sarah stepped closer, her pulse quickening. He rested a hand on the wooden grave marker. "Here lies a British naval officer—his name lost to time—who died not far from here, in a duel over a matter of the heart. A tragic misunderstanding, a flash of steel, and just like that—his life was over."

Sarah's stomach tightened. A duel?

Peter continued. "But his story doesn't end there. His dying wish was to be buried standing up—forever saluting his homeland, England." A chill swept over Sarah's skin. She immediately had a sense of familiarity with the story. She had seen him. Peter's gaze moved over the crowd. "To this day, there are those who say they've seen him—standing, watching, waiting." Sarah swallowed hard. She didn't just believe it, she *knew* it was true.

By the time they reached their final stop, the driveway leading to Hammock House, the crowd had thinned slightly—some of the more skittish tourists had quietly slipped away after the burial ground. Sarah wasn't sure if it was the night air or something else, but an unmistakable heaviness settled in her chest as she stared up the long dirt path.

The house loomed beyond the trees, its dark silhouette framed against the night sky. Sarah's breath hitched. It looked far more ominous in the darkness than in broad daylight. Not only did she see it yesterday, but she also saw it in her dreams. Peter's voice, now softer, more serious, carried over the group. "This house—this place—is one of the oldest and most haunted locations in all of North Carolina." The night pressed in around them, the distant sound of the tide lapping against the shore the only break in the silence. Sarah knew what was coming next. She just wasn't sure she was ready to hear it.

The group stood at the end of the long driveway leading to Hammock House, a respectful distance from the private property. The silhouette of the house loomed beyond the trees, partially obscured by the low fog that had begun to creep along the ground, swirling in the dim glow of nearby street lamps. Peter let the silence settle before speaking, his voice quieter now, the weight of the story pressing into the thick, humid air. "Hammock House," he began, tipping his tricorn hat slightly, "is older than this country itself. Built in the early 1700s, it has seen more than its fair share of history—pirates, betrayals, and tragedy." He turned, gesturing toward the darkened house in the distance. "And if you listen closely on certain nights, some say it still holds onto its past." The crowd shifted, some leaning in unconsciously, as Peter continued. "Many stories swirl around Hammock House, but one of the most well-known is the tale of the British naval officer, whom we just visited, where he met his untimely end right here on this property."

Sarah's breath caught in her throat. She already knew how this story ended. She had seen it. Peter's eyes gleamed as he glanced over the hushed group. "The legend says that the officer had fallen deeply in love with a young woman who lived here—a woman of great beauty and even greater misfortune. He swore to return for her after a voyage to the Caribbean, and she promised to wait for him."

A cold shiver ran down Sarah's spine. Peter's voice dropped lower. "But months passed. Then a year. And when the officer finally returned, he pulled out his spyglass from the deck of his ship and looked toward Hammock House—only to see her in the arms of another man." Sarah swallowed hard. "He rushed off his ship and made his way here, blinded by rage and heartbreak. He stormed through that very house, sword drawn, demanding to know who the stranger was." A soft murmur spread through the group. "The other man tried to explain—but the officer would hear none of it. A duel broke out, right inside the house, their swords clashing as they fought through the halls and up the stairs. The British officer drove the fight forward, blade swinging, but in his blind fury, he made one fatal mistake—" Peter paused for effect…"He stumbled." Sarah's breath hitched. "And in that moment—whether by accident or fate—his opponent's sword found its mark. The officer fell, tumbling down the staircase in a pool of his own blood."

The group was utterly silent now. Peter's expression turned grave. "It wasn't until after he had died that the truth was revealed." Sarah already knew what was coming. "The man he fought—the one he saw embracing his love—was not a rival." Peter's eyes flickered toward the house as the fog thickened around the path "It was her brother." A ripple of unease passed through the crowd. "The British officer had killed himself over a misunderstanding. And ever since that night, they say he has never left." A heavy silence stretched between them, the mist curling eerily along the path toward the house. "Some have seen him standing on the porch, his darkened expression frozen in grief and regret." Sarah's heartbeat pounded in her ears. "Others have spotted him near the upper window, gazing out toward the sea, as if still watching… still waiting… still searching for the love he lost." Peter's gaze cast upon Sarah as he spoke those chilling words. A chill swept through her body. She had felt the eyes of the storied specter pierce through her. And now, standing here, she couldn't shake the feeling that—somewhere beyond that fog—he was watching her in this very moment.

As Peter wrapped up the tour, the crowd began to disperse, voices buzzing with excitement and hushed speculation. Some guests took a final glance at Hammock House before shaking their heads and hurrying off into the night, while others lingered just long enough to approach Peter.

"Brilliant storytelling," an older man said, shaking Peter's hand and discreetly slipping him a folded bill. "Felt like I was there."

"Best ghost tour I've ever been on," a woman added, grinning as she passed him a tip.

Peter accepted each compliment with an easy, roguish charm, thanking them as if he were a seasoned performer at the end of a well-rehearsed show. Sarah, Ethan, and Tilley stood off to the side, waiting as the last of the crowd drifted away. Finally, when it was just the four of them, Peter turned to Sarah and Ethan, tilting his head curiously. "Well? What'd you think?"

Sarah hesitated, feeling the weight of what she had just heard. She wasn't sure what to say—because the story wasn't just an eerie legend to her. It was real, and she had seen it with her own eyes. Ethan, however, had no such hesitation. "That was awesome," he said, his excitement clear. "Like, I knew this town had history, but I didn't think it would be that cool."

Peter chuckled. "I do my best."

Tilley smirked. "He lives for this, you know."

Peter placed a hand over his heart in mock offense. "Madam, I am but a humble historian, merely sharing the tales of old." Sarah managed a small smile, but her mind was still spinning. Peter noticed her hesitation and raised an eyebrow. "And you, Sarah? What did you think?"

She swallowed, choosing her words carefully. "It was… a lot to take in."

Peter studied her for a moment, as if sensing there was more she wasn't saying. Then, with a knowing glint in his eye, he said, "Yeah. That one always gets people." Sarah wasn't sure if he meant the story—or something else, because even though the tour was over, she had the distinct feeling that her connection to Hammock House—and Peter- was only just beginning.

The night air was cool as Sarah and Ethan walked side by side, the sound of their footsteps blending with the distant rhythm of waves against the docks. Peter and Tilley walked alongside them, the four moving through the quiet streets of Beaufort under the glow of antique lamplight. Ethan, still energized from the tour, turned to Peter. "So, how'd you even get into doing ghost tours? You seem way too into it."

Peter smirked. "Ah, my young lad, you wound me. This is not mere enthusiasm—it is a calling."

Tilley snorted. "A calling?"

Peter ignored her and continued. "I've always loved storytelling, and when I arrived in Beaufort, I met another reenactor who introduced me to the historic ghost tours. It turned out to be the perfect fit—a way to meet people, entertain the masses, and leave a lasting impression."

Ethan grinned. "So, basically, you like being the center of attention."

Peter gasped in mock offense. "I live to educate, dear boy." Sarah chuckled despite herself. Peter was dramatic, sure, but there was something genuine about him—an ease in the way he carried himself, as if he belonged in every era of time at once.

As they reached the white picket fence of the rental cottage, Sarah and Ethan turned to face their companions. “Thanks for tonight,” Sarah said, meaning it. “It was… interesting.”

Tilley smiled. “Come by the museum in the morning. I’ll be there all day if you need something to do.”

Sarah nodded. “I will.”

Ethan, still clearly impressed, reached out to shake Peter's hand. At the last second, he slipped him a small tip, mimicking what he had seen the other tour guests do earlier. Peter glanced down at the money, then back at Ethan, his grin widening. “A fine young gentleman indeed.” With a theatrical flourish, Peter took a step back, tipping his tricorn hat dramatically, “I do hope to meet your acquaintances again very soon.” His eyes flickered toward Sarah, his expression amused yet unreadable. The glint in his gaze lingered just a second too long, as if he knew something she didn’t. Sarah held his gaze for a beat before offering a small smile. Then, with a final bow, Peter turned on his heel and disappeared down the street, his silhouette fading into the flickering lamplight. Sarah let out a breath she didn’t realize she’d been holding.

“Well,” Ethan said, pushing open the gate. “That guy is something else.” Sarah couldn’t argue with that.

But something about the way Peter had looked at her—like he saw her soul—made her stomach twist in ways she couldn't quite explain. As she and Ethan stepped inside, Sarah had the distinct feeling that this wasn't the last time their paths would cross, and she wasn't sure if that thought thrilled her or terrified her.

Chapter 16

Peter wasn't entirely sure what had just happened. He made his way back through the quiet streets of Beaufort, the cicadas humming in the trees overhead, the scent of brine and gardenias wafting on the breeze. The town had gone still in that sleepy, magical way it always did once the tourists had cleared out, and the moon had taken over the sky. He exhaled slowly, pulling off the tricorn hat and running a hand through his hair. He usually shed the character of "Peter, the Gentleman Pirate" as soon as the tour ended—like shaking off a coat—but tonight something had stuck. Something had shifted. He'd told the story of the duel at Hammock House the way he always did—dramatic, engaging, cloaked in myth and mystery. But as he walked through the night air now, it was no longer just a story. It had changed. She had changed it.

He thought of the British naval officer—the man who had sailed halfway around the world, heart full of longing, only to glimpse the woman he loved in the arms of another. Peter had always told that story with flair, with suspense, with a hint of tragic romance. But now, for the first time, he understood it. He could see it —feel it. The shock, the heartbreak, the blind, fiery rush to protect what was once his. He pictured Sarah standing in the moonlight, her gray eyes searching his face with quiet curiosity. The way she spoke—soft but certain. The way she listened, the way she observed Hammock House, taking it all in, like she already knew it.

He felt that same strange pull in his chest again. The same whisper of recognition. Peter wasn't necessarily a believer in fate. He believed in the wind and tide, in history and hard work. But tonight, something had cracked open in him. And whether he wanted to or not, he was starting to believe that some stories—the important ones—never really ended—they just waited, for someone to come along and finish them.

Chapter 17

The cottage was quiet. Ethan had already disappeared into his room, shutting the door behind him with a tired thud. Their father was still out on the boat, and their mother was somewhere downstairs, reading or watching TV. But for Sarah, sleep was the last thing on her mind. She moved through the dim hallway, the soft glow of her bedside lamp casting long shadows as she stepped into her room and closed the door. And there, on the wall above her desk, was the painting.

Hammock House.

Even in the low light, the watercolor looked exactly as she had seen it—the heavy wooden door, the long swaths of Spanish moss hanging from the trees, the darkened windows that seemed to stare right back at her. She swallowed. Tonight had confirmed what she had already known in her bones. The British officer wasn't just a story. She had seen him. And now, as she stood in her quiet room, she couldn't shake the feeling that this was only the beginning. Her mind replayed

Peter's words: Some have seen him standing on the porch, his darkened expression frozen in grief and regret.

Sarah wrapped her arms around herself, rubbing at the goosebumps rising on her skin. Had he been waiting for something? Or for someone? She turned from the painting, pulling back the covers and slipping into bed. The sheets were cool against her legs, the faint scent of sea air drifting through the open window. She tried to push the thoughts away—tried to tell herself it was just a coincidence—just a story. But deep down, she knew better. With one last glance at the painting, she switched off the lamp. Darkness settled over the room, and as she lay staring at the ceiling, listening to the distant sound of waves lapping against the docks, thoughts whispered through her mind. What if he wasn't just a random ghost? What if he wanted something from her? And with butterflies forming in the pit of her stomach, she thought about Peter—the warmth that rose up her cheeks when his eyes met hers for the first time. With that thought circling her restless mind, Sarah finally drifted off to sleep.

Chapter 18

The warm scent of freshly baked bread filled the cottage, wrapping around Sarah like a comforting blanket as she stepped into the kitchen. Her mother stood at the counter, slicing into a golden, crusty loaf, steam curling into the air as the knife pressed through the soft center. A jar of homemade preserves sat nearby, along with a small plate of butter. Sarah slid onto a stool at the kitchen island, inhaling the familiar, cozy aroma.

"Morning," her mom said without turning around. "Sleep well?"

Sarah hesitated. "Yeah."

Her mom gave her a knowing look over her shoulder. "And? How was the ghost tour?"

Sarah shrugged, reaching for a piece of bread. "It was interesting. Good stories."

Her mother smiled, clearly amused by her nonchalance. "Mm-hmm. Just stories?"

Sarah nodded, tearing off a piece of warm bread and popping it into her mouth.

Her mom chuckled. "Well, I'm glad you had fun."

Sarah chewed slowly, her mind drifting to the end of the tour, the heavy mist curling around Hammock House, the eerie weight of Peter's words hanging in the air. She shook the thought away.

Instead, she asked, "Can I take some of this to Tilley at the museum? I figured she might like some fresh bread and coffee."

Her mother brightened at the suggestion. "That's a lovely idea."

She quickly began packing a small basket, wrapping the bread in a linen cloth, and pouring coffee into a thermos. She added a few extras—a small jar of honey, a handful of blueberries from the fridge. Sarah watched, a soft warmth filling her chest. Her mother had always loved sharing food as a way of showing care. As she secured the lid of the basket, her mom glanced at her. "Oh, before I forget—Ethan's signed up for sailing lessons at Gallant's Channel today. He'll be gone for most of the day."

Sarah raised an eyebrow. "Since when does Ethan sail?"

Her mom laughed. "Since I told him he needed a hobby that wasn't video games."

Sarah smirked. At least he'd be occupied for the day. She finished her last bite of bread, then grabbed her bag, tossing in her art supplies along with the basket. "I think I'll try to find somewhere inspiring to paint," she said as she slung the bag over her shoulder.

Her mom smiled. "Sounds like a perfect way to spend the day. Have fun, sweetheart."

Sarah nodded and headed for the door. As she stepped outside, the summer air was bright and warm, the scent of salt and blooming flowers drifting through the breeze. With the basket in hand, she made her way toward the Maritime Museum, already wondering what the day had in store for her. She adjusted the strap of her bag as she walked, the basket of fresh bread and coffee swinging lightly in her grip. She could have taken the shorter route straight to the museum, but something pulled her in another direction. Instead, she turned down Ann Street, her pace slowing as she approached the Old Burial Ground. It looked different in the daylight—yet somehow, no less eerie.

The low-hanging Spanish moss swayed gently in the humid breeze, draping from the twisted branches of the ancient oak trees like ghostly curtains. The iron gate stood slightly ajar, its hinges rusted with time. A narrow dirt path wound through the graveyard, weaving between tilted headstones, some so old that their inscriptions had been worn away completely. Others leaned at odd angles, pushed up by the thick roots of the oaks, nature reclaiming what time had abandoned. Sarah swallowed as she stepped just past the gate, her gaze sweeping the rows of weathered markers until she found it.

His grave. The British officer's final resting place.

Even in the soft glow of morning, it felt heavier than the others, as if the weight of his unfinished story still pressed into the earth. Her chest tightened. The night before, she had barely been able to process the legend Peter had told. But now, standing here, she couldn't ignore the truth. She had felt his presence, his gaze, his sorrow. And now she stood before the place where he had been buried—standing upright, forever saluting a country he would never return to. Sarah exhaled slowly, shifting the basket in her hands. What was she even looking for? A sign? A feeling? A whisper of the past? Nothing happened. No flicker of movement, no ghostly figure appearing beyond the trees. Just silence. And yet…the air felt thick here, like a story waiting to be told. Sarah took a small step back, suddenly aware of how long she had been standing there. She shook off the lingering unease, turning back toward the road. The museum was waiting, and she had a feeling Tilley might have more answers than she realized.

The Maritime Museum was already buzzing with activity when Sarah arrived. The doors stood open, inviting in the morning visitors—families with excited children, older couples taking their time, and the occasional history enthusiast moving with quiet purpose. Inside, the air was cool compared to the thick summer heat outside, carrying the scent of aged wood and briny sea salt. At the front desk, Tilley sat with a stack of scavenger hunt maps, her bright expression never wavering as she handed them out to eager kids bouncing on their toes.

"Alright, pirates!" she said, grinning as she passed a map to a boy wearing a plastic pirate hat. "Find every item on this list, and you'll win a piece of Blackbeard's lost treasure!"

The boy's eyes widened. "Real treasure?"

Tilley lowered her voice conspiratorially. "Pirate treasure." She slid a small gold coin across the desk—a lightweight replica of an old Spanish doubloon. The boy's face lit up before he dashed off into the museum, waving his scavenger hunt map like a treasure map.

Sarah smirked as she stepped forward. "Are you getting a cut of this operation?"

Tilley looked up, grinning. "I wish. We'd be rich by now." She waved her hand at the museum's entrance. "Every kid that walks in here thinks they're about to uncover a chest of buried gold. And who am I to tell them otherwise?"

Sarah chuckled and held up the basket. "I brought you something."

Tilley's eyes brightened. "Ooooh, what's this?"

Sarah set the basket on the desk and pulled back the cloth, revealing the still-warm bread, a thermos of coffee, and a small jar of honey. "My mom made the bread this morning," Sarah said. "I thought you might like some."

Tilley gasped dramatically. "You are officially my favorite person." She immediately grabbed the thermos, twisting the lid off and inhaling the scent of fresh coffee. "Oh, bless you."

Sarah smiled, but her mind was still lingering on the morning's detour of the burial ground and on the British officer's grave. She kept thinking about how the air had felt heavy—expectant—as if something was waiting.

Tilley must have noticed something in Sarah's expression because she paused, setting the thermos down.

"Alright," she said, leaning on the desk. "You look like you've got something on your mind. Spill."

Sarah hesitated. Should she tell her about the grave? About the way she had felt standing there, or should she keep it to herself—at least for now? She hesitated for only a moment before deciding—Tilley needed to know. But not here. Not in front of the scavenger-hunting kids or the parents watching from the exhibit hall. As if sensing the shift in Sarah's demeanor, Tilley gave her a small nod. "Hang tight." She turned toward the woman now approaching the front desk—an older lady with bobbed white hair, slightly windblown, and wearing a navy-and-white striped sweater that looked like she had knitted herself. A gold anchor was stitched proudly onto the front. Sarah liked her instantly.

"Mrs. Adkins," Tilley greeted warmly. "You're a lifesaver."

Mrs. Adkins gave a knowing smile. "Go on, dear. I'll take it from here."

Tilley wasted no time, grabbing the basket from the counter and motioning for Sarah to follow. Sarah trailed behind her as they slipped down the museum's dimly lit hallways, past the exhibits, and toward the cozy library tucked away at the back of the building. Tilley shut the door behind them, sealing them away from the rest of the museum.

"Alright," she said, setting the basket down on the wooden table. "What's up?"

Sarah exhaled, steadying herself as she helped unpack the goodies. They set the bread, honey, and thermos of coffee between them, each pouring a cup before sitting down. For a brief moment, Sarah stared into the dark liquid, the faint scent of roasted beans and fresh-baked bread filling the quiet space. Then she looked up at Tilley. "I need to tell you something," she said, her voice just above a whisper. "But you have to promise—this stays between us."

Tilley's expression shifted, all teasing gone. She leaned forward, resting her elbows on the table. "You have my word."

Sarah took a deep breath, and then she told her everything. From the moment she first saw the British officer at Hammock House, to the dream that followed, to the pull she felt toward the Old Burial Ground that morning—right up to the unnerving heaviness that settled over her at his grave. When she finally finished, the library was silent. Tilley didn't speak right away. She simply sat there, fingers wrapped around her coffee cup, brow furrowed in deep thought. Then, after a long moment, she finally said, "Well... that's a hell of a thing."

Sarah let out a breath, half a laugh, half relief. "Yeah."

Tilley drummed her fingers against the table. "Okay. First question—are you sure you weren't just... imagining it? I mean, the ghost tour was spooky, and you were probably thinking about it a lot."

Sarah shook her head. "No. This was real. I saw him before the tour. Before I even knew his story."

Tilley nodded slowly. "Yeah, that's what I thought you'd say."

Sarah studied her. "You believe me?"

Tilley smirked, taking a slow sip of coffee before answering. "I believe that this town is full of things people can't explain." And from the way she said it, Sarah got the distinct impression that this wasn't the first time Tilley had heard something like this.

Tilley leaned back in her chair, eyes flicking toward the bookshelves that lined the cozy library. She tapped her fingers against her coffee cup, as if weighing something in her mind. Sarah waited, curiosity flickering to life. Finally, Tilley sighed. "Alright. If I'm gonna tell you this, you have to promise not to think I'm crazy."

Sarah raised an eyebrow. "I just told you I saw a ghost, and you're worried I'm going to think you're crazy?"

Tilley smirked. "Fair point." She took another sip of coffee, then set the cup down with a quiet clink. "So… this museum? It's haunted."

Sarah blinked. "What?"

Tilley nodded. "Not in the spooky-tourist-gimmick way. I mean, actually haunted."

Sarah leaned forward, intrigued. "By who?"

Tilley exhaled, staring into her cup. "No one knows for sure. But people say it's a sailor." A chill brushed over Sarah's skin. Tilley continued. "I've worked here since I was a kid—my dad being the curator and all. Spent a lot of time in this building after hours, sometimes completely alone." She hesitated before adding, "But I wasn't really alone." Sarah's pulse quickened. Tilley glanced toward the door, as if checking to make sure no one else was listening. Then, in a quieter voice, she said, "I've heard footsteps. Heavy boots on wooden floors when no one else is here. Things moving when I know I left them in one place. The sound of ropes creaking, like a ship shifting in the water." Sarah swallowed. Tilley's voice grew even softer. "But the first time I really knew something was here… was in the exhibit hall."

Sarah barely breathed. "What happened?"

Tilley smirked, but there was a flicker of unease in her eyes. "I was about thirteen, helping my dad close up one night. He was in the back office, and I was doing a final walk-through of the exhibits before locking up. Everything was fine—quiet, normal." Her fingers tapped against the wooden table. "And then… I heard whistling." Sarah's breath hitched. "A slow, shanty tune," Tilley said. "Low and deep. The kind of whistling you'd hear from an old sailor standing at the bow of a ship." A shiver ran down Sarah's spine. Tilley's smirk faded. "I froze. I knew I was the only person in the exhibit hall. But the whistling kept going, clear as day, drifting through the room like someone was standing right behind me."

Sarah exhaled slowly. "What did you do?"

"I turned around," Tilley said. "And, of course, no one was there."

Sarah's fingers tightened around her coffee cup. "Did you tell your dad?"

Tilley nodded. "Yeah. And you know what he said?" Sarah shook her head. Tilley smirked, but there was something else behind it—something thoughtful. "He just said, 'You'll get used to it.'"

Sarah blinked. "So… he knows?"

"Oh yeah," Tilley said, stretching her arms over her head before settling back down. "He's worked in this museum for over twenty years. If you ask him, he'll just say, 'The sailor doesn't bother me, so I don't bother him.'" Sarah let that sink in. "So," Tilley said, raising an eyebrow, "if you think you're the only one who's seen something in this town? Trust me—you're not."

Sarah exhaled, her nerves settling just a little. She still didn't know why the British officer had appeared to her, but at least now, she knew one thing for certain: She wasn't alone in this. Sarah sat back in her chair, absorbing Tilley's words. "So, you just… live with it?" she asked. "Knowing something's here?"

Tilley shrugged, taking another sip of coffee. "Yeah. I mean, at first, it freaked me out, but after a while…

you get used to it. It's not like the sailor ever hurt anyone. He's just—" she searched for the right word, "—there."

Sarah frowned. "But why do you think he's still hanging around?"

Tilley tilted her head thoughtfully. "Could be unfinished business. Could be he just likes it here. Maybe he never really left the sea, and this place—this museum—feels the closest to home."

Sarah shivered slightly. It was one thing to hear ghost stories, but it was another thing entirely to think of them as… people. "Is it just the museum?" Sarah asked. "Or is the whole town like this?"

Tilley smirked. "Oh, Beaufort's full of ghosts. You've heard of the British officer and Blackbeard's daughter, but there are plenty more." She paused, then grinned. "You know Mrs. Adkins? The lady who covered for me at the front desk?" Sarah nodded. "Well, her house is haunted, too."

Sarah blinked. "You're kidding."

"Nope. And not just by any ghost—a ghost dog."

Sarah's eyebrows shot up. "A dog?"

Tilley nodded, clearly enjoying Sarah's reaction. "Mrs. Adkins lives in one of the oldest houses in town. People say that back in the 1800s, the owner had this big, loyal dog—some kind of mastiff or hunting hound. When the owner died, the dog refused to leave his grave. It stayed there until it died, too."

Sarah felt a pang in her chest. "That's… kind of sad."

Tilley nodded. "Yeah. But here's where it gets weird. People started seeing the dog—even hearing it—long after it was gone."

Sarah tilted her head. "Like how?"

"Well," Tilley said, "Mrs. Adkins swears that some nights, she hears scratching at the door—like something wants to come inside. But when she opens it, there's nothing there." Sarah felt another chill run down her spine. "And sometimes," Tilley continued, "when she's walking home, she hears footsteps behind her—but it's not a person. It's four footsteps. Like paws, padding along the sidewalk. When she turns around? No one's there. But sometimes, if the streetlights are just right, she'll see a shadow of a dog standing next to her."

Sarah swallowed. "And she just… lives with that?"

Tilley shrugged. "She says it doesn't bother her. If anything, she thinks the dog's protecting her. Like it just… found a new owner." Sarah sat with that thought for a moment. "So, you see?" Tilley said, finishing off the last sip of her coffee. "Most people in Beaufort don't question the ghosts. They just coexist."

Sarah exhaled slowly. That was what unsettled her the most—not that ghosts existed, but that they were just… a part of life here. Like the tide. Like the wind. Like something constant, always there, whether you wanted it to be or not.

Tilley leaned forward, resting her elbows on the table. "So, now that you know all this… let's talk about Hammock House." Sarah straightened. If people in this town lived alongside ghosts—if some spirits just lingered because they wanted to—then maybe…maybe the British officer wasn't just waiting. Maybe he was trying to tell her something. Tilley stood, brushing off her hands as she walked toward one of the tall wooden cabinets lining the library walls. "If we're going to figure this out," she said, pulling open a drawer, "we need to start with the facts." Sarah watched as Tilley sifted through a stack of old property records, yellowed copies of the town's earliest deeds and transactions. "My dad keeps copies of all the old property deeds here," Tilley explained. "Mostly for research, but also because people love digging into their family histories.

Sometimes, we get visitors who find out their ancestors owned half the town."

Sarah leaned forward as Tilley pulled out a few carefully preserved documents. The edges were frayed, the ink faded, but still readable. Tilley spread them out on the table, pointing to one in particular. "This is the original deed for Hammock House," she said. "Built in 1700."

Sarah studied the delicate script, running her fingers lightly over the parchment. The house had been standing for over three centuries—longer than the country itself. Tilley pulled out another record, tapping her finger against the name scrawled at the bottom. "Around 1716, it was sold to E.R. Thatch, paid for in gold."

Sarah's pulse quickened. "Thatch? As in—"

Tilley nodded. "Blackbeard." A wave of goosebumps flooded over Sarah's skin.

Tilley pulled another deed from the pile, her voice turning thoughtful. "Here's where it gets interesting. The deed was transferred in late 1718 to Capt. Benjamin Thatch—believed to be Blackbeard's son." Sarah stared at the document. 1718—the year Blackbeard was killed at Ocracoke. And there, written in elegant script, was the name: Capt. Benjamin Thatch, brother of Sarah Thatch. Sarah inhaled sharply. Tilley glanced at her. "You see where I'm going with this?"

Sarah nodded slowly, her mind racing. If Sarah Thatch lived at Hammock House, and her brother, Capt. Benjamin Thatch inherited it after Blackbeard's death, then the British officer who died there—the man who had been killed in a duel of mistaken identity—might have died fighting Blackbeard's son. Sarah's heartbeat pounded in her ears. If that was true, then the story she had been told wasn't just a ghost story; it was history. And the ghost wasn't just waiting, he was waiting for an answer to *why*.

Tilley's fingers froze over the stack of documents, her breath catching as she pulled out a thin, yellowed file labeled:

AUCTION ITEMS – HAMMOCK HOUSE

Sarah glanced up from the property deeds, watching as Tilley flipped the cover open, her eyes scanning the contents. "What is it?" Sarah asked, her curiosity piquing. Tilley didn't answer right away. She squinted hard at something inside the file—then her eyes went wide. Slowly, she turned the folder toward Sarah, tapping a grainy, poor-quality photograph attached to a typed auction list. Sarah leaned in—and her breath caught in her throat. It was an old oil painting, listed among furniture, antique décor, and other heirlooms from Hammock House. The caption beneath the small photo read:

Portrait of a Young Woman, Colonial-Era. Oil on Canvas. Sold to Mr. Robert T. Davis, Harkers Island – $1,000.

But it wasn't just any young woman. Sarah's heart skipped a beat, because staring back at her from the faded, sepia-toned image was a face that looked exactly like hers. Her own wide eyes, the same shape of her lips, the familiar slope of her nose—the resemblance was undeniable. It was like looking in a mirror. Sarah felt a chill creep over her skin. Tilley's voice was barely above a whisper. "Sarah… this is you."

Sarah swallowed, trying to push down the wave of unease rising in her chest. "It can't be."

Tilley looked from the picture to Sarah, then back again. "It is."

The silence stretched between them. Sarah's fingers trembled slightly as she traced the faint outline of the portrait on the page. Who was she? And why was her face—her exact face—captured in a painting from over 300 years ago? Her heart pounded as she read the buyer's name again.

Mr. Robert T. Davis, Harkers Island.

Tilley cleared her throat, trying to steady her voice. "We need to find that painting." Sarah nodded slowly, her pulse still racing because something told her that portrait held more answers than they ever could have expected. The world around Sarah tilted slightly, a strange buzzing filling her ears—not just the hum of summer insects, but something deeper, something inside her mind. She gripped the edge of the table, trying to steady herself.

"Whoa, okay," Tilley said, immediately noticing. "Let's get you some air." Before Sarah could protest, Tilley grabbed her hand and guided her swiftly through the back door of the museum. The door creaked open, and they stepped out into the quiet parking lot, where the scent of warm pavement and blooming flowers mingled with the salty air. They sat on the curb, backs to a white picket fence that surrounded one of the many public gardens scattered throughout town. Sarah focused on the bees flitting between the flowers, their gentle hum seeming louder than usual, filling her head in a strange, rhythmic pulse. She took a deep breath, willing the uneasy feeling to settle. Tilley glanced sideways at her. "Better?"

Sarah let out a slow breath. "Yeah. Just… needed a second."

Tilley nodded. "I get it. That was a lot."

Sarah stared at her hands, still feeling the lingering tingle of recognition—not just from the portrait but from something deeper, something she couldn't yet name. Tilley gave her a light nudge with her shoulder. "C'mon. Let's shake this off. I'll grab my stuff, and we'll walk down to the boardwalk. Fresh air, boats, maybe even ice cream. Sound good?" Sarah nodded, grateful for the distraction because no matter how hard she tried to steady herself, she couldn't shake the feeling that finding that painting was only the beginning. And that whatever mystery had started the moment she stepped into Beaufort—It wasn't done with her yet.

Chapter 19

As Sarah and Tilley crossed the street from the museum, the world opened up around them. The sights and sounds of Taylor Creek filled the air—the hum of boat engines, the lapping of water against wooden pilings, the distant chatter of tourists wandering along the waterfront. The public dock was packed, every boat slip was occupied—sailboats with billowing canvas covers, sleek fishing boats with rods standing tall, and towering yachts that seemed almost out of place in the rustic charm of Beaufort.

On the creek itself, the water was alive with movement. Boaters drifted lazily, their laughter carrying across the surface. Kayakers paddled smoothly, gliding between the anchored vessels. Further out, stand-up paddleboarders balanced carefully, making their way toward the barrier island just across the creek. The town buzzed with summer energy, alive with the excitement of visitors taking in the historic charm and salty air. Sarah inhaled deeply, letting the ocean breeze carry away some of the heaviness lingering from earlier.

Then, something caught her eye. Beyond the line of boats, farther down the shoreline of the island across the creek, a small cluster of vessels floated near a stretch of golden dunes, and just beyond them, something moved. Sarah squinted. "What's everyone looking at over there?"

Tilley followed her gaze, then grinned. "Oh! Those are the wild horses of Carrot Island."

Sarah blinked, watching as a group of horses—the ones she saw when she first came into town—moved gracefully along the beach. "They're so cool!"

"Yep," Tilley said. "They've been here for centuries. People say they're descendants of Spanish mustangs from the 1500s. Some think their ancestors swam ashore after a shipwreck, others think they were left behind by early explorers."

Sarah's eyes stayed locked on the majestic creatures as they grazed on the seagrass, their manes ruffled by the wind. "Wow," she murmured. "They don't even seem to care about the boats."

"They don't," Tilley said with a chuckle. "They've seen humans come and go for generations. As long as people keep their distance, they're fine."

Sarah let her gaze linger on the wild horses, something ancient and untamed about them striking a chord deep inside her—a mystery of their own. Something left behind by time, surviving in a world that had changed around them…just like the ghosts of this town. She exhaled, letting the moment settle over her. For the first time since she had seen the portrait in the museum, her mind wasn't spinning. For now, she could just exist in the present. And somehow, that felt like exactly what she needed. The wind had shifted slightly, bringing a salty breeze down Taylor Creek as Sarah and Tilley sat on the waterfront bench, sipping their cold drinks. The rhythmic sounds of the harbor surrounded them—the creak of dock lines, the soft slap of waves against hulls, the distant squawk of seagulls circling overhead.

Tilley leaned back, enjoying the warmth of the sun on her face, but something in the distance caught her attention—a tall wooden mast, its maroon gaff-rig sail billowing slightly even as the wind calmed. A dinghy—larger than the average skiff but smaller than the modern sailboats moored nearby—was making its way down Taylor Creek, coming from the direction of Radio Island. The boat's varnished wooden hull gleamed in the late morning light, rocking gently as it cut through the channel. Tilley squinted toward the cockpit, where two figures moved with practiced ease. Her mouth curved into a knowing smile. "Looks like we might have company," she said, nudging Sarah. Sarah followed her gaze, watching as the dinghy approached. The person at the tiller was steering with confidence, following the natural bend of the creek—but what caught Sarah off guard was who it was. Ethan.

Her younger brother, usually more interested in his phone or video games, was sitting on the transom, hands steady on the tiller as he guided the boat with careful precision. His expression was focused, determined—maybe even a little thrilled. And standing at the bow, gripping the mast for balance, was Peter. Sarah felt a smile tug at her lips as he shifted his stance, his tall frame rocking easily with the motion of the boat.

His blousy pirate breeches billowed slightly in the breeze, tied just below his knees, but this time no silk stockings or leather boots, just bare, tan, muscular legs and feet. His loose linen tunic, already sun-bleached from wear, flared as he adjusted his stance. A red life jacket was buckled across his chest—an amusingly modern touch against his otherwise historic ensemble. And, of course, his tricorn hat remained firmly in place, tilted at a jaunty angle as he surveyed the dock.

As they neared, Peter grinned and waved.

"Ahoy, mateys!" he called, his voice carrying easily over the water.

Sarah rolled her eyes, but she couldn't help but laugh.

Peter turned back to Ethan, shouting something over the sound of the wind. Ethan nodded, shifting slightly as he prepared to come about. Peter dropped back into the cockpit, his movements fluid as he loosened the halyard, dropping the maroon sail halfway down the mast to reduce their speed.

Sarah could hear the slight creak of the rigging as Ethan carefully turned the tiller.

Under Peter's guidance, Ethan brought the boat around in a controlled arc, angling toward the dock with surprising ease.

Sarah exchanged a glance with Tilley.

Ethan looked like a natural.

"Not bad," Tilley murmured, impressed.

As they approached the dock, Peter released the sheet, causing the sail to luff slightly, slowing them further. With one final adjustment, Ethan guided the dinghy smoothly alongside the dock, bringing it to a perfect stop. Peter leapt onto the dock with practiced ease, moving quickly to tie off the bowline, securing the boat, and Ethan followed, stepping onto the dock with a confidence Sarah hadn't seen in him before.

Sarah smirked, crossing her arms. "Well, look at you, Captain Ethan."

Ethan grinned, still flushed with excitement. "Pretty cool, huh?"

Peter clapped a hand on Ethan's shoulder. "The lad's a natural."

Sarah arched a brow. "All you need now is your own pirate ship."

Peter chuckled. "One step at a time."

Ethan, still buzzing with adrenaline, turned to Sarah and Tilley. "So, what have you two been up to?"

Peter studied them, his usual smirk shifting into genuine curiosity.

Sarah and Tilley exchanged a look, the weight of their secret pressing between them. They had been caught up in a discovery that might change everything. And now, they had to decide whether to let Peter and Ethan in on the mystery.

Peter tilted his head, studying Sarah and Tilley with a mix of curiosity and intrigue. "Alright, you two are keeping secrets, and I don't like it. Spill."

Ethan, still grinning from the excitement of sailing, crossed his arms. "Yeah, what's going on?"

Sarah glanced at Tilley, then back at Peter. "It's… a lot."

Peter smirked. "I love 'a lot.'"

Tilley exhaled, rubbing the back of her neck. "Then you're going to need food for this."

Peter's face lit up. "Now that is something I can get behind."

Sarah chuckled, already feeling some of the tension from the morning fade.

"Royal James?" Tilley asked.

Peter beamed. "You read my mind."

The Royal James Café was Peter's favorite haunt, a local dive known for its no-frills, greasy-but-delicious burgers—easily some of the best on the Crystal Coast. It was the kind of place that was both a local favorite and a hidden gem, where the burgers were fresh, the pool tables were worn from years of play, and the history was practically baked into the wooden barstools. The four of them started making their way toward the café, the scent of grilled food and fried hushpuppies already drifting through the warm summer air.

Inside, it was exactly as Sarah expected—dimly lit, casual, and comfortably loud. The walls were covered with old photographs, ship wheels, and nautical memorabilia, making the place feel like it had been pulled straight from another time. Peter led them toward a booth in the corner, sliding in like he owned the place. Ethan followed, while Sarah and Tilley slid in on the opposite side.

A waitress—who clearly knew Peter well—arrived at the table with a smirk. "The usual, Captain?"

Peter grinned. "You know me too well, Marcy."

She jotted something down on her notepad, then glanced at the rest of the group. "Y'all getting the same, or are you feeling adventurous?"

Sarah glanced at Tilley. "If the burgers are as good as he says, I'll trust the usual."

"Same," Ethan added.

Marcy gave a satisfied nod. "Good choice. I'll get 'em right out."

As she walked away, Peter leaned forward, resting his elbows on the table. "Alright, now that we have food coming, let's get back to the important part—what the hell is going on?"

Sarah exchanged one last look with Tilley before finally saying, "We found something. Something big."

Peter's grin widened, but Sarah could tell there was real curiosity behind it. "Do tell."

Sarah took a breath. "You know how we were talking about Hammock House on the tour?"

Peter nodded, waving his hand for her to continue.

"Well…" Sarah hesitated. "It's not just a ghost story to me."

Peter's eyebrows lifted slightly. "Go on."

Ethan frowned. "Wait, what do you mean?"

Tilley jumped in. "She saw the British officer, Ethan. Before the tour. Before she even knew his story."

Ethan's jaw dropped slightly. "No way."

Sarah nodded. "Yeah. And that's not all."

Peter leaned in, clearly hooked now. "What else?"

Tilley pulled out the auction file she had tucked into her bag, flipping to the faded photograph of the colonial-era portrait.

She slid it across the table toward Peter and Ethan.

Peter picked it up, his eyes narrowing as he studied the grainy image. And then—his expression changed.

Ethan's brows furrowed as he leaned over Peter's shoulder. "Wait…"

Peter looked from the photo to Sarah, then back again. "This is you," he said, his voice quieter now.

Sarah exhaled. "Yeah."

Ethan's face scrunched in confusion. "But how is that possible? That painting is old."

"That's what we're trying to figure out," Tilley said.

Peter studied the caption beneath the photo, reading aloud. "Purchased by Robert T. Davis of Harkers Island for one thousand dollars."

He set the paper down carefully. Then he met Sarah's gaze, his usual playfulness tempered with something more serious now. "Well," he said, drumming his fingers on the table. "I'd say it's time we pay Mr. Davis a visit."

The conversation around the Royal James Café booth shifted between silence and speculation as they processed the painting. Sarah watched as Ethan leaned forward, still staring at the grainy auction photo like the answer might suddenly jump off the page.

"I mean," Ethan finally said, rubbing the back of his neck, "it's probably just... I don't know. A coincidence?"

Tilley snorted. "A coincidence?"

Ethan shrugged. "Okay, yeah, it's weird. But maybe it's just, like, one of those things where people look like someone from history."

Sarah sighed, twisting the paper wrapper of her straw into a knot. "That's what I want to believe.

But…" She tapped the paper. "This isn't just some random portrait in a museum. It came from Hammock House."

Peter had been quiet, which was unusual for him. He sat back, arms crossed, his golden-brown hair slightly tousled from the wind. His tricorn hat was tilted on the edge of the booth, and his fingers absently tapped the wooden table. When he finally spoke, his voice was thoughtful. "You know," he said, "I've heard a lot of ghost stories in this town, but I've never heard of someone finding themselves in a painting before."

Sarah sighed. "Great. Super comforting."

Peter smirked, but then shook his head. "Jokes aside, this is next-level stuff. The question is… what do we do about it?"

That hung in the air for a moment. And then, as if sensing they needed a break from the heavy mood, Peter turned to Ethan with a broad grin.

"But before we get into all that—can we take a moment to appreciate what an outstanding student your brother is, Sarah?"

Sarah blinked. "What?"

Peter clapped Ethan on the back. "I mean, did you see him out there today? Natural at the helm! I'm thrilled to watch this boy's sailing career take off!"

Ethan grinned proudly, puffing out his chest. "Not bad, huh?"

Sarah laughed. "Okay, okay. Congrats, Captain Ethan."

Ethan nodded seriously. "Thank you, thank you."

Peter leaned back, looking satisfied. "I mean, I'm just saying—it's nice to meet someone else who understands the art of the sea."

Sarah smirked. "And I suppose that means you do, too?"

Peter waggled his brows. "You suppose? Sarah, I live it."

She studied him for a moment, taking in his windswept appearance, the easy confidence in the way he moved, and—most interestingly—the silver coin on a chain around his neck.

It was worn and smooth, but the markings were unmistakable—it looked like a piece of treasure.

Sarah tilted her head. "Alright, Captain. What's your story?"

Peter's smirk deepened. "Ah, so you're interested?"

Sarah rolled her eyes. "You just made me sit through a speech about Ethan's great sailing potential. Fair's fair."

Tilley chuckled, while Peter tapped the edge of his coin, as if weighing where to begin.

"Well," he said, "it's a long tale, but I'll keep it simple. I come from a long line of sailors and watermen."

Sarah leaned in slightly. "Like, how long?"

Peter grinned. "Generations. My fifth great-grandfather lived in Montreal, where he had a foundry and a steamship line. A tug, which he built and operated, was the first sea-going vessel to reach Montreal. It proved that the St. Lawrence River was navigable to ocean-going vessels, making the port in Montreal an important shipping hub for the Midwest. My grandparents ran a sailing charter out of St. Thomas for years—real, old-school types. Salt in their veins, wind in their souls. They retired here in Beaufort."

Sarah nodded, intrigued. "And your parents?"

Peter smirked. "That's where it gets interesting. My mom and dad met in college, and after both graduating with degrees in historic preservation, they moved to Mackinac Island in Michigan's Upper Peninsula to help run the Grand Hotel."

Sarah raised a brow. "Wait—the Grand Hotel? Like, the fancy one with the giant porch?"

Peter mock gasped. "You know it?"

Sarah shrugged. "I mean, it's kind of famous."

Peter smirked. "Well, imagine growing up there—a giant, historic hotel on an island with no cars, just horses and bikes—tourists everywhere, history around every corner. It was actually pretty amazing."

Sarah could almost picture it—a childhood surrounded by water, old stories, and the kind of history people spent their lives chasing.

"But the winters?" Peter added. "Miserable. Frozen lakes, nothing to do, everything shut down. I started feeling like I was just waiting for my life to start."

Sarah watched as he fiddled with the silver coin again, his expression turning slightly distant.

"So," he continued, "when I turned 18, I told my parents I was done with the cold. I wanted to chase the sun."

He grinned, shaking off whatever thought had crossed his mind. "I already knew how to sail—been doing it since I was a kid. So, I refitted a small cabin boat and made my way down to Beaufort to stay with my grandparents. Figured I'd stay a little while, see where the wind took me."

Ethan, clearly impressed, leaned forward. "So… what's next for you?"

Peter's grin faltered just slightly.

For the first time, he didn't have an immediate, flashy response. Instead, he exhaled, tapping his fingers against his glass. "That," he said, "is the real question, isn't it?"

Sarah studied him, noticing the way his fingers lingered on the silver coin—like a nervous habit—Like he was holding onto something—A piece of history. A piece of himself. Before she could ask more, Marcy returned, setting down a tray of burgers and fries.

"Here you go, troublemakers."

Peter brightened immediately, the heavier moment slipping away as he rubbed his hands together. "Perfect timing, Marcy. You always know how to save the day."

She rolled her eyes. "Just don't start a food fight."

Peter held up his hands. "I make no promises."

As they dug into their meals, Sarah let the conversation drift, but her mind was still turning. The portrait. The house. And now, Peter's silver coin. She didn't know why—but something told her there was more to his story than he was letting on. And maybe, their stories were about to intertwine in ways neither of them expected. She wiped the salt from her fingertips and leaned forward, her eyes settling on the apparent treasure resting against Peter's chest.

"Alright," she said, gesturing to it. "I have to ask—what's the deal with the coin?"

The coin Peter wore around his neck was more than just an accessory—it was a piece of history, a tangible fragment of a world long gone. It hung from a worn leather cord, the edges of the strap darkened by sea air and time, soft from years of wear. The coin itself was a heavy, solid piece of Spanish silver, irregular in shape, its edges rough and uneven—evidence that it had once been part of a larger treasure hoard before being clipped and circulated.

The surface of the coin was weathered, yet the bold stamp of Spanish authority was still visible despite centuries beneath the sea. On one side, the faint outline of the cross of Jerusalem could be seen, divided into four quadrants, each filled with the heraldic lions and castles of Castile and León. Around the edges, remnants of the original Latin inscription curled in an uneven arc, though the letters had been softened by time.

The reverse bore the Pillars of Hercules, two towering columns with banners twisting around them—symbols of Spain's dominance over the New World trade routes. Between them, traces of the word "PLVS ULTRA"—meaning More Beyond—could still be made out, a testament to the age of exploration when Spain believed there was no limit to its empire's reach.

The coin's patina held a dull, aged luster, not the bright shine of newly minted silver, but something richer—a whisper of shipwrecks and lost fortunes, of salt water and secrets buried beneath the sea.

Peter never took it off.

Sarah had noticed it before, dangling just above the collar of his tunic when she first saw him. But now, under the golden lights of the Royal James Cafe, the coin caught the light in a way that made it look almost alive, glinting like a sliver of the past refusing to be forgotten.

Peter glanced down, as if he'd almost forgotten it was there. He rubbed his thumb across the smooth surface, his usual playful smirk fading into something more thoughtful. "This," he said, lifting it slightly so the light caught the aged markings, "is from the Atocha wreck."

Sarah's brow furrowed. "Wait—the Nuestra Señora de Atocha? The Spanish galleon that sank off the Florida Keys?"

Peter's grin returned, impressed. "Didn't take you for a shipwreck buff."

"We just studied it in European History class last semester," Sarah admitted. "The Atocha is one of the most famous treasure finds ever."

Tilley perked up, interest sparking in her expression. “Okay, now I’m curious. How’d you get your hands on that?”

Peter twirled the leather cord between his fingers. “It’s a family heirloom, in a way.”

Ethan raised an eyebrow. “You’re saying your family found the Atocha?”

Peter laughed. “Not exactly. But they helped.”

Sarah tilted her head. “How?”

Peter leaned back, stretching his arms over the booth before diving into the story: “My grandparents spent years sailing through the Caribbean, running charter expeditions out of St. Thomas. They got to know a lot of divers, treasure hunters, and old-school seafarers—including the one and only Mel Fisher.”

Sarah’s eyes widened. “THE Mel Fisher?”

Peter nodded. “Yep. The guy spent 16 years searching for the Atocha’s mother lode. He went broke more than once, fought the government over treasure claims, and lost people along the way. But he never stopped looking.”

Tilley whistled. “That’s dedication.”

Peter smirked. “Or insanity. Probably both.” He tapped his finger against the coin. “Thing is, treasure hunting isn't cheap. You need money for boats, equipment, permits… My grandparents believed in the project and used their connections to help find donors to keep it going."

Sarah listened intently, fascinated.

Peter's voice took on a proud note. "When Fisher finally found the mother lode in 1985—more than 400 million dollars in gold, silver, and emeralds—he gifted my grandparents a couple of Atocha silver coins as thanks." He held up the coin, letting it glint in the dim light of the café. "This one?" he said, grinning. "It was my granddad's."

Sarah felt a strange thrill run through her.

A piece of history, a real treasure, worn smooth from centuries beneath the sea, now resting around Peter's neck. It suited him, in a way. Something about him always felt like he belonged between worlds—part present, part past.

Ethan, still processing, shook his head. "So you're literally walking around with pirate treasure."

Peter chuckled. "Pretty much."

Tilley smirked. "Explains why you fit in so well here."

Peter winked. "Born for it."

Sarah tapped her fingers against the table, still turning it all over in her mind. A lost Spanish treasure. A ghostly British officer. A portrait of herself from centuries ago. They weren't connected. Not yet. But something about Peter's past, his connection to shipwrecks, and their shared fascination with lost history made her feel like their paths had crossed for a reason. And maybe this mystery was about to pull them all in deeper than they ever expected. Sarah took another sip of her drink, still intrigued by Peter's story.

"So, what do your grandparents do now?" she asked, watching as he absentmindedly turned the Atocha coin between his fingers.

Peter leaned back in the booth, smirking. "Still living their best lives, just in a slightly different way." He tapped the table. "My grandmother? She's a master gardener. Has a plot in the historic district, and people come from all over to admire her roses. Like, full-on gardening royalty—I'm talking newspaper articles, fancy competitions, the whole thing."

Tilley snorted. "My parents are always talking about her garden. Your grandma's roses are envied far and wide."

Peter grinned. "She does take them pretty seriously."

Sarah smiled at the thought—a woman as fiercely dedicated to flowers as treasure hunters were to lost gold.

“And your grandfather?” she asked.

Peter’s expression softened slightly. “He volunteers over at the maritime boat-building workshop, just across the street from the museum. Helps teach classes building traditional wooden boats, stuff like that.”

Sarah raised an eyebrow. “Wait—the museum has a boat-building workshop?”

Tilley nodded. “Yeah, it’s part of their living history programs. They teach people how to build old-style boats using the techniques that would have been used in the 18th and 19th centuries.”

Peter smirked. “And that, dear Sarah, is how Tilley and I first met.”

Sarah’s eyebrows lifted slightly as she turned to Tilley. “Really?”

Tilley rolled her eyes but grinned. “Yeah. It was a couple of summers ago. Peter’s granddad was running a small dinghy-building class, and Peter was assisting. I was one of the students.”

Peter nodded. “She was the best in the class—though I might have been a little biased, considering she’s the curator’s kid.”

Tilley elbowed him. “I was better than you.”

Peter clutched his chest. "Wounded."

Sarah smirked, looking between them. "So, you've known each other for a while, then."

Tilley nodded. "Yeah, and obviously, Peter being Peter, he immediately got involved with all the pirate reenactments and ghost tours."

Peter grinned. "What can I say? I like a little flair."

Sarah chuckled, shaking her head. But inside, she was still processing how interwoven everything was—how her new friends were deeply rooted in this town, its history, and its mysteries. And now, somehow, she was being pulled into it, too.

The conversation drifted for a moment, but then Peter tapped the table, his smirk fading slightly as he brought them back to the real reason they were here.

"Alright," he said, leaning forward. "Let's talk about Mr. Davis."

Tilley nodded. "Right. We know he bought the portrait at auction, and if we want answers, we need to find out where it is now."

Peter drummed his fingers against the wood. "The name Robert T. Davis sounds weirdly familiar to me."

Sarah perked up. "Really?"

Peter nodded. "Yeah. But Harkers Island is small—even smaller than Beaufort. Everybody knows everybody over there, so it's not that surprising."

Ethan frowned. "So what's the plan?"

Peter thought for a second, then grinned. "I'll ask my grandfather. He's been around here long enough, and if this guy is from Harkers Island, there's a good chance he'll know something."

Sarah exhaled, feeling a tiny flicker of hope. If they could track down the painting, maybe they'd get closer to figuring out why it existed in the first place—and what it meant for Sarah and the ghost of the British officer.

Tilley nodded. "Good. And in the meantime, I'll see if I can dig up any other auction records from Hammock House. Maybe something else was sold that could help us."

Peter clapped his hands together. "Alright, we have a plan! Now all that's left is—" He looked at Sarah with a teasing smirk. "—for you to prepare for the possibility that you're actually a time-traveling ghost girl."

Sarah threw a crumpled napkin at him. "Very helpful, Peter."

Peter laughed, dodging it easily.

But as the joking faded, Sarah sat back, staring down at the faded auction photo of the portrait. Because despite Peter's teasing…She wasn't convinced he was entirely wrong.

The salty breeze drifted through the waterfront as they stepped out of the Royal James Café, the sounds of the harbor filling the air once again. Peter stretched, letting out a contented sigh. "Nothing like a burger to fuel an afternoon at sea."

Ethan grinned. "You mean me at the helm while you stand around pretending to be a pirate?"

Peter smirked. "Semantics."

Sarah rolled her eyes. "Just put on more sunscreen, Ethan. You know Mom will lose it if you come back looking like a lobster."

Ethan groaned but dug into his bag, pulling out a bottle of sunscreen. "Fine, fine."

Together, they made their way back to the dock, the varnished and polished hull of Peter's sailing dinghy shifting slightly in the breeze as the tide moved beneath it.

Peter hopped aboard first, expertly untying the dock lines, while Ethan climbed in and took his place at the tiller. Sarah and Tilley stood on the dock, watching as Peter adjusted the sail, the wind catching it just enough to make the boat lurch slightly.

Ethan grinned over at Sarah. "See you later, Captain's Sister."

Sarah smirked. "Don't crash."

Peter gave them a theatrical salute as the dinghy drifted away from the dock, then caught the wind, picking up speed.

"Fair winds and following seas, ladies!" Peter called.

Sarah shook her head with a small laugh, watching them sail smoothly back out into Taylor Creek.

Tilley turned to her, tucking her hands into her pockets. "I've got to get back to the museum and man the front desk for the rest of the afternoon."

Sarah nodded. "Hopefully, you'll find more about Hammock House?"

Tilley smirked. "You might not know me that well yet, but I always find something." She hesitated, then added, "Until then, you should wander the shops. Maybe stop by the Olde Towne Chandler. It's one of my favorites."

Sarah arched an eyebrow. "The candle shop?"

Tilley gave her a knowing look. "Oh, it's much more than just a candle shop."

Sarah frowned, intrigued, but before she could ask more, Tilley stepped back onto the boardwalk. "I'll text you when I'm off," she called over her shoulder.

With that, they parted ways—Tilley heading toward the museum, and Sarah turning toward Front Street, the idea of the Olde Towne Chandler lingering in her mind. There was something about the way Tilley had said it—like the shop held secrets of its own, and after everything that had happened that day, Sarah had a feeling it wouldn't just be another ordinary afternoon on vacation. She gazed back at the water, Peter's sailboat picking up speed and heading back toward the mouth of the creek. In that moment, her heart fluttered slightly, and she felt inspired to capture her feelings with her paintbrush. She took a seat on the bench by the public dock beneath the live oaks and started painting a new memory she never wanted to forget. With a few loose strokes, a little sailboat with a maroon sail started to take shape on the page.

After her painting dried, long after Peter and Ethan sailed out of sight, she packed up her supplies and embarked on her next task. Sarah walked along Front Street, the sound of the harbor blending with the distant hum of conversation and the occasional chime of a shop's door opening. She wasn't in a rush. The Olde Towne Chandler lingered in the back of her mind, but something about wandering the historic district felt right. The uneven brick sidewalks, the colonial-era buildings, the salty air—everything felt timeless here, as if history was always just beneath the surface, waiting to be uncovered. But then, something caught her attention.

At first, she didn't know what had pulled her focus. She had been passing a small antiques shop, its window filled with weathered maritime artifacts—brass compasses, old ship wheels, faded navigational maps. But her eyes locked onto something deeper inside the store. A glint of silver. She stopped in her tracks.

Through the dimly lit interior, past the cluttered shelves, something in a glass display case had called to her. Sarah hesitated, then stepped inside, the old wooden floor creaking beneath her. The scent of aged books and something faintly metallic filled the space as she made her way toward the case.

And there—sitting among pocket watches, rings, and other relics—was a silver locket.

It was intricately designed, the edges smoothed with age, the metal bearing faint markings that looked strangely familiar. Sarah's fingers hovered over the glass. Why did it feel like she had seen it before?

The shopkeeper, an older man with thin-rimmed glasses and a neatly pressed vest, stepped up beside her. "Ah," he said, following her gaze. "That one's been here a long time."

Sarah swallowed. "Do you know where it came from?"

The shopkeeper nodded. "Estate sale. Some items from one of the old houses around here. Can't recall which one off the top of my head, but—" he adjusted his glasses, studying her for a moment, "—you look like you've seen it before."

Sarah's pulse quickened. Had she? She couldn't shake the feeling of recognition coiling in her chest. And something told her…this locket was connected to the mystery she had just started unraveling.

"I'll take it, please," she said.

The tiny bell above the shop door chimed softly as Sarah stepped out onto the brick sidewalk, her newly purchased locket resting in the palm of her hand. She turned it over carefully, her fingers tracing the delicate engravings on the back.

S.T.

Her heartbeat quickened. She had a feeling she already knew what the initials stood for.

Sarah Thatch.

She swallowed, her breath catching as she turned the locket over once more and gently popped it open. Inside, beneath the thin glass cover, was a small lock of hair, faded with age. The shopkeeper's words echoed in her mind.

"It was common back then. A memento… something to keep of someone special."

Sarah inhaled sharply. This wasn't just a random piece of old jewelry. It had belonged to someone. And if the initials meant what she thought they did, it had belonged to the girl in the painting—to the girl who looked exactly like her. Her fingers tightened around the locket as a rush of unease and fascination swept through her. This mystery—the portrait, the house, the ghost, the British officer's death—was only pulling her deeper, and now, she held another piece of the past in her hands…one that felt far too personal to be a coincidence. She tucked the locket into her pocket, and as she looked up, there he was! And as quickly as he appeared, he disappeared. Sarah's breath caught in her throat.

She knew what she had just seen. The flash of dark leather boots, the glint of brass buttons, the movement of a figure vanishing around the corner at the end of the alley.

It was him.
The British officer.

The same one who had stared at her from the porch of Hammock House. Her body reacted before her mind could catch up.

Go.

She took off down the alley, her feet slapping against the brick, her heart hammering against her ribs. She turned the same corner he had just disappeared behind—and stopped. Nothing. The narrow side street was completely empty, the only movement coming from the swaying Spanish moss hanging from the overhanging oak trees. No footsteps. No sign of anyone. Just silence. She spun in a slow circle, her pulse still racing.

He had been right there.

Hadn't he?

She swallowed, reaching into her pocket and clutching the locket tightly in her palm. The moment she touched it, a strange sense of recognition swept through her. A whisper of something just out of reach, something deeply familiar. She exhaled shakily and looked up toward the street ahead. The Olde Towne Chandler wasn't far now. And suddenly, she had a feeling that stopping there wasn't just a suggestion from Tilley anymore; it was a necessary step in whatever was unfolding around her. Taking one last look at the empty alley behind her, Sarah turned—and continued toward the candle shop.

Chapter 20

Sarah stood just outside the Olde Towne Chandler, her hand hovering over the iron handle of the door. For some reason, she hesitated. The air around the shop felt… different. Not in a bad way. Not in the way Hammock House had felt—heavy, unsettling, thick with an unseen presence. This was something else entirely—something older, something aware. Sarah swallowed, then exhaled slowly. *Just go in.*

She pushed the door open, and a small brass bell jingled overhead. The moment she stepped inside, the scent of beeswax, dried herbs, and something faintly smoky—like burning wood and spices—wrapped around her like a blanket. The shop was dimly lit, lined with wooden shelves overflowing with candles in glass jars, bundles of dried lavender, shelves of old books, and small bottles of what looked like hand-blended oils. It felt ancient and cozy at the same time, like stepping into a place that had existed just like this for centuries. Behind the dark wooden counter, a woman looked up. Sarah nearly took a step back—not because she was frightening, but because she was… unexpected.

The woman was middle-aged, dressed in billowy black clothing that draped around her like flowing smoke. Her dark hair was pulled into a messy, loose bun, with small sprigs of herbs and flowers woven into it as if she had been gathering them moments before and forgotten they were there. Despite her dark, witchy aesthetic, her face was warm, her eyes sharp and knowing, her smile welcoming.

"Well now," she said, her voice rich with curiosity and amusement. "I wondered when you might find your way in here."

Sarah blinked.

"What?" she asked cautiously.

The woman's smile deepened, but she didn't explain. Instead, she simply gestured toward the shop around them. "Come in, dear," she said. "I think you might find something here that was waiting for you all along."

Sarah stepped forward, her fingers still unconsciously gripping the locket in her pocket. Because somehow… she had a feeling the woman was absolutely right. Sarah let the shopkeeper's words settle, but instead of responding, she glanced around the shop, letting her feet guide her forward. The Olde Towne Chandler was unlike any store she had ever stepped into.

It was small but overflowing with history, each item carefully placed as if it belonged exactly where it had been set down—whether that had been yesterday or a hundred years ago. Shelves lined the exposed brick walls, packed with hand-poured candles, each labeled with delicate handwritten tags:

"Storm-Tossed Cedar"
"Sea Witch's Blessing"
"Fog Over the Dunes"

Sarah ran her fingers lightly along the edges of the jars, breathing in scents of salt, smoke, and wild herbs. Dried bundles of lavender, rosemary, and sage hung from the ceiling beams, swaying ever so slightly with the draft from the open door. A wooden table near the window displayed small leather-bound journals, antique keys, and tiny bottles of deep green and cobalt blue glass, filled with oils that carried mysterious names like:

"Moonlit Currents"
"Hearth and Home"
"Ebb Tide"

Sarah picked one up, rolling it between her fingers, the glass cool against her skin. There was something about this place that made her feel like she had stepped through time, like she was meant to find something here. She glanced toward the shopkeeper, who was now quietly sorting a row of tea tins behind the counter, seemingly unconcerned with Sarah's silence—as if she already knew Sarah would speak when she was ready.

Sarah exhaled slowly, finally letting go of the locket in her pocket. Then she turned back toward the counter. Because if anyone in this town might have answers about what was happening to her, she was willing to bet it was this woman.

Sarah took one last look at the shelves before finally making her way toward the counter. The shopkeeper glanced up from her quiet task of arranging tea tins, her eyes warm with expectation—as if she had been waiting for Sarah to finally speak. Sarah hesitated only for a moment before resting her hands lightly on the wooden counter.

"This place is… incredible," she said, her voice quiet but genuine. "I've never seen a shop like this before."

The woman's lips curled into a knowing smile. "That's because there isn't another shop like this."

Sarah smirked slightly, running her fingers over the smooth wooden surface of the counter. "How long have you been here?"

The woman tilted her head, as if considering how to answer. "The shop itself? Since long before my time. But me? I've been running it for a while now."

Sarah nodded, glancing at the candles, the old books, the dried herbs hanging from the rafters. "Did you always sell… all of this?"

The woman chuckled. "Not always. Places like this evolve over time—just like the people who pass through them."

Sarah studied her. There was something about the way she spoke—something layered beneath her words, as if there was more meaning than what she was actually saying. She looked down at the glass bottles of oil on the counter.

"These," she said, picking one up. "What are they for?"

The shopkeeper's eyes twinkled. "Depends on who's asking."

Sarah raised an eyebrow.

The woman leaned forward slightly, her voice playful but pointed. "Some people buy them for the scent. Some use them for rituals and intentions. Some simply feel drawn to them without knowing why."

Sarah swallowed, rolling the small bottle between her fingers. She hadn't realized until now, but she did feel drawn to this place. She set the bottle down carefully.

The shopkeeper watched her closely, then smiled again. "You're not just here to browse, are you?"

Sarah exhaled, feeling that strange, electric pull in her chest again.

“No,” she admitted. “I think… I’m looking for answers.”

The shopkeeper’s smile didn’t fade. Instead, she simply nodded.

“Well then,” she said, placing her hands gently on the counter. “Why don’t you tell me what it is you’re trying to find?”

Sarah exhaled slowly, her fingers brushing against the locket still tucked safely in her pocket. She wasn’t sure why, but standing here—in this dimly lit shop that smelled of wax, herbs, and something older than time itself—she felt like she could trust this woman. She pulled the locket from her pocket, holding it in her palm for a moment before carefully setting it down on the counter.

“I bought this a few minutes ago,” she said, her voice quieter now. “Something about it… I don’t know. It felt familiar.”

The shopkeeper’s eyes flicked to the locket, her expression unreadable as she reached forward, gently picking it up. Her fingers brushed across the engraved initials—S.T. She didn’t react right away, just studied it, running her thumb over the smooth, timeworn surface.

Sarah watched, feeling like she was holding her breath, though she wasn’t sure why.

Finally, the woman looked back up at her, those sharp, knowing eyes locking onto hers.

"And have you figured out why it feels familiar?"

Sarah swallowed.

"Maybe."

And just like that, everything spilled out of her.

She told the woman everything—about seeing the British officer on the porch of Hammock House, about the ghost tour, about finding the painting at the museum, and how the girl in the portrait looked exactly like her. She told her about the auction records, about Robert T. Davis, about the strange, unsettling pull she felt toward this mystery—as if she was being guided toward something she didn't yet understand.

The shopkeeper listened, silent and still, fingers still resting lightly on the locket.

When Sarah finally finished, her pulse was racing. She had just told a complete stranger everything. And yet, she didn't regret it.

The woman exhaled softly, her expression thoughtful, unreadable.

Then, she finally spoke.

"Well," she murmured, her voice carrying an undeniable weight. "It sounds like the past is calling you, my dear." She turned the locket over once more, brushing her fingers along the engraved initials. "And I have a feeling," she added, "this isn't the only thing that's found its way back to you."

Sarah's heart skipped a beat. Because deep down… She knew the woman was right.

The shopkeeper held the locket between her fingers, turning it over carefully, almost reverently. Sarah felt a strange weight settle in her chest, anticipation pressing against her ribs. The woman's eyes flicked up to meet hers.

"This isn't just any locket, Sarah," she said softly. "This was made to hold onto something—someone." She tapped a fingernail lightly against the glass window inside, where the small lock of hair rested beneath its delicate casing.

"A memento," Sarah murmured, remembering what the antiques dealer had told her.

The shopkeeper nodded. "A mourning locket. In the past, when someone lost someone dear to them, they would keep a piece of them close—woven into jewelry, pressed into keepsakes, locked away in something precious enough to last lifetimes."

Sarah's fingers twitched. "So… this belonged to someone grieving?"

The woman nodded slowly. "And if I had to guess—" she turned the locket back over, running a finger across the engraved initials—"the one who mourned was likely the one whose initials are carved here."

Sarah's throat tightened.

S.T.

Sarah Thatch.

Her mind raced. If Sarah Thatch owned this locket, and it held a piece of someone she lost…Then whose hair was inside? Before she could voice the question, the shopkeeper spoke again.

"You said the British officer appeared to you at Hammock House."

Sarah nodded, pulse quickening.

The woman exhaled slowly, tapping the locket once more.

"Perhaps this belonged to her—to Sarah Thatch. And perhaps, inside it, she carried a piece of the man she lost."

Sarah's stomach dropped. The British officer. The man who had died in that house. Could it be—? She reached for the locket instinctively, her fingers trembling slightly as she clutched it in her palm.

The shopkeeper studied her closely, her voice gentle but firm.

“The past doesn’t always stay buried,” she said. “Sometimes, it finds its way back.”

Sarah swallowed hard. Because the truth was—It already had.

The shopkeeper let Sarah sit with the weight of her words for a moment before finally extending her hand.

“I believe introductions are in order,” she said with a small smile. “My name is India Reed.”

Sarah shook her hand, her mind still swirling. “Sarah.”

India chuckled softly. “Yes, I know.”

Sarah blinked. There was something about the way she said it—not just an acknowledgment of her name, but something deeper, as if India had known more than she was letting on. Sarah hesitated, then asked, “You said the past doesn’t always stay buried. Does that mean you believe in all of this? Ghosts? The idea that… that something is trying to find me?”

India gave her a knowing look, then walked around the counter, motioning for Sarah to follow her deeper into the shop.

Sarah followed as India stopped beside an old wooden table stacked with leather-bound journals and aged parchment maps, placing her hand gently on the surface.

"There is an old story," India said, her voice soft but deliberate, "one that has been whispered through time, passed down in fragments."

Sarah swallowed, suddenly certain she was about to hear something she wasn't sure she was ready for.

India continued, "You know of the duel at Hammock House, yes?"

Sarah nodded. "Peter told it on the ghost tour."

India sighed. "Then you know how it ends."

Sarah's stomach twisted. "The British officer was killed," she murmured.

"Yes," India said. "But he died before he ever knew the truth."

Sarah felt her breath catch.

India's fingers traced the grain of the table. "The man he fought—his supposed rival—was not another suitor."

Sarah already knew where this was going. "It was Sarah Thatch's brother," she whispered.

India nodded. “He never lived long enough to understand his mistake. He died believing that the woman he loved had betrayed him.”

The words hit Sarah harder than she expected. She looked down at the locket in her hand, its small weight suddenly feeling monumental. “If this belonged to Sarah Thatch,” she said slowly, “and if she was mourning him… then maybe…” She couldn’t finish the sentence.

India did. “He may be showing himself to you because he thinks you are her.”

Sarah’s heart pounded in her chest.

India’s voice was gentle, but firm. “If you bear her face, it’s possible his spirit, still lost in time, believes that you are his long-lost love. And after centuries of waiting, he may be yearning to be reunited with her in the afterlife.”

The thought terrified her. And yet… A part of her ached at the tragedy of it. A soul, trapped in grief and longing, forever searching for something just out of reach, and now, he had found her. Sarah’s grip on the locket tightened, her mind still reeling from everything India had just told her. The specter in the hammocks thought she was Sarah Thatch. He was seeking something—maybe her, maybe peace—but he was still wandering, lost in the echoes of time. She swallowed hard. “What… what am I supposed to do?”

India studied her for a long moment before stepping around the counter and leaning against the wooden table. "You have a very special gift, Sarah," she said, her voice calm but firm. "One that few possess—the ability to see into another world."

Sarah felt a chill creep up her spine.

India continued, "Not everyone can see what you see. Not everyone can feel the weight of the past pressing against the present." She gestured to the locket in Sarah's hand. "That's why these things find you."

Sarah's pulse pounded in her ears.

India's expression softened slightly. "But you must understand, while this is a gift, it can also be dangerous."

Sarah frowned. "Dangerous how?"

India exhaled. "Opening yourself up to the spirit world doesn't just mean you can see those who are lost. It also means they can see you."

Sarah's stomach twisted.

India's voice dropped slightly, a warning laced in her tone. "Not all spirits are kind, Sarah. Some may wish you harm. Some may try to use you for their own unfinished business. And some… may not even be what they appear to be."

Sarah's fingers tightened around the locket. "So what do I do?"

India's gaze met hers, unwavering. "You must be very careful in how you choose to use your gift. Just because a spirit calls to you, does not mean you have to answer."

Sarah swallowed, the weight of India's words pressing down on her. Something told her this wasn't the last time the British officer would appear to her. Perhaps next time, knowing what he died believing, he might be more threatening.

India moved with quiet certainty, guiding Sarah through the back of the shop.

Sarah followed, her eyes adjusting to the dim light as they passed cauldrons, drying herbs, shelves lined with jars of unknown contents, and bundles of dipped candles hanging from the low rafters. The air was thick with earthy scents—lavender, rosemary, something slightly smoky—but none of it felt overwhelming. Instead, it felt ancient, intentional. India reached the back door, pushing open the creaky screened entrance that led to a small enclosed garden. Sarah stepped outside, blinking as the warm summer air pressed against her skin.

The garden was lush and orderly, each patch of green carefully labeled with handwritten markers. Some plants Sarah recognized—basil, thyme, chamomile—

while others had names she'd never seen before. India walked toward the fence line, where a patch of vibrant green leaves grew in a neat cluster. She reached down, pinching off a small sprig, then turned and pressed it into Sarah's palm. "Sage," she said simply. Sarah glanced down at the soft, velvety leaves, rolling them between her fingers. The scent was strong and unmistakable. "It's one of the most powerful herbs for protection," India continued. "But not just any sage—this kind must be fresh. The moment it dries, it loses its strength, and more must be pinched to renew the protection." Sarah looked up, the weight of the moment settling over her.

India met her gaze, serious now. "Carry it with you. Keep it close. If you ever feel that something isn't right—if a presence feels too strong or too… wrong—crush a few leaves in your hand. The energy will shift, and whatever is near will know it's not welcome."

Sarah swallowed, nodding. Deep down, she knew this wasn't just advice; it was a warning. Something was coming, and whether she was ready or not, she had to be prepared. She stood in the quiet garden, the fresh sage leaves still resting in her palm, their scent grounding her in the present. Everything India had told her—the warnings, the truths, the history she was now tangled in—felt like too much to process at once. She inhaled deeply, trying to steady her thoughts. But just as she was beginning to collect herself, her phone buzzed in her pocket. She pulled it out and saw a message from Tilley:

Hey! Gotta head home to help Mom with dinner —company coming over. Let's catch up tomorrow!

Sarah exhaled slowly, staring at the screen for a moment before typing back:

Sounds good. Talk soon!

As soon as she hit send, she glanced back toward India, who was watching her with quiet understanding.

"Everything alright?" India asked.

Sarah nodded. "Yeah. Just… my friend had to head home."

India hummed in acknowledgment, then gestured toward the shop's back door. "Come. Let's get you back inside."

Sarah followed, stepping through the creaky screen door once more, feeling the weight of the locket in her pocket and the sage in her hand. Somehow, she knew—this wasn't over. And when she met up with Tilley again, she would have a lot to tell her.

Chapter 21

As Sarah stepped onto the porch of the rental cottage, she could already smell the rich, buttery aroma of garlic and lemon drifting through the open windows. It was warm and inviting, grounding her in something real, something normal—after an afternoon that had been anything but.

She pushed open the door and stepped inside. Her dad was leaning against the counter, a cold drink in hand, his face bright red from the sun.

Sarah's eyebrows lifted. "Dad… did you forget sunscreen?"

Her father sighed dramatically. "I didn't forget, I just underestimated how strong the sun was."

Her mom, who was tossing a summer salad at the kitchen counter, smirked without looking up. "He said, like he hasn't been living by the ocean a good portion of his life."

Sarah chuckled, setting her bag down. "Well, at least it looks like you caught something."

Her dad grinned. "Oh, we did. And you're going to love it."

From the oven, the fresh fish broiled to perfection, its savory scent filling every corner of the cottage.

Sarah turned toward the living room, where Ethan was sprawled on the sofa, a book about sailboats open in his lap.

She recognized it had Peter's name written on the cover in black Sharpie on a piece of masking tape. "Peter let you borrow that?" she asked.

Ethan nodded enthusiastically, barely looking up. "Yeah, he said I needed to know my vessels if I'm going to crew his dinghy tomorrow."

Sarah smirked. "Oh, so you're part of the crew now?"

Ethan grinned. "Obviously."

Their mom chuckled, setting the salad bowl on the table. "At this rate, I wouldn't be surprised if Peter ropes you into the reenactments next."

Ethan perked up. "You think he needs a first mate?"

Sarah rolled her eyes. "Let's get through one sailing lesson before you join the pirate fleet."

Their dad chuckled, ruffling Ethan's hair as he passed. "I'll bet you'd make a great sailor, buddy."

Sarah took a deep breath, absorbing the warmth of home, the comfort of family. For a few moments, the weight of the locket, the ghost, and everything else faded into the background. At least for tonight… She was just Sarah, sitting down for dinner with her family. But deep down, she knew—the past was still waiting for her. And soon enough, she'd have to face it again.

The small dining table was set simply—plates, silverware, a bowl of summer salad in the center, and the perfectly broiled fish that Sarah's dad had caught earlier that day. The warm glow of the kitchen lights made the space feel cozy, the scent of lemon, garlic, and fresh herbs filling the air as Sarah settled into her seat. Ethan was still flipping through Peter's book, only looking up when their mom set a glass of water in front of him.

"Put the book down and eat," she said, giving him a pointed look.

Ethan sighed but obeyed, carefully placing the book next to his plate before reaching for a piece of fish.

Their dad sat down with a contented sigh, shaking his head. "I'll tell you what, nothing makes you hungrier than a full day on the water."

Sarah smirked. "Or maybe it's the sunburn that's draining all your energy."

Her mom chuckled, but their dad groaned, reaching up to rub his reddened forehead. "I know, I know. I already got the lecture."

"You deserve the lecture," their mom said, passing him a plate. "You'd think after years of fishing, you'd learn by now."

Ethan grinned. "At least I remembered sunscreen."

Their dad shot him a look. "Alright, sailor."

Sarah took a bite of fish, the flaky texture melting in her mouth, the buttery citrus flavor making her realize just how hungry she actually was. As they ate, Ethan launched into a full breakdown of his sailing plans for the next day, animatedly describing everything Peter had told him—about how to read the wind, how to properly trim the sails, and how one day, he was going to have a boat of his own.

Sarah's mom smiled as she listened. "Sounds like Peter is a good teacher."

Ethan nodded enthusiastically. "Yeah! And he said that once I get better, we could try something bigger than the dinghy."

Their dad smirked. "Should we start calling you Captain Ethan?"

Ethan grinned proudly, but then his expression turned thoughtful. "Hey, Dad, have you ever been to Harkers Island?"

Sarah nearly choked on her water.

Her dad paused, raising an eyebrow. "Yeah, plenty of times. Why?"

Ethan shrugged, not noticing Sarah tensing slightly. "Peter was talking about it today. Said his grandpa knows just about everyone over there."

Their dad nodded. "Not surprising. Harkers is a small, tight-knit community, mostly old fishing families. If you grew up around these waters, you probably know someone from there."

Sarah kept her expression neutral, but her mind was racing. Was it possible her dad might know something about Robert T. Davis? She hesitated, debating whether to ask, but before she could decide, her mom turned her attention to Sarah.

"So, what about you? Did you end up meeting up with Tilley today?"

Sarah nodded, choosing her words carefully. "Yeah. She was at the museum, so I stopped by for a bit. We grabbed coffee and walked around."

It wasn't technically a lie, but she wasn't about to unload everything at the dinner table—not yet.

Her mom smiled. "I'm glad you made a friend. Tilley seems nice."

Sarah poked at her salad, feeling a familiar twist of unease in her stomach. If her mom knew what she and Tilley had actually been up to—digging through deeds, auction records, and haunted history—she'd probably insist they stay far away from Hammock House entirely. And Sarah wasn't ready for that conversation.

"Yeah," she said instead. "She's great."

Her dad leaned back, his plate nearly empty. "You two gonna hang out again tomorrow?"

Sarah hesitated, remembering Tilley's text.

"She has family stuff tonight," she said. "But yeah, we'll probably meet up."

Ethan perked up. "You should come sailing with us!"

Sarah smirked. "We just started talking about me getting on a boat, and now you think I should be a deckhand?"

Ethan grinned. "First mate."

Their dad chuckled, pushing his chair back. "Well, if she doesn't go sailing, she can always come fishing with me. We'll see if she can catch something bigger than what I brought in today."

Sarah smiled, but her thoughts were already drifting. Because while a peaceful day on the water sounded nice…She had a feeling her next move wasn't going to be that simple.

As they finished dinner, there was a loud knock on the screen door. Their dad opened the door and greeted the guest with a warm welcome. Sarah stepped away from the table, wiping her hands on a napkin as she took in Peter's unexpectedly casual appearance.

Gone was the tricorn hat, the blousy pirate breeches, the historic waistcoat—tonight, Peter looked like any other guy spending his summer by the water, dressed in a simple t-shirt and board shorts, barefoot on the wooden porch.

Sarah smirked. "I almost didn't recognize you without the pirate costume."

Peter grinned. "Yeah, I figured I'd give the townspeople a break from my overwhelming presence—at least for one night."

Ethan beamed, still riding high from their sailing earlier. He held out a fist, and Peter bumped it without hesitation.

"Can't wait for tomorrow," Peter said. "Hope you're ready to take the helm again, Captain."

Ethan sat up straighter, his face lighting up. "I'll be ready."

Peter turned his attention to Sarah, his expression shifting just slightly—still playful, but with something unspoken beneath it.

"Hey, you up for a walk?" he asked, turning to her parents. "I was thinking about showing her some of the older spots in town—places that don't make the ghost tour."

Her dad shrugged, glancing at Sarah's mom, who seemed pleased by the unexpected visit.

"That okay with you, sweetheart?" her mom asked.

Sarah hesitated for a fraction of a second, but then nodded.

"Yeah," she said. "That sounds good."

Peter flashed his signature mischievous grin, then stepped back off the porch, waiting for her. Sarah grabbed a light jacket from the chair by the door, slipping it over her shoulders as she followed him onto the brick path. The warm glow from the cottage faded behind them, and soon, it was just the two of them, stepping into the softly lit streets of historic Beaufort.

Peter walked beside Sarah, his hands tucked casually into his pockets, the warm summer air wrapping around them as they strolled down the quiet historic streets.

"So," he said, casting her a sideways glance, "other than being haunted by a coastal specter, how are you liking it here?"

Sarah let out a small laugh. "Honestly? I really like it."

She looked around at the charming colonial-era homes, the flickering glow of lanterns on porches, the soft sound of waves drifting in from the waterfront.

"The town is beautiful," she continued. "The people are warm and friendly. It's the kind of place that makes you feel like you belong, even if you've only been here a short time."

Peter smirked, that familiar glint of mischief in his eye. "I think the locals like you, too."

Sarah rolled her eyes but felt the warmth rise to her cheeks. "Oh yeah? I've only been here a week."

Peter shrugged, flashing a knowing grin. "What can I say? Some people just fit here."

Sarah shook her head, but before she could reply, Peter's expression shifted slightly—still easygoing, but with something more intentional behind it.

"I actually asked my grandad about Mr. Davis today," he said, glancing at her.

Sarah's attention sharpened immediately.

"And?"

Peter nodded. "Turns out, my grandad knew him—the late Mr. Davis. He passed away about ten years ago."

Sarah's brows furrowed. "So he wouldn't have the painting anymore."

"No," Peter agreed. "But get this—he had a daughter, Theresa, and she still lives around here. Well, not here exactly, but over by Fort Macon, right on the beach."

Sarah's mind raced. "So you think she has the portrait now?"

Peter shrugged. "Makes sense. My grandad said that after Mr. Davis passed, his house on Harkers Island was sold. If the painting was still in the family, Theresa would've been the one to take it."

Sarah nodded slowly, her fingers instinctively brushing over the locket in her pocket. A new lead. A name, a location, a possible connection to everything she had uncovered so far. She looked up at Peter, feeling the excitement bubbling just beneath the surface.

"We have to find a way to talk to her," she said.

Peter grinned, his eyes glinting in the soft glow of a streetlamp. "I thought you might suggest that."

Peter led Sarah down the boardwalk, past the last of the bustling waterfront shops and restaurants, until they reached the quieter, more secluded end.

The water lapped gently against the wooden pilings, reflecting the golden glow of the dock lights. The breeze carried the familiar scent of salt and distant marsh grass, the rhythmic sound of waves filling the space between them.

"This is it," Peter said, stopping near the edge of the pier. "This is where the 18th-century dock would have been."

Sarah looked around, trying to picture the past layered over the present—the modern sailboats replaced by tall-masted ships, the soft hum of conversation replaced by the shouts of sailors and creaking rigging.

Peter turned, his gaze shifting toward the direction of Hammock House.

"It was here," he continued, his voice quieter now, "that the British officer stood aboard his ship, looking toward Hammock House through his spyglass."

Sarah followed his line of sight, but the view was blocked—modern homes and buildings now crowded the space where open land once stood.

But back then…She closed her eyes for a brief moment, letting her imagination pull her into the past. She could almost see it—the way Hammock House stood alone on the knoll, watching over the town like a silent sentinel. No buildings in its way. No barriers. Just a clear, open view to the house on the hill. And from his ship, the officer would have seen—A sharp pang settled in her chest. He would have seen her. Or rather, Sarah Thatch—the woman he had longed for, dreamed of, and unknowingly condemned himself over. Sarah opened her eyes again, the present rushing back to meet her. Peter was watching her carefully.

"Hard to imagine now, isn't it?" he said. "How different it must've looked back then."

Sarah nodded, still feeling the lingering echo of the past pressing against her.

"He saw something that broke him," she murmured.

Peter exhaled. "And it set everything in motion."

Sarah shivered, even though the summer air was still warm. Because standing here, knowing what had happened next, she couldn't shake the feeling that the British officer's story wasn't finished yet. And somehow…She was part of it now.

Peter and Sarah walked back through the quiet streets, the energy of the waterfront shifting as the town settled into the late evening hush.

Peter stretched his arms above his head, letting out a content sigh. "I gotta meet Ethan bright and early at Gallants Channel tomorrow. The kid's already halfway to thinking he's a full-fledged sailor."

Sarah chuckled. "He's obsessed. You've created a monster."

Peter smirked. "Yeah, well, I like his enthusiasm. He's got a natural instinct for it."

They walked a little farther, the rhythmic lapping of the creek filling the space between them, before Sarah glanced over at Peter.

"So… who actually owns Hammock House now?"

Peter's expression darkened slightly, his easy grin fading into something more serious.

"Well," he said, slipping his hands into his pockets. "That's the thing. A lot of people have owned Hammock House over the years. Or, at least, they've tried to."

Sarah frowned. "What do you mean?"

Peter glanced at her. "Every person who's bought it with the idea of fixing it up, restoring it, living there—they don't last."

Sarah's pulse ticked up a notch. "Why not?"

Peter sighed. "Something in that house doesn't want to be disturbed. Every owner who's tried to take it on? They've been run off by something. Strange noises, things moving on their own, shadows in the hallways—enough to scare them out."

A chill crawled up Sarah's spine.

"How long do they usually last?" she asked.

Peter let out a short laugh. "Months. Maybe a year at best. But the last owners? They didn't even make it that long."

Sarah's brow furrowed. "What happened to them?"

Peter shook his head. "Packed up in the middle of the night. Didn't even tell anyone they were leaving—just loaded a moving truck before sunrise and disappeared."

Sarah swallowed. "That bad?"

Peter nodded. "Bad enough that they left the house in foreclosure and refused to talk about why."

A cold prickle settled at the back of Sarah's neck.

"So why hasn't it gone back on the market?"

Peter hesitated before answering. "Rumor has it, the bank doesn't want to deal with it anymore. They're supposedly considering turning it over to a big hotel developer, much to the Historical Society's chagrin, but the Historical Society doesn't have the funds to take on a project of that magnitude."

Sarah's breath hitched. "So… if that happens, would it be turned into an inn?"

Peter smirked. "They'd probably bulldoze it. What it needs is someone with deep pockets who loves the history of it, but good luck finding someone willing to step foot in it long enough to make that happen."

Sarah pressed her lips together, her mind swirling with thoughts. If the house itself was rejecting people, then the presence inside was strong. And now, that presence had noticed her.

As they reached the cottage, Peter stretched once more, flashing her a grin. "Well, M'Lady, thanks for the walk."

Sarah shook her head with a small laugh, blush rising in her cheeks. "You're impossible."

Peter gave a mock bow, then stepped back. "See you around, Sarah Thatch."

She froze for half a second. When she looked up at him, his expression was unreadable, his eyes twinkling. Before she could respond, he turned on his heel and vanished down the street, whistling softly as he went. Sarah stood there for a long moment, her pulse uneven, her thoughts spinning. Because somehow, she had a feeling…Peter knew a lot more than he was letting on. She lingered on the porch, watching Peter's retreating figure as he disappeared into the dimly lit street. His last words echoed in her head.

See you around, Sarah Thatch.

He had said it playfully, almost teasingly—but there was something about the way he'd looked at her, something too knowing. Did he actually believe there was a connection between her and Sarah Thatch? Or was he just messing with her? And why did the idea unsettle yet excite her more than it should have? She exhaled and turned toward the door, slipping inside the quiet warmth of the cottage.

Chapter 22

The living room was dark now, except for the soft glow of the kitchen light and the muffled hum of the dishwasher running. Her parents had gone to bed, and she could hear Ethan's soft snores from his room. She set her bag down near the entryway, slipping her sandals off as she moved quietly through the house, her mind still spinning with everything Peter had told her. Hammock House had driven away every owner it ever had. The last family fled before sunrise, their belongings barely packed. And now, the house stood empty—waiting.

Sarah shivered, hugging her arms around herself as she stepped into her room, closing the door behind her. She turned on the small bedside lamp, casting a warm glow over the walls. Her eyes immediately landed on the painting she had taped up earlier—her own sketch of Hammock House, the one she had drawn without meaning to, almost like the image had forced itself onto the page.

She swallowed hard. Was the house calling to her? Was that why the British officer had appeared to her first—because it was always meant to pull her in? She reached into her pocket and pulled out the locket, turning it over in her palm. The engraved initials gleamed faintly in the soft light.

S.T.

Sarah Thatch.

She ran her thumb over the metal, feeling the coolness of it against her skin, then popped it open, staring at the fragile lock of hair inside. India had said it was likely a mourning locket. That Sarah Thatch had kept a piece of the man she lost inside. But if that was true, why did it find its way to Sarah now?

She inhaled deeply and gently snapped the locket shut, setting it down on the small nightstand beside her bed. Tomorrow, she would meet up with Tilley and tell her everything she had learned. Tomorrow, she would figure out what she was supposed to do next. But for tonight, she just needed to sleep.

She climbed into bed, pulling the covers over her shoulders, her eyes still drifting toward the sketch of Hammock House. The shadows in the room stretched along the walls, and for a brief moment, she thought she saw a figure standing just beyond the edges of the paper—watching. She blinked, and it was gone. Sarah closed her eyes and forced herself to breathe. Even as she drifted off, she knew—the past wasn't finished with her yet.

Chapter 23

The dream always began the same way. Sarah stood at the edge of the path, looking up at Hammock House, its aged white walls and dark, empty windows staring back at her like hollow eyes. The air was thick and heavy, the summer night filled with the rhythmic chirping of cicadas and the occasional distant crash of waves against the shore. But no matter how warm the night was, the air around the house felt cold.

A low fog curled along the ground, clinging to the wooden steps that led up to the front porch. Spanish moss swayed like ghostly fingers from the live oak hammocks surrounding the house, framing it like a portrait suspended in time. She didn't want to move. She wanted to turn away, to wake up. But she couldn't. Because the door was open. Not wide open—just slightly ajar, as if it had been left that way on purpose. Sarah's heartbeat thundered in her ears. Then, like a whisper carried on the salt-tinged wind, she heard it.

"Sarah…"

She gasped. The voice was soft, distant—but undeniably real. She took a step forward, the damp earth cool beneath her bare feet. The house loomed above her, waiting. Her fingers trembled as she reached for the brass doorknob, its aged metal cool and solid beneath her touch. She pushed the door open, and it creaked on its ancient hinges, revealing only darkness beyond.

The moment she crossed the threshold, the temperature dropped. The summer air outside vanished. Inside, it was cold, silent, heavy—as if the very air carried centuries of secrets. Sarah's breath was shallow as she stepped further inside. Somewhere in the darkness, a voice whispered again.

"Sarah, I have longed for you."

Her spine stiffened, a chill rushing over her skin. Her eyes adjusted to the dim light, revealing a long wooden hallway stretching before her. At the end of the hall, a large window stood open, allowing the moonlight to spill onto the floor in a pale, silvery glow. She moved forward, her steps silent on the aged floorboards. A set of stairs emerged from the darkness, leading up to the second floor. Then—another whisper.

"Sarah…"

But this time, it came from above.

Her hands trembled as she gripped the wooden railing. She didn't want to go up, but she had to. Her bare feet made no sound as she climbed the stairs, the air growing colder with each step. The second-floor landing was also illuminated by the pale glow of moonlight, spilling through another window.

And standing at the top of the staircase—waiting for her—

Was him.

The ghost of Hammock House.

His tall figure was bathed in shadows, but his face was illuminated just enough for her to see the anger, the betrayal, the fire in his eyes.

"How could you, Sarah?"

The accusation hung in the air, thick and sharp like a blade. She didn't move. She didn't run. Unlike before, when she had been paralyzed by fear, this time, she stood her ground. Her mouth opened, but before she could speak, he was gone. The air in the house shifted, thickening.

Then—

The sound of swords clashing. Loud, violent, chaotic. Steel scraping against steel, echoing through the stairwell. The heavy pounding of footsteps—racing up and down the stairs, moving between floors, chasing, fleeing, fighting.

Sarah spun around, her heart slamming against her ribs. Then—silence. A deep, suffocating silence followed by a sensation—warm and wet beneath her feet. Slowly, she looked down. Her breath caught in her throat. Beneath her bare feet, moonlight reflected against deep, crimson red—it was blood.

Warm, fresh blood pooled around her toes. A scream ripped from her throat—And she bolted upright in bed, gasping for air. Sunlight filtered through the sheer curtains, casting a warm glow over her room. But the terror still clung to her, the vivid sensation of blood beneath her feet refusing to fade. It was just a dream. And yet—It wasn't. She knew it wasn't. Hammock House wasn't finished with her yet. And neither was he.

Sarah sat in bed for a long moment, her breath still uneven, her skin cool with lingering fear. The dream had felt too real, too detailed, as if she had been transported through time—not just witnessing the past but living it. She rubbed her hands over her arms, trying to shake off the chill that clung to her despite the warm rays of morning sunlight spilling into the room.

It was just a dream, she told herself. But even as she said it, she knew better. The house was pulling her in. The British officer wasn't just an apparition. He wanted something—he needed something. And she had a sinking feeling that he wasn't going to stop until she figured out what it was.

Taking a deep breath, she threw off the covers and forced herself to get ready. She splashed cool water on her face, trying to wash away the exhaustion that still weighed on her. She dressed quickly, slipping into comfortable clothes and securing her sketchbook and watercolors in her bag—she had a feeling she might want them today. Then, without hesitation, she grabbed her phone and set off to find Tilley. She needed to tell her everything—The dream. The blood. The accusing words of the British officer. Because if anyone could help her piece together what was happening, it was Tilley.

Chapter 24

Sarah pushed open the door to The Salt & Cedar, a small but cozy coffee shop nestled across from the Royal James Café. The rich scent of freshly brewed coffee and warm pastries wrapped around her as she stepped inside, her pulse still a little uneven from the weight of her dream.

Tilley was already there, sitting by the window with a croissant half-eaten on a plate and a steaming mug of coffee in front of her. She looked up as Sarah entered, her eyes immediately narrowing with curiosity.

"Okay," Tilley said as soon as Sarah slid into the chair across from her. "You look like you've seen a ghost."

Sarah huffed a dry laugh, setting her bag down. "Funny you should say that."

Tilley's brow arched. "Oh?"

Sarah wrapped her hands around the warm ceramic mug the barista had just placed in front of her, letting the heat ground her before taking a breath. Then, in careful detail, she recounted the dream—how it had felt like she had been inside the past, how she had heard the officer's voice, full of betrayal, and how she had stood there frozen in place rather than running away this time. When she described the clashing swords, the footsteps racing up the stairs, and the blood pooling around her feet, Tilley visibly shivered.

"That is…" Tilley paused, setting her croissant down. "That is seriously unsettling."

Sarah exhaled sharply. "Yeah. And the worst part? It felt real. I could feel the air in the house, the cold of the stairwell, the weight of everything happening around me. It was like I was actually there."

Tilley chewed her bottom lip, staring into her coffee for a long moment. "So, you think it was just a dream? Or something else?"

Sarah swallowed hard. "I think it was more than a dream. I think it was a memory—one that keeps pulling me back."

Tilley's eyes flickered with understanding. "And the officer…"

Sarah nodded. "He's not finished with me."

The air between them felt heavier now, the reality of what Sarah was experiencing settling in.

Tilley leaned forward, lowering her voice slightly. “Alright. So if this was a real memory, we need to figure out why you’re seeing it—and what you’re supposed to do next.”

Sarah nodded. “I was hoping you’d say that.”

Tilley smirked. “Of course you were.”

She took another sip of her coffee, then tapped a thoughtful finger against the rim of the mug.

“I think it’s time we start getting serious about finding out exactly what happened in that duel.”

Sarah swallowed. “You mean go through more museum records?”

Tilley shook her head. “I mean, we track down that painting.”

Sarah’s eyes widened.

Tilley looked at her knowingly. “If we find that portrait, and we get a better look at Sarah Thatch, maybe we’ll understand why you’re the one being pulled into this.”

Sarah stared at her, her heartbeat picking up again. Because deep down, she knew Tilley was right. And the next step in solving this mystery…was finding Sarah Thatch’s face.

Tilley pulled out her phone and tapped her fingers against the screen thoughtfully. “You know… I have a feeling this won’t be as hard as we think.”

Sarah raised an eyebrow. “Why’s that?”

Tilley smirked. “Because Theresa Davis isn’t some mystery woman living off the grid—she’s actually pretty involved with the Maritime Museum.”

Sarah blinked. “Wait. Really?”

Tilley nodded. “Yeah. She’s a longtime patron and has volunteered at a bunch of museum events—especially the annual fundraising gala.” She glanced up, already pulling up the museum’s member directory. “I’ll bet we can find her contact info in, like, two seconds.”

Sarah leaned in as Tilley scrolled through a list of names on her phone. And sure enough—there she was. *Theresa Davis Guthrie. Patron. Former volunteer. Last known address: a beachfront home near Fort Macon.*

Sarah exhaled. “Well. That was… almost too easy.”

Tilley grinned. “Sometimes it pays to have museum connections.”

Sarah bit her lip, staring at the name. “So… what do we do now?”

Tilley tapped the screen. "I think we should call her. We can tell her we're researching colonial history for the museum. That part's not even a lie."

Sarah hesitated. "And if she still has the painting?"

Tilley looked up, her expression serious now. "Then we ask if we can see it."

A beat of silence passed between them. Sarah wasn't sure what she expected when she started this journey, but now that they were one step away from finding the portrait, she felt uneasy—like something was about to shift. But there was no turning back now.

Sarah nodded slowly, gripping her coffee cup. "Okay. Let's call her." Tilley grinned, then hit the dial button. Sarah held her breath as the phone rang.

Once.

Twice.

Then—

A woman's voice, warm and poised, answered on the other end. "Hello, this is Theresa."

Tilley straightened in her seat as the voice on the other end of the line answered. Her accent was thick and unmistakable, the rolling Hoi Toider brogue giving her words a distinct rhythm—something between Outer Banks maritime dialect and old-world Elizabethan

English, shaped by generations of islanders. Tilley put on her best polite, professional voice. "Hi, Mrs. Guthrie. My name's Abigail Tillman, and I'm calling with my friend and colleague, Sarah Whitaker. We're reaching out on behalf of the Maritime Museum in Beaufort."

"Oh, well, isn't that nice?" Theresa said, her voice warm but curious. "Y'all puttin' on another fundraiser?"

Sarah could almost hear the smile in her voice—a woman who had spent years in the museum's circles, volunteering, attending events, and keeping up with the community.

"Yes, ma'am, it is getting close to that time for our annual gala, and we look forward to you joining us," Tilley said smoothly. "But right now, I'm actually doing some historical research, specifically about Hammock House and some of its past residents. We came across some museum records that said your father, Mr. Davis, had purchased a colonial-era painting at an auction years ago—one that we believe might be of Sarah Thatch."

There was a brief pause on the other end.

Sarah held her breath.

Then, Theresa exhaled, her tone shifting slightly. "Well, now. That is somethin'."

Tilley shot Sarah a look—this was a good sign.

“I reckon you’re talkin‘ ’bout that big ol’ portrait my daddy bought back when I was still livin’ on Harkers Island,” Theresa continued. “Lord, I hadn’t thought ‘bout that in a long while.”

Sarah leaned forward, listening intently as Theresa went on.

“Daddy had a love for that kinda thing—old stories, old history,” she said fondly. “Used to tell us young’uns about that girl in the paintin’ and how she met a tragic end. Said she was caught up in a bad storm o’ love an’ revenge.”

Sarah’s skin prickled. Theresa knew the story. Tilley took the chance to press further. “Do you still have the portrait, Mrs. Guthrie?”

Another pause. Then, in a knowing tone, Theresa said, “Well, now, I might.” Sarah’s heart skipped. “I’ll tell ya what,” Theresa continued, her voice warm but firm. “I’d be more’n happy to have y’all come by an’ see it for yourselves. I reckon it’s got a story worth tellin’.” Sarah felt her pulse quicken. This was it. The next piece of the puzzle.

Tilley grinned, jotting down an address on a napkin. “We’d love that, Mrs. Guthrie. When’s a good time?”

“Oh, anytime later this morning or early afternoon will do,” Theresa said. “House isn’t hard to find. Big ol’ place out near Fort Macon, right on the ocean. I'll have some sweet tea waitin' for ya."

Sarah finally found her voice. "Thank you, Mrs. Guthrie. We really appreciate it."

"Oh, honey, ain't nothin' to it," Theresa said kindly. "Reckon if y'all are chasin' down ghosts, you might as well see the face of one."

The call ended, and for a moment, Sarah and Tilley just sat there. The words hung heavy in the air. *See the face of one*. Sarah swallowed hard, because deep down, she already knew—when she saw the portrait with her own eyes, she wouldn't just be looking at Sarah Thatch, she would be looking at herself.

Tilley set her phone down on the table, exhaling as she stared at the address she had just scribbled on the napkin. Across from her, Sarah sat quietly, fingers absently tracing the rim of her coffee cup.

For a long moment, neither of them spoke. Then, finally, Tilley leaned back in her chair and gave Sarah a look. "Okay. This is getting real now."

Sarah let out a shaky breath. "I know."

Tilley tapped the napkin. "We're about to see the portrait. We're about to see her. This could be the proof that ties all of this together—why you're being haunted, why you're having those dreams, why he thinks you're her."

Sarah nodded but still looked deep in thought, her mind circling back to how they even got here. Because the only reason she even knew about Theresa Davis Guthrie…Was because of Peter.

She looked up at Tilley. “It’s kind of crazy, isn’t it? How fast this all came together?”

Tilley frowned slightly. “What do you mean?”

Sarah hesitated. “Think about it. I only found out about Theresa’s connection to the painting because Peter talked to his grandfather. If he hadn’t done that, we wouldn’t even know where to look.”

Tilley tilted her head. “Yeah, I guess that’s true…”

Sarah bit her lip. “But how did Peter know exactly what to ask his grandfather? He heard about the painting at lunch, sure, but it’s like he just knew it was *that* important.”

Tilley crossed her arms, considering it. “He’s really taken with you, Sarah. I can tell, I’ve never seen him like this.”

Sarah blushed. “Really, you think?. I don’t know, I think he’s just really good at following a hunch.”

Tilley smirked. “I mean, the guy does spend half his life telling ghost stories. Maybe he just has an instinct for this kind of thing," she said in a slightly sarcastic tone.

Sarah wanted to believe that, but the way Peter had looked at her last night before he left—the way he had called her Sarah Thatch—it still lingered in her mind.

Tilley picked up her coffee, taking a sip. "Okay, let's be real for a minute. You look just like that small catalog photo of the painting, Sarah. I'm sure Peter's trying to work out what in the world is going on—I know I am!"

Sarah sighed. "I don't know, but something tells me this mystery is way bigger than just Hammock House. And I think Peter is going to be a part of it whether we ask him to be or not."

Tilley nodded thoughtfully, then nudged the napkin toward Sarah. "Well, for now, let's focus on this. We finally have a lead. We're about to see a portrait of a girl who may or may not have the same face as you. That's enough to keep us busy for one day."

Sarah exhaled, then gave a small nod. "You're right. One thing at a time."

She finished the last sip of her coffee and set the cup down.

"Let's go meet Theresa Guthrie."

Chapter 25

As they stepped out of the coffee shop, Tilley stretched her arms over her head and let out a satisfied sigh. "Man, it's a perfect day."

Sarah glanced up at the sky, the deep blue nearly cloudless, the air warm but not stifling. The occasional soft sea breeze drifted through the streets, carrying the faint scent of salt and marsh grass. "Yeah," Sarah agreed. "It's beautiful."

Tilley shot her a curious look. "You like boating?"

Sarah hesitated. "I mean… I guess? I haven't been on the water much, so I don't really know. My dad can't get enough of it, and we've seen how Ethan has taken to it."

Tilley grinned. "Then today's the day to find out."

Sarah raised an eyebrow. "Why?"

Tilley grabbed her arm, already pulling her toward the waterfront. "Because it's way more fun to go by boat! And my dad's Parker is right there at the dock."

Sarah blinked. "Wait, we're taking a boat to Theresa's?"

Tilley nodded eagerly. "Yeah! There's dockage on the Intracoastal Waterway side, just across the road from her house. Plus, this weather is too nice to waste on driving. No wind, no chop—it'll be a smooth ride."

Sarah felt a thrill of excitement. She hadn't expected a detour on the water, but the idea of cruising along the coast, past the islands and salt marshes, was strangely inviting.

"Okay," she said, smiling. "Let's do it."

Tilley whooped, picking up the pace as they hurried toward the docks.

It didn't take long to reach Mr. Tillman's boat, a 21-foot Parker center console, sitting tied up at the Beaufort town docks. The boat was sleek, well-maintained, and built right in town—a sturdy vessel, made for both fishing and exploring the coastal waters.

Tilley jumped aboard with ease, tossing her bag onto the seat before turning to Sarah. "Come on, Captain Thatch, hop aboard." Sarah rolled her eyes at the nickname but climbed in carefully, steadying herself on the T-top frame as the boat gently rocked beneath her feet. Tilley fired up the Yamaha outboard, the smooth hum of the engine filling the quiet morning air.

Sarah grinned. “Okay, I already like this.”

Tilley winked. “Just wait ‘til we get moving.”

With that, Tilley eased the Parker away from the dock, her movements smooth and confident as she shifted the throttle forward. Sarah took in the view as they drifted past the docks, small waterfront cottages, grander historic homes, and the lively marina filled with boats of all sizes. They were careful motoring through Taylor Creek, slowly idling past the sailboats moored in the waterway. A little farther down the creek, she spotted Carrot Island again, where a few of the wild horses grazed along the shoreline, their tawny coats illuminated by the morning sun. “This is amazing,” Sarah murmured, watching the scenery drift by.

Tilley grinned. “Yeah, you get a whole different view of town from the water.”

They continued past the moored boats and kayakers paddling along the edge of the marsh until the creek opened up toward Beaufort Inlet. Ahead, the Intracoastal Waterway stretched wide and bright, the sun catching the ripples in the water. Tilley checked over her shoulder, making sure they had a clear path, then eased the throttle forward. The boat picked up speed, skimming across the blue-green expanse as they crossed toward Atlantic Beach. The mainland was on one side, a long barrier island on the other, where sandy dunes and tall sea oats lined the edge of Bogue Banks.

Sarah grinned, her heart thrumming with exhilaration. The gentle rocking of the boat, the salty breeze, the vast openness of the water—she loved it.

Tilley glanced over at her, smirking. “Told you this was the best way to travel.”

Sarah laughed, nodding. “You win. This is way better than driving.” As they coasted along, the breeze tangled through Sarah’s hair, and she felt a lightness in her chest that she hadn’t felt since arriving in Beaufort. For a moment, she wasn’t thinking about ghosts, haunted houses, or eerie dreams. For a moment, she was just a girl on the water, chasing adventure. And she kind of loved it.

They passed a few fishing boats and a small fleet of shrimp trawlers, their nets hoisted high, ready for the day’s catch. A couple of jet skis zipped past in the distance, their wakes breaking the glassy surface of the water. Before long, Tilley pointed toward the shoreline ahead. “There. That’s our dock.” Sarah followed her gaze, spotting a small private dock tucked along the Intracoastal side of Atlantic Beach. Just beyond it, she could see the tall dunes and beachfront houses, one of which belonged to Theresa Guthrie.

Tilley slowed their speed as they approached, the boat settling back into a gentle glide as they pulled up to the dock. Sarah’s pulse quickened with anticipation, because they weren’t just arriving at Theresa’s house—they were arriving at the next piece of the puzzle—and

Sarah had a feeling whatever they found inside was going to change everything.

Tilley skillfully maneuvered the Parker toward the dock, bringing the boat in smoothly alongside the weathered wooden pilings. She shifted the throttle into neutral and let the boat drift the last few feet before tying it off with a quick, practiced motion. Sarah stood, gripping the T-top frame as she took in their surroundings. The dock stretched over the calm water, the pilings lined with clusters of barnacles and oyster shells clinging just below the surface. Beyond the dock, a private boardwalk led through a patch of low-lying salt marsh, where seabirds flitted between the tall grasses, their calls sharp in the morning air.

Just past the boardwalk, Theresa Guthrie's house stood tall against the backdrop of the Atlantic. It was a beautiful, sprawling coastal home, painted soft dune-gray with crisp white trim, perched high on pilings as if standing guard over the ocean beyond. A long wraparound porch framed the front, rocking chairs neatly arranged to take in the breeze from the sound side. The roof was metal, glinting in the sunlight, and a weathered wooden sign above the doorway read "Seafarer's Rest." The place had character. It wasn't new and polished like some of the modern beachfront houses, but it had the kind of timeless, lived-in charm that only came from decades of being well-loved. Sarah inhaled the fresh, salty air, feeling the ocean's presence all around her. It was different here than in Beaufort—more exposed, more open, maybe because the sea itself was closer, more powerful. "This place is beautiful," Sarah murmured.

Tilley nodded as she secured the last dock line. "Yeah, not bad for a retired nurse, huh?" Sarah took another look at the house. Even in its serenity, there was something about the house that felt significant, like it had been waiting for them. Tilley stepped onto the dock first, holding out a hand to help Sarah off the boat. Sarah took it, steadying herself as she climbed onto the planks, the sun-warmed wood solid beneath her feet.

The air smelled of the ocean, sun, and something faintly floral, and as they started down the boardwalk toward the house, Sarah could see the shifting dunes just beyond the yard, the waves of the Atlantic crashing softly in the distance. The beach felt isolated, peaceful —but full of history. Just as they reached the bottom of the porch steps, the screen door creaked open. Sarah looked up to see Theresa Guthrie standing in the doorway, waiting for them.

She was a tall, striking woman in her late sixties, with silver-streaked blonde hair pulled into a loose braid over her shoulder. She wore a breezy linen shirt, faded denim capris, and a pair of well-worn sandals, her sun-kissed skin evidence of a lifetime spent near the water. Her eyes, a sharp ocean blue, studied the girls with keen curiosity. A knowing smile tugged at the corners of her mouth. "Well now," Theresa drawled, her Hoi Toider accent thick and melodic, "y'all made good time, didn't ya?" She propped a hand on her hip, looking between Sarah and Tilley like she was already sizing them up. Sarah opened her mouth to respond, but before she could, Theresa gestured toward the porch.

"Come on in, girls," she said, stepping back to hold the door open. "I got a fresh pitcher of sweet tea and a story or two I reckon y'all might wanna hear." Sarah exchanged a glance with Tilley, then followed Theresa inside because the answers they had been searching for…might finally be within reach.

As Sarah stepped over the threshold of Seafarer's Rest, the coolness of the house enveloped her, a stark contrast to the warm coastal air outside. The home smelled of aged wood, and something faintly sweet—perhaps vanilla and citrus, lingering from a candle long burned out. The interior was just as charming as the exterior—a blend of nautical antiques and cozy, lived-in comfort. The floors were wide-planked oak, worn smooth by decades of footsteps. The walls were adorned with old maritime maps, framed black-and-white photographs of sailors and fishing boats, and a wooden ship's wheel mounted above the stone fireplace. A long bookshelf stretched along one side of the living room, filled with leather-bound volumes, historical accounts of the Carolina coast, and well-loved novels. A breeze fluttered through the sheer white curtains, carrying the distant sound of crashing waves from beyond the dunes.

Sarah took it all in, feeling impossibly small in a house that seemed to breathe with history. Theresa led them past the living room into the kitchen, which opened onto the back porch overlooking the ocean. The space was bright and airy, with white cabinets, blue tile backsplash, and an old butcher block island. On the counter, a glass pitcher of sweet tea sat sweating beside three mason jar glasses, ice cubes already clinking inside. Theresa motioned for them to sit at the kitchen table, its surface a well-worn farmhouse-style wood, softened by time. Sarah took a seat, still absorbing everything around her.

Tilley, ever the one to break the silence, grinned. "I love your house, Mrs. Guthrie. Feels like stepping into another time."

Theresa chuckled as she poured the tea. "Oh, honey, I been collectin' old things for as long as I been breathin'. But if you ask my husband, he'll tell ya it's just an excuse not to throw anything away." She set a glass in front of Sarah, then paused, mid-movement, her sharp blue eyes lingering on Sarah's face. Sarah felt the weight of her gaze, watching as Theresa's expression shifted—curiosity flickering into something deeper. A look of recognition.

Theresa slowly sank into the chair across from Sarah, gripping her glass lightly, her eyes searching Sarah's face as if trying to make sense of something. "Lord, have mercy," she murmured.

Tilley glanced between them. "What is it?"

Theresa exhaled sharply, shaking her head like she had seen a ghost. "I haven't seen that portrait in a long time… but, darlin'—you got her face." Sarah's breath hitched. Theresa leaned in slightly, studying her. "The shape of your eyes… your jawline… even the way you carry yourself." She let out a slow breath. "It's uncanny." Sarah's pulse quickened because Theresa wasn't saying she resembled Sarah Thatch; she was saying she was identical to her.

Tilley's eyes widened. "I knew it."

Theresa sat back, folding her arms. "I don't know what it means, child, but I got the strangest feelin' that portrait found its way to me for a reason."

Sarah swallowed hard. "May we see it?"

Theresa nodded. "Come on, then." She pushed back from the table, leading them down a short hallway lined with more framed photos—some old, some modern, all with the ocean in the background. At the end of the hall, she opened a door into what looked like a small study. Inside, an old wooden steamer chest rested against the far wall, its surface smooth with age. Theresa walked over and lifted the lid, revealing a carefully wrapped canvas inside. She pulled it out, turning it around with deliberate care.

And there she was. Sarah Thatch. The portrait was hauntingly beautiful—an oil painting, its colors still rich despite the centuries. The young woman in the painting had long, dark curls cascading over her shoulders, her skin fair, her eyes strikingly familiar.

Sarah stared at herself, or her reflection from another time. A strange chill crept up her spine. It was her—it was exactly her.

Tilley let out a breath. "Well… if we needed confirmation, I think we just got it."

Theresa, still watching Sarah carefully, muttered, "I don't believe in coincidences, honey." She tilted her head slightly. "I think you got a past that's tryin' to call you back."

She didn't know if she was ready to answer, but something told her…she might not have a choice. She couldn't tear her eyes away from the portrait. It was her—or rather, Sarah Thatch—but the resemblance was so exact, so uncanny, that it felt like looking into a mirror distorted by time. The painted girl's dark curls framed her face in soft waves, her gaze steady, almost knowing, as if she were looking through the centuries, straight at Sarah now. She swallowed hard, forcing herself to breathe, to focus. Her pulse was still uneven, her thoughts racing. This was proof. Proof that something—or someone—was pulling her into the past. Proof that the British officer's ghost wasn't appearing to her by chance.

Tilley was the first to break the silence. "Sarah," she said gently. "You okay?"

Sarah blinked, tearing her gaze away from the painting to look at her friend. "Yeah. I just… I don't know what to do with this."

Theresa, who had been studying Sarah's reaction with quiet understanding, sighed and carefully turned the portrait around in her hands. "Well, darlin'," she said, "before you try to figure out what to do with it, there's somethin' else you oughta see." Sarah and Tilley leaned in as Theresa pointed to the back of the canvas.

The wooden frame was aged, its surface slightly rough from time. But in the corner, beneath a layer of dust and faint remnants of varnish, was a delicate inscription—handwritten in old ink, nearly faded but still legible.

For my darling, whom I long to see.

Sarah's breath hitched. The words sent a chill through her, as if they were whispered across time, meant for her ears alone. She reached out but stopped short, hovering just over the inscription, afraid to touch it—afraid of what it might mean.

Tilley read the words aloud, her voice barely above a whisper. "For my darling, whom I long to see…" She turned to Theresa. "Who do you think wrote it?"

Theresa's gaze remained locked on Sarah. "My guess?" she murmured. "I think she did."

Sarah's fingers curled into her palm. For the first time since this all began, she wasn't sure if the British officer was haunting her out of anger, love, or both. Sarah forced herself to breathe, the weight of the moment pressing down on her as she stared at the delicate inscription on the back of the canvas.

"For my darling, whom I long to see."

The words carried centuries of longing, a whisper of a love lost to time.

Theresa ran a thoughtful hand along the edge of the frame, her gaze distant as if piecing together a puzzle long forgotten. "I got a feelin'," she said slowly, "that this wasn't a gift from the officer."

Sarah looked at her sharply. "What do you mean?"

Theresa tapped a finger against the canvas. "I think Sarah Thatch had this painted for him. Somethin' to send him off with when he went back to England."

Tilley frowned. "So, like a keepsake?"

Theresa nodded. "A way for him to have a piece of her while they were apart. Women back then did that sort of thing—had miniatures or portraits painted to send to their betrothed if they were travelin' far."

Sarah felt a shiver travel up her spine. "So how did it end up back in Beaufort?" she asked.

Theresa's expression turned solemn. "Well, that's the part that gives me a bad feelin'. If she gave it to him before he left, and he brought it back…"

Tilley caught on first, her eyes widening. "That means he still had it in his possession when he died."

Theresa nodded grimly. "And it likely wasn't returned to Hammock House until after his death."

Sarah swallowed hard. The image of the British officer clutching the painting while an ocean separated him from his love sent a shiver down Sarah's spine.. Had he looked at it one last time before he stormed up to Hammock House in a jealous rage? Had he held onto it, even in death?

Sarah's fingers instinctively brushed over the locket in her pocket, the weight of it suddenly heavier than before. The portrait, the locket, his spirit calling out to her. Everything was connected. But there was still one question she couldn't shake: had the officer brought the painting back as a token of love, or as a reminder of his betrayal, and why had it stayed hidden for so long?

Sarah and Tilley exchanged a glance before turning back to Theresa, who had settled into the chair beside the antique chest, still holding the portrait as if it contained all the secrets of the past.

Tilley was the first to ask the question lingering between them. "Mrs. Guthrie, do you know why your father wanted this painting so badly?"

Theresa exhaled, running her fingers over the edge of the canvas, her eyes thoughtful. "I wondered the same thing after he passed."

Sarah leaned in. "And? Did you ever find out?"

Theresa nodded slowly. "I started diggin' into our family history, askin' myself what it was about this particular paintin' that got Daddy so intrigued. Turns out… he had a very good reason." She looked at Sarah, her blue eyes sharp with meaning. "Through genealogical research, I found out that my daddy—Robert Davis—was a direct descendant of Sarah Thatch's brother."

Sarah's face fell in shock.

Tilley sat up straighter. "Wait—you mean he was actually related to her?"

Theresa nodded. "That's right. Sarah Thatch's brother—the one caught in the duel—had children. His line kept goin', passin' down through the years, all the way to Daddy."

Sarah's mind reeled. Robert Davis had been Sarah Thatch's kin! Had he known? Had he felt the same eerie pull to the past that she was feeling now?

"He must have known about the connection," Theresa continued, tapping the frame of the painting. "Why else would he be so intrigued by it when it came up for auction? He paid a hefty price for it. More than most would have given for an unidentified colonial-era portrait."

Sarah shivered. "Maybe he wasn't just buying a painting. Maybe he was saving it so that one day it might be brought back home, to Hammock House, where he thought it belonged."

Tilley nodded, her expression serious. "And if he knew… maybe he knew more about the story of Sarah Thatch than we do."

Theresa gave them both a meaningful look. "If you ask me, I think y'all are followin' the same trail my daddy started. Only difference is, you're in it deeper than he ever was."

Sarah swallowed, the weight of the past pressing heavier against her because Theresa was right. Robert Davis had been searching for something, and now, she was picking up where he left off.

Tilley leaned forward, her eyes gleaming with excitement, as if something had just clicked into place in her mind. "You know," she said, voice brimming with inspiration, "this painting—and the story behind it—is exactly what the museum needs right now."

Theresa raised an eyebrow. "Oh?"

Sarah glanced at Tilley curiously. "What are you thinking?"

Tilley grinned, the kind of grin that meant she was about to hatch a big plan. "I'm thinking… this could be the centerpiece of a fundraiser."

Theresa and Sarah both looked at her in surprise. "A fundraiser?" Sarah repeated.

Tilley nodded. "Not just any fundraiser—a historic preservation effort. What if we crowdfunded to raise enough money for the museum to purchase Hammock House?"

Theresa's eyebrows shot up. "You wanna buy the house?"

Tilley leaned in, her enthusiasm growing. "Not me, but the museum! Think about it: Hammock House is sitting there, abandoned, falling into ruin, and everyone who's tried to restore it has been run off. But if we can turn it into a museum property, restore it to its original condition, and tie it into the local history, it could become a historical landmark." Sarah's mind raced. It was bold. It was ambitious. And it was kind of perfect.

Theresa folded her arms, her expression thoughtful. "That's a mighty big idea, sugar."

Tilley nodded, unfazed. "Yeah, but big ideas happen all the time when people believe in them. The museum has connections, the historical society would be involved, and if we start a crowdfunding campaign, people from all over—locals, history buffs, tourists—could contribute."

Sarah could see it now: the museum hosting events and tours, visitors walking through a fully restored

Hammock House, hearing the real stories of its past instead of just the whispered legends and ghost tales.

Theresa sat back, clearly intrigued, tapping her fingers against the table. "Well," she said slowly, "I do love a good historical project." She gave Sarah a pointed look. "And somethin' tells me you're already more tied up in this house than you ever planned to be."

Sarah swallowed but nodded. "Yeah. I think that's an understatement."

Theresa chuckled, then exhaled deeply. "Alright, I'll tell ya what. If y'all can make this happen—if you can get the museum involved and find a way to bring in the funding—I'll donate this portrait."

Sarah's eyes widened. "You'd give it to the museum?"

Theresa smiled. "Yep. I reckon it belongs there, right over the mantel at Hammock House; right where she should've been all along."

Tilley beamed. "This is huge. We have to go straight to my mom about this—I bet she'll love the idea!"

Sarah's heart was pounding, excitement and uncertainty swirling together. The painting. The house. The fundraiser. It was all coming together. But as thrilled as she was, she couldn't shake the feeling that Hammock House wasn't going to let its secrets go without a fight. And the British officer—would he finally be at peace, or was she about to stir something even deeper?

Chapter 26

Tilley pushed the throttle forward, and the Parker lifted slightly as they picked up speed, gliding effortlessly across the Intracoastal Waterway back toward Beaufort. The air was warm and fresh, the breeze whipping through Sarah's hair as she gazed out at the passing scenery—marshy inlets, trawlers rocking in the distance, the occasional dolphin surfacing in the wake of a passing boat.

Tilley, still high on excitement, grinned as she looked over at Sarah. "Can you believe it? If we actually pull this off, we could be a part of history."

Sarah nodded, though her expression was more pensive than thrilled. "Yeah… it's incredible. But there's something else we need to think about."

Tilley's smile faded slightly. "What's that?"

Sarah grabbed a handhold tightly as they began to hit a little chop in the waterway. "If we're going to restore Hammock House, we can't ignore the reason why it's haunted. The officer and Sarah Thatch—they need to be put to rest."

Tilley's hands tightened slightly on the wheel, her expression turning serious. "You mean, before we do anything with the house?"

Sarah nodded. "I just—I feel it. Whatever happened between them, it's unfinished. And if we stir up the past without settling it first, I don't know what could happen."

Tilley exhaled. "So… you think we need to figure out what actually happened before we get too deep into this?"

Sarah turned to her, her expression firm. "Not just figure it out. Set it right, and the sooner, the better."

Tilley thought about it for a long moment, then nodded. "Alright. First, we get my parents on board with the fundraiser. Then? We figure out how to end the haunting." Sarah swallowed, staring ahead as Beaufort's harbor came into view. Because something told her—ending it wouldn't be as easy as it sounded.

As Beaufort's waterfront came into view, Sarah noticed a larger sailboat with a sky-blue hull cutting gracefully through the water, its white sails catching the wind perfectly as it headed toward the inlet. It took her a moment, but then she recognized the two figures on board the Flying Scot. Peter was reclined on the bench, arms crossed, looking completely at ease, while Ethan was on the tiller, his posture focused but relaxed.

When Tilley realized who it was, she shot them a wide grin. "Would you look at that? Your brother's out here single-handing that boat like a pro."

Sarah blinked. "Wait—he's actually sailing it alone?"

Tilley nodded, already adjusting the throttle to pull the Parker alongside them. "Yep. Peter's just supervising."

As they approached, Peter turned his head and grinned. "Ahoy, there! Look who decided to take a pleasure cruise," he smiled as he looked at Sarah.

Tilley smirked. "I was going to say how impressive it is that Ethan's single-handing, but now I see you're just making him do all the work."

Peter feigned offense, placing a hand over his heart. "I'll have you know I am actively supervising. This is important training. The boy's gotta earn his sea legs."

Ethan, confident at the helm, rolled his eyes but couldn't hide the proud smile on his face. "Honestly, I think I'm getting the hang of it."

Sarah laughed. "I bet you are." She turned to Peter. "So, where exactly are you two heading?"

Peter motioned toward the inlet and beyond. "Thought we'd take a trip out toward Shackleford Banks, and perhaps on to Cape Lookout if the seas cooperate—Let Ethan stretch his skills a bit with some open water. We are well provisioned to enjoy a superb repast with seaside entertainments complete with Beanie Weenies and canned chicken salad."

Tilley gave Ethan a nod of approval. "Well, I gotta say—I'm impressed. Not bad for a kid who just started."

Ethan grinned. "Thanks. Peter says I've got natural instincts."

Peter lowered his sunglasses and winked. "That, or you just listen well—which is more than I can say for most people I try to teach."

Tilley laughed, while Sarah shook her head, amused. Peter turned his attention back to the girls. "And what about you two? You looked like you were on a mission just now." Sarah and Tilley exchanged a knowing glance.

Tilley crossed her arms, teasingly. "Oh, just planning to save a historic house, uncover a centuries-old mystery, and maybe put a ghost to rest. You know—the usual."

Peter raised an eyebrow. "Now you have my attention."

Sarah chuckled. “Good. Because we might need your help sooner rather than later.”

Peter smirked. “Well, in that case, I’d better get Ethan back in one piece so I can hear all about it.”

Ethan rolled his eyes. “I am right here, you know.”

Sarah laughed, shaking her head. “Alright, well, you two be safe out there.”

Tilley revved the engine lightly, readying to pull away. “Try not to get lost at sea!”

Peter gave them a mock salute. “We make no promises.”

With that, Sarah and Tilley turned the boat back toward town, while Ethan and Peter continued their course toward Shackleford, their sail tight, catching the wind once more.

Sarah exhaled, turning to Tilley. “Alright. Now, let’s go convince your dad and mom we need to buy a haunted house.”

Tilley smirked. “No big deal, right?” They both laughed, though deep down, Sarah knew—The hardest part was yet to come.

Chapter 27

Sarah and Tilley hurried through the museum, bypassing the main exhibits and slipping through a staff-only door that led to the Queen Anne's Revenge conservation lab. The air inside was cool and dry, filled with the faint scent of aged metal and chemicals used for preservation. Large water tanks lined the walls, filled with artifacts still undergoing desalination, while long stainless-steel tables held various pieces of Blackbeard's infamous ship—timbers, cannonballs, pottery shards, and encrusted relics pulled from the seafloor.

At the center of the room, Margaret Tillman, Tilley's mother and the Director of Operations for the Queen Anne's Revenge exhibit, sat next to a large, heavily concreted cannon, its surface coated in centuries of hardened marine growth. An assistant was carefully prepping electrolysis equipment, getting ready to begin the long process of removing the concretion to reveal the iron underneath. Margaret glanced up as the girls entered, arching an eyebrow. "Let me guess—you need something."

Tilley grinned. "What gave it away?"

Margaret smirked before turning back to the cannon, checking the wires attached to the metal frame surrounding it. "This had better be good, because I'm about to spend the next several months trying to convince this cannon to give up the secrets it's been keeping for over three hundred years." Tilley launched into the pitch, her words quick and passionate—explaining how Hammock House had been sitting abandoned for years, how private owners had been driven away, and how it was one of the most historically significant buildings in Beaufort.

Margaret didn't interrupt. She simply listened, her amber eyes studying Tilley with practiced patience. When Tilley finished, she set down her tools and turned to face them fully. "You want the museum to purchase and restore Hammock House?"

Sarah nodded. "Yes. We'd launch a crowdfunding campaign to raise money for the restoration. And we already have a major artifact to feature—the portrait of Sarah Thatch."

Margaret's eyes flickered with interest. "The portrait still exists?"

Tilley nodded. "We saw it today. And Sarah looks exactly like her."

Margaret's lips pressed together, her mind clearly calculating. "Mom, you already know the connection Hammock House has to Blackbeard," Tilley continued. "It's even pictured in the Queen Anne's Revenge exhibit—you've personally made sure that connection is emphasized in the museum."

Margaret nodded. "Of course. The house was linked to Blackbeard's inner circle, possibly under his birth name, Edward Thatch. It's long been rumored that Sarah Thatch was either his daughter or a close relative." She sighed, shifting her weight slightly. "The historical significance is undeniable. But a project of this size?" She folded her arms. "The bank still owns the property, and they haven't exactly been eager to list it for sale."

Sarah took a step forward. "But if the museum shows interest, and there's a strong public backing, they might be willing to work something out. No private owner has lasted long there—maybe the town would rather see it in the hands of a historical institution."

Margaret was silent for a long moment as she sat in pensive thought, then let out a small chuckle. "I have to admit… the idea of preserving the only known building in the state that was once tied to Blackbeard himself is very appealing."

The door opened and in walked a tall, broad-shouldered man in his mid-fifties. He wore a well-worn work shirt with the museum's logo embroidered on the pocket, and he had the same keen eyes as his daughter.

"Dad! I'm glad you're here! We were just telling mom about our mission to save Hammock House." Dr. Tillman looked at the girls with a puzzled expression and then glanced over at Margaret.

"They've hatched quite an impressive plan for a restoration project of the old Hammock House, David," said Margaret. If we can get all our ducks in a row, it could be an incredible extension for the QAR project. I think we need to approach the bank."

"I certainly wasn't expecting this, but it's a nice surprise that you girls are so enthusiastic about historical preservation. I presume you have a plan in place for how you'll pull this rabbit out of the hat?" Dr. Tillman asked.

"Indeed, we do!" Said Tilley. "Mom can fill you in. We're on a mission."

David and Margaret looked at each other, exchanging playful smiles. Tilley beamed. "So... does that mean you'll at least consider reaching out to the bank?"

Margaret let out a long breath, shaking her head with both amusement and resignation. "Let me see what I can do. I have my hands full at the moment, but I'll try to get a meeting set up this week."

Sarah exchanged a thrilled glance with Tilley. They weren't just chasing ghost stories anymore; they were about to make history. With Margaret's tentative approval, Sarah and Tilley wasted no time.

After leaving the lab, they headed to the museum's library, where they could spread out their notes and begin drafting a plan for the crowdfunding campaign. Tilley pulled out her laptop, flipping it open as Sarah grabbed a legal pad and pen from the desk. "Alright," Tilley said, cracking her knuckles. "If we're gonna do this right, we need a solid plan. First—who's our target audience?"

Sarah thought for a moment. "Definitely local history enthusiasts. People who love Beaufort's maritime past."

Tilley nodded. "And ghost story fanatics. You know the haunted history angle is going to bring in a ton of interest."

Sarah scribbled down *history buffs + ghost enthusiasts*. "What about tourists? People who visit every year and love the town?"

Tilley grinned. "Yes! We could partner with local businesses to help spread the word. Shops, restaurants—heck, even the ghost tour groups would probably be on board."

Sarah jotted down local business partnerships. "And we need to focus on the museum's credibility. People will be more likely to donate if they know a respected historical institution is backing the project."

Tilley pointed at her. "Exactly. So we need a convincing campaign page—something that tells the whole story of Hammock House, but also why it needs to be saved."

Sarah tapped her pen against the paper. "We should include the portrait of Sarah Thatch. That's a huge selling point. And maybe we can even get Theresa to do a short video discussing her ancestral ties to the property and the painting."

Tilley's eyes lit up. "Ooh, I love that! A personal connection makes the story stronger."

She started typing quickly. "Alright, we need:

- A compelling introduction
- The history of Hammock House (Blackbeard connection, duels, ghost stories)
- Why it's in danger of being lost
- What the museum plans to do
- What donors get in return."

Sarah paused. "Wait—what do donors get?"

Tilley grinned. "That's where we get creative. We could do tiered donations with special rewards. Like, for $25, you get a limited-edition print of the painting. For $100, you get a private ghost tour of the house once it's restored."

Sarah's excitement grew. "And for a really big donation, like $1,000, someone could get their name on a plaque inside Hammock House!"

Tilley nodded enthusiastically. "Now that's a legacy."

The girls worked furiously, bouncing ideas back and forth as they began drafting the campaign page. They weren't just trying to save a house, they were about to bring history back to life, and the whole world was about to hear their story.

Tilley pulled her phone out, dialed, and put Theresa on speakerphone, setting her phone between them on the museum library table as Sarah flipped through their campaign notes.

"So, what do you think?" Tilley asked eagerly. "Does it sound solid?"

Theresa hummed thoughtfully on the other end. "Y'all have a great start," she said. "But you're thinkin' too small."

Sarah frowned. "What do you mean?"

"You're focusing too much on just local donors," Theresa explained. "And don't get me wrong—Beaufort loves its history, but Hammock House isn't just some small-town relic. People all over the country, and even the world, know about it."

Sarah glanced at Tilley, who looked intrigued. "Because of the ghost stories?"

Theresa chuckled. "That, and Blackbeard. Honey, tales about him and that house have been published in books, articles, and even TV specials for decades. It's got name recognition far beyond the Crystal Coast."

Tilley nodded, her wheels already turning. "So, you think we should go national with the campaign?"

"I know you should," Theresa replied. "You'd be surprised how many people—historians, ghost hunters, maritime enthusiasts—would be interested in saving a place like Hammock House."

Sarah's heart picked up pace. A national campaign. It hadn't even crossed their minds, but now that Theresa had said it, it made perfect sense. "You could reach out to ghost hunting groups, maritime museums, even Blackbeard historians. National Geographic and the History Channel are always running content about the infamous pirate," Theresa continued. "The bigger the audience, the better your chances."

Tilley grinned. "This just got way bigger than I thought."

Theresa laughed. "Well, sugar, history's only worth as much as the people willing to save it." Sarah absorbed the weight of that statement, realizing just how far this could go. Not just saving Hammock House, but bringing its story to the world.

Tilley ended the call and turned to Sarah. "Looks like we need to go even bigger."

Sarah nodded. "And we need the Ghost with the Most's take on this," referring affectionately to Peter.

Chapter 28

Later that afternoon, Sarah and Tilley made their way toward the docks, knowing exactly where to find him.

As they approached, they spotted Peter near the public slip, sitting on the edge of the dock with his feet dangling over the water. His tricorn hat rested beside him, and he was tying a fresh knot in one of his boat lines, completely absorbed in the task.

"Hey, Captain," Tilley called. "Got a minute?"

Peter glanced up, a grin spreading across his face. "For you two? Always." He patted the dock beside him, and Sarah and Tilley sat down, the wood warm beneath them from the afternoon sun. The faint smell of diesel and the tide filled the air as they listened to the gentle lapping of water against the hulls of nearby boats. "So," Peter said, leaning back on his hands. "What's the latest? Are we throwing a haunted masquerade fundraiser, or do I need to start auctioning off ghost-hunting tours?"

Tilley rolled her eyes. “Not quite, but you’re not far off. We called Theresa Guthrie this afternoon to tell her what we were thinking, and she gave us a huge idea.”

Sarah nodded. “We were thinking too small with our crowdfunding campaign—just focusing on local support, but Theresa reminded us that Hammock House is famous.”

Peter raised an eyebrow. “Famous?”

Tilley smirked. “You, of all people, should know this.”

Peter chuckled. “I mean, yeah, it’s *infamous.* You can’t step foot in Beaufort without hearing stories about Blackbeard, ghost duels, and British officers haunting the place.”

Sarah leaned forward. “Exactly. And that means it’s not just a local treasure—it’s something all different kinds of people across the country know about.”

Tilley nodded. “Theresa thinks we should go national with the fundraiser, like Nat Geo big Market it to history lovers, ghost hunters, maritime enthusiasts, and anyone obsessed with Blackbeard and his lost legacy.”

Peter let out a low whistle, clearly impressed. “That’s… actually brilliant.” He pulled at the silver coin around his neck, lost in thought. “You know, you’re right. There are tons of people who would donate just to be a part of saving something tied to Blackbeard."

Sarah exhaled. "So… do you think it's doable?"

Peter's signature grin returned. "Oh, it's more than doable. I think you're about to start something way bigger than you ever imagined."

Tilley clapped her hands together. "Then let's make this happen."

Peter sat up straighter. "You're gonna need a good hook—something that'll grab people's attention immediately."

Sarah thought for a moment. "Maybe a campaign slogan?"

Peter nodded. "Yeah, something that ties in the mystery, the history, and the urgency."

Tilley grinned. "How about 'Save the Legend: Restore Hammock House'?"

Peter tilted his head. "Not bad… but what about something with Blackbeard's name in it? That's what draws people in."

Sarah tapped her fingers against the dock. "What if we went with something like' …Blackbeard's Lost Legacy: Save Hammock House'?"

Peter snapped his fingers. "Now that has a nice ring to it."

Tilley nodded enthusiastically. "It tells people exactly why it's important!"

Sarah felt a rush of excitement. "Then that's what we'll use. We'll make it about history, mystery, and Blackbeard's connection."

Peter leaned back, crossing his arms. "You know… I might actually have a few connections that could help boost this."

Sarah's eyes widened. "You do?"

Peter smirked. "Let's just say I know some folks who run popular maritime history blogs and ghost tourism networks. If we can get them to share the campaign, we could bring in way more people."

Tilley pointed at him. "See? This is why we needed you."

Peter grinned proudly. "I do tend to be useful." He cut his eyes over to Sarah, his mood changing from exuberant and confident to something almost shy, in a boy-like way. "By the way, Sarah, my student had to cancel his sailing lesson tomorrow. Ethan mentioned you were really interested in seeing Cape Lookout Lighthouse and maybe the wild horses. I'd like to take you there if you'd like to partake in an adventure on the high seas."

"I'd love to," she said as she felt the butterflies return. "How about I pack lunch?"

Peter smiled, noticing Tilley playfully rolling her eyes. "I'll see you tomorrow morning, right here."

Chapter 29

The morning sun shimmered on Taylor Creek as Peter helped Sarah into the cockpit of the Flying Scot, his hand warm and steady as she climbed aboard. The boat bobbed gently beside the dock, its white sail furled and ready, its tall mast reaching confidently toward the pale blue sky.

"You're sure this is okay?" she asked, glancing toward the horizon where the barrier islands stretched like a thin ribbon of dunes and marsh.

Peter grinned, stepping down beside her. "Ethan said you've been wanting to see the lighthouse. Thought we'd make a day of it since the weather is perfect—just the right amount of wind. Horses, adventure, and sandwiches— just can't beat it!"

They set off just after breakfast, the wind catching the mainsail and sending them gliding smoothly into the waterway. The air was clean and fresh, scented with a hint of marsh mud and distant pine, and the cries of gulls overhead completed the feeling that they were sailing into another world. Sarah sat forward facing the bow, her face turned toward the breeze, her dark hair whipping around her shoulders, eyes alight with wonder.

It took a little over an hour to reach the cape. The tall black-and-white diamond-patterned lighthouse of Cape Lookout stood like a sentinel above the dunes, its shadow long and familiar in Peter's memory. As they turned into the channel and neared the shore, Sarah's hand went to her heart.

"Oh," she breathed. "It's even more beautiful than I imagined."

The beach was deserted but for a distant group of wild horses wandering in the sea oats, their manes windblown, their movements slow and graceful. Sarah stared at them in awe, and Peter dropped anchor just off the white sandy beach, pulling the boat gently into the shallows.

They waded barefoot to the beach and set up a picnic under the shade of a weathered cedar, spreading a blanket over the warm sand. Lunch was simple—fruit, sandwiches, a thermos of sweet tea—but it tasted better here, with the waves lapping softly and the breeze whispering through the dune grass.

As they ate, Sarah glanced over at Peter, brushing the sand off her fingertips.

"So tell me," she said. "How did you do it? Sail from Michigan all the way here—by yourself?"

Peter leaned back on his elbows, gazing toward the water for a moment before answering. "Well, my mom ran guest services and my dad handled logistics and scheduling for the Grand Hotel. I used to sneak through the back halls and ballrooms like a ghost. It felt like living inside a history book, but the winters were brutal, and it was way too quiet for me." He paused and smiled, eyes squinting against the sun. "So when I turned eighteen, I took the little cabin boat I'd been fixing up for years, rigged her best I could, and headed south. I waited until I graduated and set out in late spring, pretty much as quickly as I could take my cap and gown off. I took my time, hugging the Great Lakes, down the riverways, then the ICW. A couple of months later, I dropped anchor in Beaufort. Of course, my grandparents were here, but when I first sailed into the New River from Adams Creek, I knew I was home."

Sarah tilted her head. "Because of the water?"

"Because of the past," Peter said. "It's everywhere here. In the wood, in the wind. I started helping my grandfather with the museum's boatbuilding classes on the weekends, then teaching sailing in the summers. And the ghost tours…" He laughed, shaking his head. "Well, that was just me trying to make history fun. But turns out, I like telling stories, especially when they matter." He glanced over at her then, his expression shifting.

Sarah had pulled out her little tin of watercolors and her sketchbook, her brush already dancing along its surface. She barely looked up as she worked—just flicked her gaze at him every now and then, then back down, her fingers moving swiftly and confidently. When she finally turned the paper around to show him, Peter stilled. It was him—sitting barefoot in the sand, a quiet smile on his face, wind tousling his hair, the lighthouse rising ghostlike behind him. But it wasn't just his likeness she'd captured. It was *him*. The shape of his thoughts. The curve of his feeling.

"I…" he began, but his voice caught.

Sarah looked at him, her gray eyes soft and open. "I can paint lots of things," she said quietly. "But I only paint people like this when I feel like I can really see them." Peter looked from the portrait back to her, the air between them thick with something unsaid, something ancient and new all at once. He didn't need to say a word. She already knew.

He reached for her hand, brushing his thumb lightly across her knuckles. "Then I hope you'll keep painting me," he said. "Because I'm not sure I've ever been seen like that before." They sat together in silence after that, the waves quietly lapping the shore, the lighthouse casting its long, steady gaze over them—like it, too, had been waiting for this moment.

The late afternoon light turned the world golden as Peter raised the anchor and hoisted the sail. The wind had shifted slightly, just enough to fill the canvas and send the boat slicing gently through the shallows. Sarah sat near the tiller, her knees tucked to her chest, her damp hair curling from the salt air. The painting she'd made of Peter was tucked carefully back into her sketchbook, now zipped inside her bag. She kept stealing glances at him—at how he handled the lines, how natural he was on the water, how the sun glinted off the silver coin he wore around his neck.

He caught her watching and grinned, that easy smile she was beginning to recognize as something that belonged only to her. "Perfect sailing weather," he said. "We'll be back before the tide changes."

Sarah smiled and let the words drift over her like the wind. The boat skimmed across the water, leaving a soft wake behind it. The wild horses on the island grew smaller in the distance until they disappeared entirely into the dunes. As they crossed into the inlet, Morehead City, Radio Island, and Beaufort came slowly back into view—the church steeples, the old rooftops, the colorful boats docked at the waterfront like toys. The familiar shape of the Maritime Museum's watercraft center stood stoically near the shoreline, its cedar-shake facade now touched with gold from the descending sun. Sarah leaned over the edge of the boat and trailed her fingers through the water, letting the salt cling to her skin. She felt different. Lighter, maybe. Or, like something inside her had shifted.

Peter was quiet now, his gaze focused on the horizon. She sensed he was giving her space to think, but she also knew he was waiting. For what, she wasn't entirely sure—but the thought comforted her. "You've really built a life here," she said at last. "A real one. Not just summer jobs and stories."

Peter looked at her and nodded. "I like building things that last. Boats, stories…maybe even something more than that." Their eyes met, and a current passed between them that had nothing to do with the tide.

As they entered Taylor Creek, the sky turned lavender, and the first street lamps flickered on. The town was winding down, settling into its quiet coastal hush. Peter expertly guided the boat alongside the dock, slowing just enough for Sarah to reach over and loop the dock line around the piling. When they stepped onto the dock, the world felt still in a new way. Like it was waiting.

He didn't say goodbye right away. He stood there, one hand on the dock rail, the other brushing the back of his neck like he was working up to something. "Thanks for coming out today," he said. "I know you've got a lot going on—with the house and the ghost and everything else—but… I liked having you out there. Just us, the ocean…and the horses."

Sarah smiled. "Me too." She stepped forward and reached up to smooth a windblown curl from his forehead—just a small gesture, but it made Peter go still. Then, with the softest smile, she turned and stepped off the dock toward home, her sandals tapping gently against the planks.

Peter watched her go, that silver coin catching the last of the light as it rested against his tanned chest. Just before Sarah reached the edge of the dock, she looked back over her shoulder. He was still standing there, smiling. And she realized something with absolute certainty—Whatever happened next, they were in this together.

Chapter 30

Sarah took a deep breath, feeling the weight of everything falling into place. This wasn't just a wild idea anymore. This was real. Soon, the whole world was going to hear about Blackbeard's Lost Legacy. The house potentially held a deeper connection to the infamous pirate, the possibility of his daughter's portrait hanging above the mantle in its rightful place, the connection to locals in the community whose ancestors have settled the area for centuries, with the possibility his blood still coursing through their veins, made the site a relic. It was an incredible feat for the state to uncover the wreck of the Queen Anne's Revenge, where the contents of the ship can be viewed behind glass at the Maritime Museum, but to walk upon the same floors, within the same walls that held Edward Thatch and his children, was palpable in almost a spiritual sense.

Tilley was practically glowing with excitement as they wrapped up their conversation at the Salt and Cedar. Peter was already making lists of contacts, and she was scheming campaign strategies in her head.

Sarah, however, felt something else stirring deep inside her, a pull—an unsettled feeling she couldn't shake. The fundraiser was important. But so was the ghost of Hammock House, and Sarah knew she couldn't move forward without understanding what he wanted from her. As the sun dipped lower over Beaufort, she excused herself from Tilley's planning frenzy, said goodbye to her friends, and wandered down the narrow brick alleys, her thoughts swirling like the breeze through the moss-draped oaks.

She needed to talk to India Reed.

The Olde Towne Chandler was just as she left it—the scent of beeswax, aged paper, and dried herbs filling the air as soon as she stepped through the door. India was behind the counter, carefully tying twine around a bundle of dried lavender. She glanced up, her piercing eyes immediately reading the storm in Sarah's expression. She set the bundle aside. "You've seen something, haven't you?"

Sarah exhaled. "More than that. I've discovered something."

India motioned for her to follow, leading her through the dimly lit shop to the cozy back parlor, where the scent of burning sage lingered. Sarah sat on the plush velvet chair, clutching the locket in her pocket, and told India everything—the portrait of Sarah Thatch, the inscription, the fundraiser to restore Hammock House.

India listened without interrupting, her sharp gaze never leaving Sarah's face. When Sarah finally finished, India let out a slow breath. "So," she murmured. "You're bringing the house back to life."

Sarah hesitated. "That's the plan."

India leaned forward, steepling her fingers. "And what about the gentleman spirit?"

Sarah swallowed. "I don't know. That's why I'm here."

India studied her for a moment. "The past doesn't rest just because we decide to restore it, Sarah. If his ghost is still reaching for you, there's something he's still waiting for."

Sarah nodded. "I know. And I think it has something to do with how he died—and what he never understood."

India was silent for a long moment, then she stood, walked to a wooden cabinet, and pulled out a small, leather-bound book. She handed it to Sarah. "This belonged to my grandmother. It's filled with old stories, rituals, and ways to commune with restless spirits."

Sarah ran her fingers over the worn cover, her heart pounding. "You think I need to… talk to him?"

India's gaze was unwavering. "I think you need to listen."

A chill crawled up Sarah's spine. She had sensed it before. But now she knew for certain—she had to seek him out. She was the only one who could hear what he had to say. Sarah kept the book tucked away in her bag for the rest of the evening, the weight of it pressing against her thoughts even as she sat at dinner with her family.

Chapter 31

Her father was raving about Ethan's sailing progress, and her mother was talking about trying out a new recipe for the next day's meal, but Sarah found herself distracted, nodding along without really listening. The book was waiting. And something inside her knew that once she opened it, there would be no turning back.

As soon as dinner was finished, she excused herself, muttering something about being tired from the long day. She slipped upstairs to her room, closing the door behind her, and pulled the book from her bag. The cover was worn and smooth, the deep brown leather cracked from age. The pages inside were thick, yellowed parchment, filled with small, spidery handwriting and the occasional illustration of symbols and herbs. Sarah settled against her pillows, pulling the lamp on her nightstand closer. The dim light cast long shadows on the pages as she carefully turned to the first section.

Communing with the Restless

Her pulse quickened as she scanned the words, written in an old-fashioned script.

Spirits tethered to this world linger not without cause. Some remain for vengeance, some for love, and others because their final truth was never revealed.

Sarah swallowed. *Final truth.* That was what haunted the British officer—his death, his misunderstanding, his belief that Sarah Thatch betrayed him. She kept reading.

To hear the whispers of those who have not moved on, one must open their senses, not their fears. The dead speak not in words, but in impressions, visions, and echoes of memory. To understand them, one must be willing to listen.

Sarah bit her lip. *Visions.* She had already seen Hammock House in her dreams, had already felt the ghost's presence pull her toward something unresolved. She turned the page.

A Ritual for the Unseen

A small sketch of a candle, a mirror, and a sprig of sage was drawn in the margins. The instructions beneath were clear but eerie.

At the hour when the veil is thin, light a candle and set a mirror before you. Burn fresh sage to guard your spirit. Speak the name of the lost, and they may answer in whispers, in flickers of candlelight, or in shadows not yet at rest.

Sarah's breath hitched. It sounded simple, but she knew nothing about how this was going to be easy. She closed the book, running her fingers over the cover, heart pounding. If she wanted answers…She would have to face him again, and this time, she had to be ready to listen. She closed the book carefully, setting it on her nightstand as she exhaled a deep breath.

She wasn't ready. Not yet. The idea of calling out to a spirit—summoning the British officer directly—felt too soon, too dangerous. She needed to understand more. She needed to be sure. For now, she would wait. Instead of turning off the lamp, she let its soft glow illuminate the room as she lay back against the pillows, staring up at the ceiling. Her mind replayed everything she had learned—the painting, the inscription, the duel, and the officer's tragic misunderstanding. Had he clung to this world simply because he had died believing a lie, or was there something more binding him here? Sarah turned onto her side, the locket still tucked safely in her pocket. The weight of it was comforting—like she wasn't entirely alone in this.

She wouldn't rush it. Tomorrow, she would figure out her next step, and soon enough, she would hear his story the way it was meant to be told. But tonight, she would let herself rest for as long as her dreams allowed.

As the wind whispered through the cottage windows and the moonlight spilled like silver across the floorboards of her room, Sarah drifted into sleep with the weight of everything pressing gently at the edge of her thoughts—Hammock House, the handsome apparition, the locket, the painting, the ritual they were preparing for. But, her mind pulled her somewhere else—somewhere deeper—a time different from the present.

She found herself walking barefoot along a windswept beach under a velvet-black sky, stars pulsing above like watchful eyes. The sand was cool beneath her feet, the scent of sea oats and old wood rising with the tide. Far ahead, a tall ship sat anchored offshore—its sails furled, its hull dark against the horizon. Lanterns flickered along the deck, casting a golden path across the water.

She turned inland, drawn by a sound—soft laughter, the hush of voices carried on the wind. And there he was, Peter. Not exactly as she knew him now—a little older somehow, leaner, and dressed in a pale linen shirt half-unbuttoned, sleeves rolled to his elbows. His dark breeches were tucked into leather boots, and his sun-kissed hair was tied back at the nape of his neck with a bit of black ribbon. He was sitting on the edge of a weathered dock, a spyglass in one hand, a half-smile on his face as he turned toward her.

"I was wondering when you'd come back," he said, as if they'd spoken only hours before.

Sarah stood frozen, unable to speak at first. But in her dream, her heart knew something her waking mind didn't. "Do I know you?" she whispered.

Peter rose slowly and crossed the sand to her. When he reached her, he lifted his hand, brushing a stray wisp of hair from her cheek. His fingers were warm. "You've always known me," he murmured. "Even when the world forgot."

The wind picked up, catching the edges of her dress —an old-fashioned gown the color of fog, with fine embroidery at the cuffs. She hadn't noticed it before, but she was dressed like someone from centuries ago. Peter took her hand and led her up the beach, past dunes and sea oats, toward a small gathering beneath the wide porch of a candlelit tavern. Voices were singing softly, the smell of roasted meat, the faint clink of glasses. He pulled her close and spun her gently in a slow, quiet dance just beneath the stars.

"I've waited so long to see you again," he whispered, his voice husky with emotion. "I think I've lived lifetimes searching for this moment."

Sarah rested her head against his shoulder, her pulse humming like the tide, and she whispered back, "Then don't let go."

"I won't," he said. "Not this time."

But even as she held on to him, the dream began to shift. The stars flickered. The air grew colder. In the distance, she saw the tall figure of Captain James Thorne, standing at the edge of the sea. He stared at them, face cast in shadow, but his eyes burned with something ancient—longing, jealousy, grief.

Peter turned toward the figure, his jaw tightening. "You have to go," he said to her gently. "There's something only you can do."

"What is this place?" she asked, trembling.

Peter kissed her forehead softly. "It's the memory of a promise. And you're the only one who can make it right."

The wind howled. The dream darkened. Sarah tried to hold on to Peter's hand, but he was already fading, like sea foam beneath her fingers.

Slowly, darkness enveloped the corners of her vision before swallowing everything into the abyss. She could feel her spirit being pulled back from the depths of a bygone time. Her senses began to come back to her— the morning light spilling through the window, the sounds of birds chirping, and the fragrance of summer flowers in the air. Her hand was still clenched, as if she'd been holding on to something. Or someone. She tried to savor whatever she could of the dream or memory before she finally opened her eyes.

Chapter 32

That morning, Sarah walked through town with purpose, heading straight for the Salt and Cedar where she and Tilley had agreed to meet. The warm scent of fresh-brewed coffee and pastries drifted through the air as Sarah stepped inside, scanning the small crowd. Tilley was already there, seated in the corner booth, sipping on an iced latte while flipping through her phone. She looked up as Sarah approached and grinned. "You look like someone with secrets to spill."

Sarah slid into the booth, setting her bag beside her. "That obvious?"

Tilley smirked. "You've got that look—like something big just clicked into place, but you don't know what to do with it yet."

Sarah let out a breath. "That's… pretty much exactly it."

She hesitated for a second, then pulled India's book from her bag, placing it between them on the table.

Tilley's eyebrows lifted. "Okay… what's this?"

Sarah lowered her voice. "A book from India Reed. It belonged to her grandmother—filled with old stories, rituals, and ways to commune with restless spirits."

Tilley's eyes widened as she reached for it, carefully flipping through the aged pages. "So, like, actual instructions on how to talk to ghosts?"

Sarah nodded. "Yeah, and there's a section about spirits that are tied to unfinished business."

Tilley leaned in, lowering her voice to match Sarah's. "Like your ghost of Hammock House."

Sarah tapped a passage in the book. "Exactly. It says that some spirits stay behind because their final truth was never revealed."

Tilley sat back, eyes full of intrigue. "That makes so much sense. I mean, we already know he died believing a lie."

Sarah nodded. "And I think that's why he keeps appearing to me—why I keep feeling him. He's not just haunting Hammock House. He's searching for Sarah Thatch."

Tilley drummed her fingers on the table, thinking. "So… what does the book say about actually communicating with him?"

Sarah hesitated. "There's a ritual."

Tilley's brows shot up. "A ritual?"

Sarah nodded, explaining the details—the candle, the mirror, the sage—everything that would supposedly help her hear the spirit more clearly.

Tilley whistled. "And you're gonna do this?"

Sarah exhaled. "Eventually, but… I need to be ready. This isn't just some spooky encounter—this is his story, and I have to be sure I'm listening the right way."

Tilley studied her for a moment, then nodded, respecting her hesitation. "Well," she said, closing the book gently, "then let's make sure you have everything you need before you try it." Sarah smiled, feeling an overwhelming sense of relief. She wasn't alone in this—Tilley was in her corner, ready to help her uncover the truth. And soon, the past would finally speak.

Tilley tapped her fingers against the table, brows furrowed. "Okay, so before we even think about performing this ritual, we have one major problem…"

Sarah sighed. "We have to get inside Hammock House."

Tilley nodded. "And since it's private property—bank-owned, and still very much off-limits—we can't just walk up to the front door and waltz in."

Sarah chewed on her lip, thinking. "Has anyone ever gone inside since it was abandoned?"

Tilley tilted her head. "I'm sure people have tried. The last owners left in the dead of night, and rumor has it the bank has it sealed up pretty well. However, it does still have the original doors and windows."

Sarah frowned. "So… there might be a way in?"

Tilley shrugged. "Maybe. But it's not like I can just ask my mom for the keys. Even if she's looking into acquiring the house for the museum, we're not at that point yet."

Sarah exhaled, thinking through their options. "What about Peter?"

Tilley gave her a knowing smirk. "Ahh, now you're thinking like a local."

Sarah rolled her eyes. "I mean, he seems like the kind of person who… knows things about places he probably shouldn't know."

Tilley laughed. "Oh, he definitely does." She leaned forward. "And honestly? If anyone can figure out how to get inside a centuries-old building, it's Peter."

Sarah hesitated. "Do you think he'd help?"

Tilley smirked. "Let's just say Peter's always up for an adventure. And if we tell him we're solving a real mystery? He won't be able to resist." Sarah still felt a small knot of nervousness in her stomach. Breaking into an abandoned haunted house wasn't exactly something she'd ever pictured herself doing. But if this was the only way to find the truth…she was willing to take the risk.

Tilley pulled out her phone. "Should I text Peter now?"

Sarah took a breath. "Yeah. Let's see what he says."

Tilley typed out a quick message, thumbs flying over the screen.

Tilley: *Hey, Captain. Need your expertise. Hypothetically... if someone wanted to get inside Hammock House, how would they do it?*

She set her phone down on the table and smirked at Sarah. "Now we wait."

Sarah exhaled, tapping her fingers on her coffee cup. "You think he'll go for it?"

Tilley grinned. "Peter lives for this kind of thing. He's probably already imagining himself as the lead character in some historic ghost-hunting, swashbuckling adventure."

Just then, her phone buzzed. She flipped it over, and her smirk faltered slightly.

Peter: *Not funny, Tilley.*

Sarah raised an eyebrow. "Not the reaction I was expecting."

Tilley quickly typed back.

Tilley: *I'm serious. We need to get in. We think it's the key to solving the mystery of the haunting.*

A moment passed before another reply came through.

Peter: *That place isn't just haunted—it's cursed. People don't last there for a reason. I don't mess with that kind of stuff.*

Sarah felt a slight chill creep up her spine. She had assumed Peter would be all in, but his hesitation made something feel… different.

Tilley glanced at Sarah before responding.

Tilley: *We aren't trying to stay there forever. Just long enough to get some answers.*

Peter's reply came a few seconds later.

Peter: *Look, I believe in ghosts, but I also believe in not tempting fate, and let's not forget, its ILLEGAL!*

Sarah took a deep breath, then nodded at Tilley. "Tell him we need to do this."

Tilley nodded and typed.

Tilley: *We're not asking you to break in, necessarily; we just need your sage wisdom on finding a way inside.*

There was a long pause before the screen lit up again.

Peter: *I'm not saying I'm going to help you trespass, but meet me at the docks at sunset. We'll talk.*

Tilley grinned. "And that, my friend, is what we call progress."

Sarah exhaled, heart pounding. This was really happening. They were one step closer to uncovering the truth, and something inside her knew Hammock House was waiting for them.

Chapter 33

Sarah and Tilley sat on a bench near the boardwalk, the sun starting its slow descent toward the horizon. The smell of each chef's culinary delights from the waterfront restaurants wafted through the salt air, mixed with the distant hum of summer tourists still milling about town. "We need a solid excuse," Sarah muttered. "Something that makes sense, but won't raise too many questions."

Tilley smirked. "Oh, I've got one."

Sarah arched a brow. "Let's hear it."

Tilley leaned forward conspiratorially. "We tell our parents we're helping Peter with a ghost tour."

Sarah hesitated. "But… there isn't a ghost tour tonight."

Tilley waved a hand. "Doesn't matter. We say it's a special practice run—just us helping Peter test some new scares for an upcoming event."

Sarah considered it. “So… basically, we’re dressing up and jumping out at people for fun?”

Tilley grinned. “Exactly. It’s something Peter would actually do, and it’s not so out of character for us that they’d question it too much.”

Sarah chewed on her lip. “Okay. And what if they ask where we’re doing this?”

Tilley thought for a moment. “We say we’re using different spots around town—the Old Burial Ground, the docks, maybe even near the museum. We don’t mention Hammock House.”

Sarah sighed in relief. “That might actually work.”

Tilley stood, brushing off her shorts. “Come on, let’s go test it out.”

Back at the cottage, Sarah found her parents sitting on the front porch, enjoying the warm breeze off the water. Her mother looked up as she approached. “You’re home early. I thought you’d still be out with Tilley.”

Sarah forced a casual shrug, adjusting the strap of her bag. “Yeah, we just finished working on something. Actually, I wanted to ask if I could go out again tonight.”

Her dad glanced at her. “Doing what?”

Sarah rehearsed the story in her head before saying, "Peter's testing some new scares for his ghost tour, and he asked if Tilley and I would help."

Her mom smiled. "That sounds fun. What would you be doing?"

Sarah kept her voice light. "Just, you know, jumping out at people, adding a little extra spook factor. It's a practice run, so we'll be moving around to different locations."

Her dad chuckled. "And people pay for this?"

Sarah grinned. "You'd be surprised."

Her mom hesitated for a moment, then nodded. "Alright. Just don't stay out too late."

Sarah exhaled in relief, forcing herself not to look too eager. "Thanks! I'll be back before midnight."

Her dad smirked. "Just don't bring any ghosts home with you."

Sarah swallowed hard. If only he knew.

As Sarah walked back toward the boardwalk to meet Tilley, her phone buzzed.

Tilley: *Mission accomplished. Parents totally bought it. Meet you at the docks.*

Sarah smiled. Step one was done. Now came the hard part—convincing Peter to help them break into Hammock House. Something told her…this was going to be one interesting night. She met Tilley just past the boardwalk, where the docks stretched out into the shimmering waters of Taylor Creek. Tilley was already there, leaning against a piling, watching the boats sway with the gentle evening tide. She looked up as Sarah approached, her expression serious.

"Well, our cover story worked," Tilley said. "Now we just have to convince Peter that this is totally worth the risk."

Sarah exhaled. "Yeah… I obviously don't want us to get caught, but I hope he'll get on board."

Tilley crossed her arms. "He will"

Sarah arched a brow. "You sound sure."

Tilley smirked. "Peter likes to act all cautious and responsible, but deep down? He lives for this kind of thing."

Sarah sighed. "Still, we should be prepared in case he needs more convincing."

Tilley nodded. "Agreed. Let's run through what we know."

Sarah mentally sorted through the pieces. "Okay. We know Hammock House has been abandoned for years. The last owners fled in the middle of the night, and no one has successfully stayed there since."

Tilley added, "And we know that the bank owns it, it's locked up, but I can't imagine they have it secured like Fort Knox—it doesn't even have an alarm system."

Sarah nodded. "Right. But we don't know if all the doors and windows are locked."

Tilley shrugged. "That's where Peter comes in. He's a pirate—he might know a way in that we don't," she said with a chuckle.

Sarah bit her lip. "And if we get inside… I have to figure out how to communicate with the British officer."

Tilley glanced at Sarah's bag, where she knew India's book was tucked away. "Are you sure you're ready for that?"

Sarah hesitated. "I don't know. But I have to try."

Tilley nodded in understanding. "Okay. And if Peter asks why we need to do this?"

Sarah exhaled. "We tell him… the ghost won't leave me alone. I need to find out what he wants, and this is the only way."

Tilley smirked. "A little dramatic, but hey—it's true."

Sarah couldn't help but grin. "So, what's the backup plan if Peter refuses?"

Tilley thought for a moment. "We go to Hammock House anyway and figure it out ourselves."

Sarah laughed. "Of course, that's your answer."

Tilley grinned. "Look, we've come this far. No way we're stopping now."

Just then, the sound of footsteps on the dock made them both turn. Peter had arrived. He wasn't in his usual pirate attire—tonight, he wore a simple dark T-shirt, cargo shorts, and a familiar mischievous glint in his eyes. "Alright," he said, stuffing his hands in his pockets as he came to a stop in front of them. "Tell me why I should risk finding my way onto the gallows."

Sarah and Tilley exchanged a glance. It was time to convince the pirate to take the plunge. Sarah took a breath, steadying herself as she faced Peter. She knew she had to get this right—no dramatics, no hesitation, just the truth.

Peter crossed his arms, watching her carefully. "So. You two really want to do this?"

Sarah nodded. "Yes."

Peter sighed, glancing out over the darkening water. "You do realize how many people have tried to stay in that house and failed, right?"

Sarah held his gaze. "I do."

Peter studied her for a long moment, as if weighing whether she truly understood what she was asking. "Then tell me why. Why is this so important to you?"

Sarah felt the weight of the moment, but she didn't look away. "Because it won't leave me alone," she admitted. "The ghost. The house. It's all pulling me toward something—something I don't understand yet. But I have to do it, otherwise I don't think it's going to stop."

Peter raised an eyebrow. "What do you mean 'pulling you'?"

Sarah hesitated. Then, she reached into her bag and pulled out India's book, flipping to the passage about spirits bound to unfinished business.

"This," she said, showing him the page. "This is why."

Peter leaned in, scanning the words, his expression growing more serious.

Tilley spoke up. "The British officer didn't just die at Hammock House—he died believing a lie. The only way to release his spirit is to reveal the truth to him… then he can move on!"

Peter glanced at Sarah. "You think?"

Sarah exhaled. "I know."

For the first time, Peter didn't look like he was about to make a joke or brush it off. He just looked… thoughtful. "So you don't just want to see a ghost," he said finally. "You want to set one free."

Sarah nodded. Peter ran a hand through his sun-bleached hair, looking away for a second. "Man, this is not what I signed up for when I agreed to give ghost tours…"

Tilley grinned. "But come on, you love it."

Peter let out a breath, shaking his head with a small, reluctant smirk. "I hate that you're right."

He looked back at Sarah. "Alright. If you're serious about this, I'll help. But…" He pointed at her. "If things get weird—I mean, really weird—we're out, got it?"

Sarah smiled, relief flooding her chest. "Got it."

Peter sighed dramatically, throwing his hands in the air. "Alright, fine. Let's break into a haunted house." Tilley cheered, and Sarah felt the excitement build in her chest. They had their plan. They had their team.

And soon… they would finally step inside Hammock House.

With Peter finally on board, Sarah, Tilley, and Peter hurried through the darkening streets of Beaufort, making their way toward the Olde Towne Chandler. The shop's warm glow spilled onto the quiet brick alleyway, the scent of wax, dried herbs, and something faintly floral lingering in the air. Tilley pulled open the heavy wooden door, the small brass bell above it jingling as they stepped inside. India looked up from behind the counter, already raising an eyebrow at them. "Let me guess," she said dryly. "You're here for candles." She smiled at them with a twinkling in her eyes.

Sarah approached, placing India's book on the counter. "We're doing it. Tonight."

India's sharp gaze flickered between Sarah, Tilley, and Peter. "And I take it this one"—she gestured to Peter—"has finally been convinced to join the madness?"

Peter smirked, raising both hands in surrender. "Against my better judgment, m'lady."

India exhaled, then gave them a small, knowing nod. "Alright. What do you need?"

Sarah quickly listed the items:

- A white candle for illumination
- Fresh sage for protection
- A small mirror for reflection

- A piece of iron for grounding

India moved with purpose, pulling the items from various shelves and cabinets, her motions quick but deliberate. As she placed them on the counter, she gave Sarah a pointed look. "This isn't just about calling him, you understand? It's about listening. Let him speak. Don't push. Don't demand. Just listen."

Sarah swallowed and nodded. "I understand."

India's gaze softened slightly. "Good. Because if you do this right, Sarah…" She paused. "He might finally find peace." Sarah took a deep breath, accepting the weight of what she was about to do.

Peter cleared his throat. "Uh… just making sure—there's no, like, way this could go horribly wrong, right?"

India gave him a long, unreadable look. Then, finally, she smiled. "That depends entirely on her."

Sarah felt the chill settle over her. She had everything she needed. Now, all that was left…was to step into Hammock House.

Chapter 34

After gathering their supplies, Sarah, Tilley, and Peter left the Olde Towne Chandler, stepping into the warm night air. The streets of Beaufort were quieter now, the last of the tourists lingering along the waterfront, their laughter and conversations distant against the lapping of the tide.

Peter stopped at the edge of the alley, arms crossed. "Alright, before we go charging into one of the most notoriously haunted houses in town, let's make sure we actually know what we're doing."

Sarah nodded. "Agreed."

Tilley looked around, spotting an empty bench near the docks. "Let's sit for a second and go over the plan."

They moved quickly, settling onto the wooden bench with the distant sound of boat rigging clanking softly against masts in the harbor. Peter leaned forward, elbows on his knees. "First things first—how exactly are we getting in?"

Tilley tapped her chin. "The house has been abandoned for a while, so there's a chance at least one of the doors or windows isn't completely secured."

Peter frowned. "Or… we break in?"

Sarah shot him a look. "We're not breaking anything. If we can't get in without damaging property, we leave."

Peter sighed dramatically. "Fine. But if there's a loose window or something, I'm taking that as an invitation."

Sarah ignored him and turned to Tilley. "Once we're inside, we set up the ritual as quickly as possible. I don't want to be in there longer than necessary."

Tilley nodded. "Agreed. So what's the setup?"

Sarah pulled India's book from her bag and flipped to the page on the ritual for requesting a ghost's presence. "We'll need to find a space in the house that feels… charged. Somewhere the spirit is strongest."

Peter muttered under his breath, "Fantastic."

Sarah continued, ignoring his sarcasm. "We'll light the candle, burn the sage for protection, set up the mirror, and I'll speak to him."

Tilley glanced at the book. "And then we listen."

Sarah nodded, feeling the weight of those words. "We listen."

Peter tapped his fingers against his knee. "And what if something goes wrong?"

Tilley smirked. "Oh, now you're worried?"

Peter gave her a look. "You're the one who originally told me the last owners literally fled in the middle of the night."

Sarah exhaled. "If things feel dangerous, we leave immediately. No, trying to push it. No heroics."

Peter considered that, then finally nodded. "Alright. Sounds reasonable."

Tilley grinned. "Look at that—he's on board."

Peter rolled his eyes. "Yeah, yeah. Let's just make sure we don't get ourselves added to the next version of this town's ghost tour."

Sarah felt her pulse quicken. It was time. She met both of their eyes. "Let's go." And with that, they rose from the bench and began the walk toward the notorious house—toward the unknown, toward the past, and toward the ghost that had been waiting for her all along.

As they walked toward Hammock House, the reality of what they were about to do settled in Sarah's chest like a weight. This wasn't just a ghost hunt; it wasn't about seeing him, it was about giving him the truth he never had in life. She would present herself as Sarah Thatch. If he showed himself, she would let him speak first—listen to him, hear his sorrow, his anger, his longing. And only when the time was right… she would tell him the truth. She glanced at Peter and Tilley, who were both unusually quiet as they walked alongside her.

Tilley broke the silence first. "You're really sure about this?"

Sarah nodded. "It's the only way."

Peter exhaled, rubbing the back of his neck. "You're braver than me, that's for sure."

Sarah gave a small smile. "I don't feel brave."

Tilley smirked. "That's how you know you're actually brave."

Peter shot her a look. "That made zero sense."

Tilley shrugged. "Made sense to me."

Sarah let out a breathy laugh, the moment of levity easing some of her nerves. But as they turned onto the darkened, overgrown path leading to Hammock House, all humor faded. The towering dormers of the house loomed ahead, dark and waiting, its silhouette stark against the backdrop of the star-flecked sky. A soft breeze rustled the Spanish moss, sending a whisper through the trees. Sarah slowed her steps, feeling the pull grow stronger, an unseen force urging her forward. She wasn't sure if it was fear or something else entirely, but she knew one thing for certain— He was waiting for her.

The closer they got to the old building, the quieter the world became. The night felt unnaturally still—as if the wind itself had chosen to hold its breath. Even the distant hum of the town had faded, leaving only the sound of their footsteps crunching softly against the dirt path. Sarah's heartbeat thudded in her ears, steady but heavy.

Time had not been kind to the old house. The wooden planks of the porch were warped from centuries of humid sea air, the shutters hung slightly askew, and the third-story dormer windows gaped like hollow eyes, staring down at them with a silent, knowing gaze. Spanish moss draped from the gnarled oak trees surrounding the house, their twisted limbs casting long, reaching shadows across the ground.

Peter let out a low whistle. "Whew… this place really knows how to set a mood."

Tilley shot him a look. "Not helping."

Sarah barely heard them. Her pulse quickened as she stepped off the road and onto the overgrown front lawn, her sneakers brushing against tall blades of grass that swayed ever so slightly—though there was no breeze. She could feel it. The energy was different here. Charged. Watchful. A tension sat thick in the air, pressing down on her chest. She wasn't just approaching a house; she was walking into a story that had never ended. Something shifted near the house—a faint movement in the shadows beneath the porch. She stopped cold, her breath catching; she knew that shape…that tall, broad figure.

That dark silhouette standing just behind the porch railing, motionless, watching. He was there. He had been waiting for her…and this time…she would not run.

Sarah's breath caught as she locked eyes with the shadowed figure on the porch. The British officer stood perfectly still, his dark coat blending into the night, his face just barely illuminated by the faint glow of the moonlight. She could feel the weight of his unwavering stare, cold and full of something unreadable—pain, anger, longing? A shiver crawled down her spine, but she forced herself to stay rooted to the spot, her hands clenched into fists to keep them from trembling. Then, as if sensing her hesitation, he vanished. Not with a dramatic gust of wind or a flash of light—he simply blinked out of existence, dissolving into the darkness like a shadow retreating into itself. Sarah exhaled shakily.

Tilley touched her arm. "Did you see something?"

Sarah nodded. "He's here."

Peter let out a slow breath. "Something's here, that's for sure."

But there was no time to stand frozen in fear. They had come here for a reason, and they needed to get inside before the weight of the moment made them second-guess everything. Sarah squared her shoulders. "Let's find a way in."

Tilley gestured toward the house. "The front door is obviously locked, and I doubt the bank is leaving keys under the mat."

Peter tilted his head, scanning the darkened windows. "If we're lucky, one of the side doors or windows might not be secured. It's an old house—something's bound to be loose."

Tilley motioned for them to follow as she crept around the side of the house, careful to keep her footsteps quiet on the overgrown path.

The side porch was in worse condition than the front—wooden slats missing from the railing, vines creeping up the posts as if nature itself was trying to reclaim the house. Peter tested the back door handle, giving it a firm tug. It was locked. He sighed. "Figures."

Sarah scanned the side of the house, her eyes landing on a window slightly ajar just beneath the awning. "There," she whispered, pointing.

Peter followed her gaze, then grinned. "Well, well. Looks like we just got an invitation."

Tilley rolled her eyes. "That's not an invitation, that's just old wood shifting."

Peter ignored her and stepped up onto the porch, testing the stability of the window. It groaned slightly, but didn't budge much further.

Sarah grabbed the edge and helped gently pry it open, the aged frame protesting with a soft creak. It was just wide enough for them to slip inside—one at a time.

Peter looked at them, his usual smirk faltering slightly. "Last chance to back out."

Sarah shook her head. "No turning back now."

Tilley exhaled. "Might as well make history."

Peter chuckled under his breath and held his hand out in front of him. "Alright then, ladies first." With one last deep breath, Sarah climbed through the window, dropping down into the darkness beyond. As she landed softly inside the house, a deep chill settled over her skin. The air was thick, unmoving—not just cold, but ancient, heavy, charged. It felt as if time had stopped here, the house suspended in a world that no longer belonged to the living. She took a slow breath, her eyes adjusting to the oppressive darkness. It was just like her dream.

The air smelled of damp wood, dust, and something faintly metallic—blood, her mind whispered. The walls loomed tall and shadowed, their surfaces warped and peeling from years of abandonment. Cobwebs clung to the corners, and the wooden floor beneath her feet creaked under the slightest shift of weight. A narrow hallway stretched out before her, just as she had seen in her dream. At the far end, a tall window let in a sliver of moonlight, spilling a soft, silver glow onto the warped floorboards. Her heart pounded as she took a cautious step forward. It felt like she had stepped into a memory, reliving a moment that wasn't her own. The whisper of a voice drifted through her mind, carried on an unseen current—

"Sarah…"

She froze. It was not her name being spoken; it was *hers*. Sarah Thatch. The girl whom the British officer had died believing he had lost. Her chest tightened. He was here. The moment she had been waiting for—the moment she had been drawn to—was finally happening, but she wasn't sure if she was ready.

A soft rustling sound behind her startled her back to the present. Tilley was climbing through the window, followed by Peter, both of them landing with barely a sound as they scanned the darkness around them.

Tilley's eyes widened as she took in the eerie silence, the sheer stillness of the place. "Wow… this is way worse than I imagined."

Peter exhaled, shoving his hands into his pockets as if trying to act casual. "Yep. Definitely haunted."

Sarah turned back toward the hall, her fingers brushing against the locket in her pocket. She had come here to face him, to let him speak. Now, there was no turning back. She turned to Peter and Tilley, her voice steady but urgent. "We need to go upstairs."

Tilley hesitated. "Upstairs? Why?"

Sarah swallowed, glancing down at the floor beneath her feet—solid, but somehow still echoing with something unseen. "In my dream," she murmured, "I was on the second-floor landing. That's where I saw him. And that's where I… where I felt—" She cut herself off. She didn't need to say it. Where she had stood in his blood. Tilley and Peter exchanged a look, both clearly unsettled.

Peter ran a hand through his hair. "Well. That's… not horrifying at all."

Tilley exhaled. "Okay. Upstairs it is."

Sarah turned toward the staircase, barely visible in the dark. The wooden banister was warped with age, the steps covered in a thin layer of dust, untouched by time but thick with presence. The three of them moved carefully, footsteps light, the house creaking beneath them as if protesting their presence. Sarah's pulse quickened with every step. This was the same path the British officer had taken in his final moments as he and his opponent raced through the house and up the stairs in a frenzy of flashing steel. As they reached the second-floor landing, a cold draft slid past Sarah's skin, making the fine hairs on her arms stand on end. She didn't have to say it, she knew this was the spot.

Peter let out a slow breath. "Alright. We're here. Now what?"

Sarah reached into her bag, fingers brushing against India's book, the candle, the sage, the iron key, and the mirror. "We set up the ritual," she said softly. Her hand trembled slightly, but she steeled herself. This was it, it was time to face him.

The second-floor landing was bathed in cold silver moonlight, casting long shadows that flickered against the walls as the three of them moved. Sarah took a steadying breath, kneeling on the aged wooden planks where she had stood in blood in her dream. She carefully pulled out the candle, the mirror, an old iron skeleton key, and the bundle of fresh sage. Tilley knelt beside her, helping arrange everything in a careful circle, while Peter stood nearby, his arms crossed, glancing uneasily around the empty house.

Sarah placed the mirror directly in front of her, angling it to catch the glow of the moonlight filtering through the window. The white candle was set at the center of the space, its wick ready to be lit.

Tilley handed Sarah the small bundle of sage. "You light it first, then the candle."

Sarah nodded, taking a deep breath before pulling out the matches. She struck one, the tiny flame flaring to life, and touched it carefully to the edge of the sage bundle. A thin ribbon of smoke curled into the air, carrying the earthy, crisp scent of burning herbs. Sarah let the smoke drift over her hands, her face, her shoulders—India had told her it was for protection, a barrier between herself and anything that meant her harm. Then, she pulled out another match and struck it to light the candle. The small golden flame flickered, casting an eerie glow against the mirror's surface.

Peter let out a slow breath. "Okay… now what?"

Sarah held her breath for a moment, then spoke softly.

"James."

As the name passed her lips, she realized no one had known his name, no one had told her who he really was. She just knew, and then the air in the room shifted. The candle flickered sharply, the temperature around them plunging. The house groaned, as if something long dormant had just awakened.

Tilley's breath hitched. "Did you feel that?"

Sarah nodded, her eyes locked onto the mirror's surface, waiting. She spoke again.

"James Thorne."

The moment she said his full name, a soft gust of wind blew through the landing—impossible, unnatural, like a breath from the past. Peter swore under his breath, taking an instinctive step back. Then, a shadow moved in the mirror. Sarah's stomach twisted. She wasn't looking at her own reflection anymore—something else was there. Someone who had been watching—waiting.

Moonlight poured through the broken window on the second-floor landing, dancing across the old wooden floorboards. The house creaked and groaned with age as if it were holding its breath. Sarah held on to the post at the second-floor landing to keep her knees from buckling. Peter stood a step behind her, tall and quiet, every muscle in his frame tight with anticipation, and Tilley knelt near the wall with the lantern, watching, wide-eyed but steady. Sarah's breath turned icy in her throat as the creaking of the third-floor landing echoed through the house. Slowly—dreadfully—she lifted her gaze. There, at the top of the stairs, stood the phantom of the British officer.

Captain James Thorne.

He was exactly as she had seen him before—his crisp military coat adorned with gold buttons and epaulets, his leather boots planted firmly on the worn wooden floorboards, his sword hanging at his side like an extension of his very being. But it was his face that sent a shudder through her. It was cold and dark, his sharp features twisted with emotion—anger, grief, betrayal. His eyes burned with an intensity that sent ice through her veins. He was now completely visible to Peter and Tilley, both staring at him in shock. Peter cursed under his breath. Tilley grabbed Sarah's wrist. "Oh my god…" she whispered.

But Sarah couldn't look away. The officer's gaze locked onto hers, as if searching—as if trying to see past time itself. And then—his voice came, low and broken, full of something deep and unresolved.

"Sarah."

Captain Thorne stared down at her, his face half-illuminated, half-consumed by darkness. His chest rose and fell as if he was truly breathing, as if he had never stopped. His eyes locked—those burning eyes that haunted her dreams. But then they shifted, they moved to Peter.

The captain's entire body stiffened. His expression twisted—grief, rage, heartbreak all battling for control. "You," he snarled. His voice was low and thunderous, like a storm approaching across an open sea. "You dare return here… by her side?"

Peter stepped forward, instinctively placing himself slightly in front of Sarah, grabbing her hand tightly.

"Who is he, Sarah?" James demanded, voice shaking with fury. "What is he to you?"

Sarah's mouth opened, but the captain wasn't looking at her anymore. He was fully focused on Peter now, and his torment deepened with every breath. The flickering lantern light caught the gold braid on his shoulder, the polished hilt of his sword, the agony behind his eyes.

"I saw you," James growled, descending a step. "That day. Through my glass. Holding her, stealing her from me. And now—" his voice cracked with anguish, "you stand here again, mocking me, standing at her side like before?"

"James," Sarah said, stepping forward gently, "you're mistaken. This isn't—"

"—Silence!" he thundered, his voice echoing down the staircase like cannon fire. "Do not defend him! Not again!"

Peter stood his ground, his gaze fixed on the ghostly figure. He could feel the fury radiating from the landing above—he could feel a storm of torment in the stairwell pressing in on all sides.

The air escaped Sarah's lungs. James thought Peter was Sarah Thatch's brother— the man who caused him to go completely mad. The man who killed him. And now the cycle threatened to repeat.

"James, listen to me," Sarah said softly, raising her voice only enough to reach his ears.

His eyes darted back to hers, full of pain. "He looks at you… as I once did."

She swallowed. "He sees me. Just as you once saw Sarah. But I am not her."

Silence fell between them.

James' apparition wavered—his form flickering like candlelight on the edge of wind. The fury in his eyes faltered, just a little. He began to descend the stairs, slowly, as the boards creaked beneath his ghostly aura. He stood just above Sarah, his expression softer, yet full of sorrow. He extended his right hand and brushed it by her cheek—her body now ice cold, "I have dreamed of your face all this time," he said, voice gentler now, lost. "I thought I had been given a second chance… but you came back only to be lost to me again."

"No," Sarah whispered. "I came back so you could be free. So you could know the truth. So you could find peace."

Sarah did not move. She had called him here, and now he was laying bare his torment. This was his truth, and she had to let him speak it. Even as the air grew heavier, the room colder, and the phantom of James Thorne stepped closer…closer to the truth he had never been given.

The candle flame twisted, the air thickened, and the room felt smaller, as if the walls of Hammock House were closing in around them. Sarah remained still, her breath barely leaving her lips. She could feel Tilley tensed beside her, feel Peter's uncertainty lingering in the air, but none of that mattered, because James Thorne's torment had not yet been spent.

His dark, piercing eyes locked onto her—seeing through her, searching, remembering. "I sailed through storms I never thought I would survive for you." His voice was a low, bitter rasp, filled with something ancient and unrelenting. "I betrayed my King and country for you. It was you I dreamed of—you I longed for. I clutched your letters to my chest on cold nights, held onto your words when I had nothing else. And when my ship finally turned home—" He faltered, his jaw tightening. "I searched for this dwelling through my glass from the deck, and there you were." His voice dropped into something fractured, something haunted. "But not alone."

His expression darkened, his shoulders tensing, his hands clenched as if he could still see it—still reliving the moment over and over, trapped in the endless cycle of his final heartbreak. "Another man's arms around you. Another man's hands upon you." A gust of wind tore through the hallway, strong enough to make the candle gutter, its flame flickering wildly before steadying again. "I was a fool." His mouth curled downward, pain flickering across his ghostly face. "To think I was enough. To believe you would keep your word."

Sarah felt her chest tighten, the weight of his misplaced sorrow pressing against her like the weight of the ocean. He had spent three hundred years believing this lie—believing Sarah Thatch had betrayed him, believing he had died in vain. And now, finally, he was demanding an answer.

Behind her, Peter remained silent, letting her speak. His presence was steady, like the Cape Lookout Light in the fog.

Sarah, letting go of Peter's hand, climbed a step slowly toward the specter.

"The man you fought was her brother, James. Not your rival. He had just returned from sea, the same as you. You fought over a misunderstanding that cost you and Sarah Thatch everything." The captain's shoulders dropped ever so slightly. His sword clattered softly to the wooden step. She watched as tears began to flood his eyes.

Sarah reached into her pocket and took out the locket, holding it up to the moonlight. "She waited for you. She kept this with her always, a lock of your hair, a piece of you inside. She never stopped loving you, James."

His jaw tightened, his form wavering slightly. Memories colliding. The moment of his death replaying in his mind—but this time, with the knowledge he had never allowed himself to see. "No." His voice was weaker now, his anger fading into something far more fragile. "You mean to tell me… I fell upon a blade meant only to defend… and I have spent purgatory in torment for nothing?" James staggered back a step, his dark boots hovering over the worn wood. His features were knotted with disbelief, as if he couldn't bring himself to accept the truth after all these years. "I—" He stopped, his brows furrowing. "But … the fight—"

Sarah swallowed. "You drew your sword on a man who meant no harm. He tried to explain, James. But you would not listen." She felt the weight of his grief, the way it clung to the walls, the air, the space between them. "Not for nothing." She stepped closer still, her tone tender but firm. "For love. For what you believed was true. But now, James… now you know."

His eyes searched hers, his form wavering slightly, as if his grip on this place—on this world—was finally loosening. For the first time, his expression was not angry. Not betrayed. Just… lost. "Sarah…" he murmured, his voice breaking on the name.

Sarah loosened her grip on the locket she had purchased at the antique shop. Slowly, she held it out toward him, "She longed for you, too."

James Thorne stared at the locket, his entire form flickering, as if something within him had just broken free. A deep shuddering breath left his lips, and for the first time in three hundred years…Captain James Thorne began to let go. His breath hitched, his ghostly form wavering as he stared at the locket in Sarah's outstretched hand. His storm-dark eyes lifted to meet hers, filled with something no longer burning rage or grief—but something softer, sadder… something breaking free.

"I have been lost in the dark for so long," he whispered. The candlelight flickered, the shadows along the walls shifting like waves upon the sea. "I have called for you… waited for you…" His voice cracked, his expression filled with awe and disbelief. "And you have come."

Sarah opened her mouth to speak, to tell him that she was not the woman he loved, that she was only here to set him free, but before she could say a word, a soft, glowing presence emerged beside her. A presence she had not called… but one that had been waiting.

A young woman stepped from the darkness, her form illuminated in silver light, her face delicate, kind, hauntingly identical to Sarah's. She gasped—It was her…the real Sarah Thatch. Her spirit stood just beyond the flickering candlelight, her long gown flowing like mist, her hair cascading in waves over her shoulders. Her soft eyes glistened with unshed tears as she gazed at James. "My love," she whispered, her voice carrying through the house like a song on the wind.

James staggered back, his hands trembling. His cold, sharp expression melted, his knees nearly buckling beneath him as he beheld her at last. "Sarah?" His voice was barely a breath.

She took one graceful step forward, the light around her growing brighter, warmer. "I did wait for you, James," she murmured. "I have waited all this time… for this moment. For us to be together again."

A shudder passed through James' form, his entire being flickering with raw, unfathomable emotion "It is you, you're real." He looked at her as if afraid she might fade away like a cruel illusion.

Sarah Thatch smiled. "As real as the love we have always shared."

James let out a breathless, broken laugh, one of relief, of surrender. The house groaned softly, as if it too was releasing something it had held for far too long. Sarah Thatch reached out her hand. "Come with me, my darling." Her voice was like the hush of the tide, gentle and knowing. "Come home with me."

James stared at her, his chest rising and falling with an emotion too great to name. And then, for the first time since he had returned from Kingston, since he had drawn his sword in a battle that never should have happened, he stepped forward. Slowly, his trembling hand lifted, reaching toward hers. The moment their fingers touched, a golden light spread through the room, bright and soft as the rising sun. Captain Thorne let out a long, shuddering breath—And then, with one final look at the woman he had died waiting for, he and Sarah Thatch faded together into the light.

The golden light slowly faded, leaving only the soft glow of the candle between them. The air in the house, once so thick and heavy with grief, now felt… lighter—warmer—alive. Sarah stared at the empty space where James Thorne and Sarah Thatch had stood, her heart still racing, her hands trembling at her sides. She had felt it—the shift, the release, the peace. They were gone. No longer bound to this house, no longer trapped in a story that had ended centuries ago.

Tilley let out a long, shaky breath, breaking the silence first. "Did that just… actually happen?"

Peter was still frozen, wide-eyed, his mouth slightly open as if he wanted to say something but had no idea where to start. Finally, he let out a low whistle, running a hand through his hair. "I mean… wow. That was—wow."

Sarah exhaled, finally able to breathe again. She closed her eyes for a moment, pressing a hand to her chest to steady herself. "It's over," she whispered.

Tilley shook her head in disbelief. "They actually… moved on."

Peter let out a dry laugh, still stunned. "Yeah. Guess your ghost problem just—poof—solved itself."

Sarah didn't laugh. She felt different. As if something deep inside her had changed, as if she had just witnessed something she would never be able to explain, but had always been meant to see. She looked around the old, darkened house, now feeling more empty than eerie. No cold breath of the past lingering at her heels. No eyes watching her from the shadows. Just… silence. And for the first time since setting foot onto this property, Sarah knew—the house was finally at peace.

Tilley shook her head again, still trying to process everything. "I can't believe it. All this time, and no one ever thought to just… tell him the truth."

Sarah smiled softly. "Maybe he was just waiting for someone to listen."

Peter exhaled, rubbing the back of his neck. "Well, whatever just happened… I think it's safe to say this is officially the best ghost story in Beaufort."

Tilley smirked. "And no one is ever gonna believe it."

Sarah chuckled, finally feeling some of the tension leave her body. "Probably not."

Peter gestured toward the window. "Alright, so… since we didn't die, can we maybe leave before the house changes its mind and decides to trap us here?"

Sarah and Tilley laughed, and without another word, they gathered their things. Sarah needed to take one last glance at the now quiet and still landing. She stood frozen at the bottom of the stairs, her breath still shaky, her hand still clutching the locket. Beside her, the lantern flickered low. Tilley looked from Sarah to Peter, then back up the stairs as if expecting something else to appear. But the house had settled into itself now —quiet and watching. "I… I think I'll wait outside," Tilley said gently, her voice barely above a whisper. She offered Sarah a soft smile, touched her arm, and then turned toward the open window. Her footsteps were light, respectful.

For a long moment, it was just Sarah and Peter. He stepped closer, his shoes barely making a sound against the old wooden planks. She still hadn't moved. The moonlight painted her in a soft glow, like something out of a memory—her gray eyes unfocused, her expression dazed and tender. "Sarah," Peter said quietly. She blinked, and when her eyes met his, he saw the storm still inside them. He reached for her without hesitation, his calloused palms cradling her face. His thumbs gently brushed her cheeks, anchoring her back to the present. "You okay?" he asked, his voice husky but soft. She nodded slowly, but a tear slipped from the corner of her eye anyway. Peter leaned forward and pressed his lips to her forehead—warm, steady, protective. The kind of kiss that said *you're not alone now*. The kind that said *I see you. I see all of you.*

Sarah exhaled, her breath catching in the hollow of her throat. She let herself lean into his touch for just a moment longer. Peter pulled back, his hands still on her cheeks. "Let's get out of here," he murmured. "You've done enough for one night." She nodded again.

As they turned toward the window, the house remained still behind them, the shadows calm, the staircase no longer a place of tragedy, but one of closure. Peter steadied Sarah's arm, stepping aside, letting her go first. She paused as she climbed through the window, casting one last look over her shoulder.

"Rest now," she whispered to the house, and then she stepped outside.

Peter followed, closing the window behind them—firmly, but with quiet reverence—leaving Hammock House at peace for the first time in three hundred years. The air outside felt cleaner, the night sky somehow brighter, though the moon still hung heavy above them. The trio walked silently, each of them lost in their thoughts, the shadows of Hammock House growing smaller behind them. Sarah's mind was still racing, trying to make sense of everything—of the ghostly encounter, the feelings that had come over her, the revelation of the truth. It all felt like it had happened to someone else, yet it had been her all along.

Finally, Peter broke the silence, his voice rough, almost as if he were still processing it all. "Well, I'll admit… I didn't think it'd end like that."

Tilley laughed lightly, but there was a tiredness in her voice. "Neither did I. It's strange, isn't it? How something so… heavy… can just be lifted with a few words."

Sarah nodded, turning toward her two friends. "It's over. They're together now… at peace."

Peter let out a long breath, glancing back toward the house. "I know I'm the best tour guide of the dearly departed, but I don't know if I'll ever get used to the idea of ghosts actually being… real."

Tilley grinned. "Oh, don't worry. We'll find some new way to freak you out before the week's up."

Peter rolled his eyes but smiled. "If you could've seen your face when the two of them faded away… I think you might be scarred for life."

Sarah smiled softly, but there was something a little sad in her eyes. "I'll never forget it. I've never felt something like that—like… the weight of history was lifting."

Tilley, usually the more lighthearted of the two, looked over at Sarah with a serious expression. "You did it. You gave them the peace they needed."

Peter added, "That's not something a lot of people get to do. You helped them."

Sarah looked down, taking in the quiet, warm, humid air around them. "I didn't do it alone."

Tilley reached over and gave her a light nudge. "You still had to walk in there, face him, listen to him."

Peter looked up at the stars. "I think… all of us did. Maybe we weren't meant to just be here for the ghost stories, but to help make history right."

Sarah stopped walking, looking back over her shoulder at Hammock House one final time. She didn't feel the fear anymore—just a deep, peaceful stillness that seemed to stretch out in all directions. “It feels like the town itself is breathing a little easier.”

Tilley glanced at her. “Maybe we all are.”

With one last glance toward the house, they turned and started walking toward the quiet town, their hearts lighter, and the house’s spirits finally free from the shadows.

Chapter 35

Two days had passed since the night at Hammock House, and in that time, life in Beaufort had begun to settle back into its usual rhythm. The summer sun shone bright, the streets were filled with tourists, and the sea breeze carried the familiar scent of the surrounding marshes and blooming gardenias. For Sarah, though, something felt different. It was as if the air was clearer, the weight that had lingered in the town finally lifted. She still thought about Captain James Thorne and Sarah Thatch, about the love that had waited three hundred years to be reunited. She had been a part of setting them free, and no matter where life took her, she knew she would carry that moment forever. But now, it was time to look ahead.

That afternoon, Sarah, Tilley, and Peter met up at their usual spot—a shaded table outside the Salt and Cedar, across from the Royal James Café. Peter arrived last, dropping into a chair with his usual easygoing grin. "Alright, ghostbusters. What's next?"

Tilley set her iced coffee down with purpose, her eyes lighting up. "The fundraiser. We're doing this."

Sarah nodded, feeling a spark of excitement. "If we raise enough money, the museum could buy Hammock House and finally restore it."

Peter leaned back in his chair, arms crossed. "And, you know, maybe keep it from getting haunted again. Just a thought."

Tilley smirked. "You know you'd love it if it were still haunted."

Peter shrugged. "Would make for a great business opportunity."

Sarah rolled her eyes. "Well, we want it to be a part of history, not just another ghost story."

Tilley pulled out a notebook and flipped open to a fresh page. "Okay, so we need to strategize. We have Theresa Guthrie's support, and she's willing to donate the portrait of Sarah Thatch if we pull this off."

Peter nodded. "And my grandad is on board—he's been talking to some of his old maritime buddies who love historical preservation projects."

Sarah leaned in. "Then let's start planning. We need to reach as many people as possible—locals, historians, even ghost-hunters. If we do this right… we could really save Hammock House."

For the first time in days, there was no shadow hanging over them, no mystery waiting in the dark. Just a new adventure, a new purpose, and as they began mapping out their plan, Sarah knew—this summer in Beaufort had changed everything.

The next few days were a whirlwind of preparation. Sarah, Tilley, and Peter had poured over their plans, reaching out to local historians, museum patrons, and community leaders. But all their efforts hinged on one major event—the annual Maritime Museum fundraising gala that was set to take place at one of the town's historic waterfront venues—The Harvey W. Smith Watercraft Center. The event was a big deal. Prominent members of the community, museum benefactors, and town officials would be in attendance. More importantly, so would Mr. Alden Mercer, the head of the bank that currently owned Hammock House.

"If we're going to convince anyone that the house belongs to the town," Tilley said, "it has to be him.

Chapter 36

The sun had just dipped below the horizon, casting a rosy-gold glow over the waterfront as the crowd gathered at the Maritime Museum's Annual Gala. Twinkle lights shimmered above the open-air tent, strung from mast to mast of decorative sailing poles, casting a warm glow over linen-covered tables and glass lantern centerpieces. The sound of a live string quartet drifted through the evening air, mingling with the faint scent of magnolia and jasmine from the blooming gardens across the street.

The moment Sarah stepped inside the Harvey W. Smith Watercraft Center, she felt transported into another world. The space where wainwrights built wooden boats with primitive tools of the past was elegantly decorated, with chandeliers casting golden light across the hardwood floors. Small wooden dinghies in progress were displayed around the perimeter of the building, and tools, organized methodically, hung on the walls where each project was placed. The scent of freshly cut flowers and ocean air drifting through the open balcony doors filled the space.

The string quartet played softly in the corner, the lilting notes of a violin carrying through the air as guests in formal attire mingled, laughed, and exchanged pleasantries over glasses of wine, champagne, and cider.

Peter stood near the back, dressed in a navy blazer, his sun-kissed hair slightly tamed, though a few strands refused to stay put. He wore his leather cord with the Atocha coin, now polished and gleaming against the crisp white of his shirt. He hadn't seen Sarah yet, and though he tried to keep up a conversation with Dr. David Tillman and one of the museum donors, he found his eyes continually drifting toward the entrance. Then —he saw her, and the world went very still.

Sarah stepped through the massive barn doors, walking between her parents and Ethan, but Peter only saw her. The delicate sea-glass green of her dress shimmered in the low light, catching the reflection of the harbor like moving water. Her long, dark hair was swept back in soft waves, a few tendrils curling around her face, and her gray eyes sparkled like silver beneath the twinkling lights. She was breathtaking. It wasn't just the dress, nor was it just the candlelight in her eyes. It was *her*—the way she held herself with quiet strength, her grace and intelligence and something timeless, something that made Peter feel like he was standing in two centuries at once. His breath caught, and for a moment he forgot what he was supposed to say to the person in front of him.

Sarah's eyes found his across the crowd. Her lips curled into the softest smile, as if she already knew what he was thinking. Peter took a step toward her, weaving through guests and wine glasses and laughter until he reached her side. "You look…" He shook his head, his voice quieter than he intended. "You look like a vision, Sarah Thatch."

She laughed, her cheeks flushing. "That's not my last name."

He leaned in slightly, his voice a little lower. "It was once."

Sarah glanced up at him, and he reached out to brush a stray hair behind her ear, his fingers grazing her cheek. "I didn't think I could be more taken with you than I already was," he said honestly. "But here you are —and I am."

She looked down, her smile shy and warm, then met his gaze again. "Let's make tonight count."

"We will," Peter said, offering his arm. "Let's go change the future of Hammock House."

And together, under the stars, chandeliers, and sea breeze of the magical gala, they stepped into the crowd —two hearts that had somehow found their way back to each other, across centuries and storms, ready to honor the past by saving what remained of it.

Peter guided Sarah through the soft hum of conversation and clinking glasses, his hand lightly resting at the small of her back. String lights glittered above them like a constellation suspended in time, casting gentle shadows across linen tablecloths and polished wood underfoot. Servers wove through the crowd with silver trays of crab cakes, bacon-wrapped scallops, and flutes of champagne and sparkling cider. The scent of lemon, rosemary, and ocean air mingled in a way that was purely Beaufort—elegant, breezy, and touched with old-world charm.

At the far side of the building, just beneath a banner that read "Blackbeard's Lost Legacy—Save Hammock House", Sarah spotted Tilley, who was talking animatedly with one of the museum's board members. She wore a midnight blue dress that swished around her knees and a necklace shaped like a ship's wheel that sparkled every time she turned her head. She noticed Sarah and Peter approaching and immediately broke into a grin.

"There she is!" Tilley beamed, slipping away from the conversation and throwing her arms around Sarah in an enthusiastic hug. "Oh my gosh, look at you! You look like you just stepped out of a Jane Austen novel."

Sarah laughed. "You clean up pretty well yourself."

Tilley leaned in, eyes wide. "You have no idea how many people have already come up to me asking about Hammock House. We've got bank execs, history buffs, and ghost story lovers all buzzing about it. I think tonight might really change everything."

Peter gave a subtle nod. "We're ready if we need to speak. Mercer said he'd stop by our table before the auction portion starts."

"I've got your materials in the binder," Tilley said, motioning toward a side table tucked beside the stage where a stack of museum presentation packets sat. "If anyone needs to see the restoration proposal or property records, we've got it all in black and white."

Sarah glanced around the room again. "It's kind of surreal, isn't it? Everyone dressed up, music playing, drinks flowing—and all of it… all of this… might actually help save that house."

Peter looked over at her with a soft smile. "You're part of something bigger now, Sarah. And the best part is, it's only the beginning."

Tilley squeezed Sarah's hand. "We're doing it, Thatch. You're not just connected to history—you're helping make it."

As the sun finally dipped beyond the horizon and the lanterns lit with a golden glow, the three of them stood side by side—Sarah, Tilley, and Peter—each changed by what they had uncovered, and more determined than ever to honor the past by preserving the future. In the wind that whispered through the gala and over the harbor, it felt like Hammock House was listening.

Peter adjusted his jacket, looking quite debonaire and unusually polished for someone who spent most of his time in pirate attire. "Alright, ladies, let's work some magic."

Tilley smirked. "By the way, I didn't know you owned real clothes."

"Only for special occasions," Peter shot back, flashing a grin. "And this, my friends, is very special."

Tilley, in her navy dress that made her look every bit the daughter of a museum director, straightened the portfolio in her arms—inside were historic photos, the property deeds, and carefully written arguments on why Hammock House deserved to be preserved.

"This isn't just about making our case," she reminded them. "It's about making Mr. Mercer want to be a part of something bigger than a real estate deal."

Sarah took a deep breath. They could do this. They had to. With one last glance at each other, they stepped inside the gala, ready to make their pitch to the man who held the future of Hammock House in his hands.

Beyond the large room, an open-air veranda overlooked the moonlit creek where sailboats and yachts gently bobbed in their slips. The glow of dock lights reflected off the water, shimmering like stars fallen from the sky. Sarah couldn't help but feel a little out of place among the finely dressed crowd, but Tilley and Peter seemed completely at ease—Tilley because she had grown up around these kinds of events, and Peter because he had never cared much for social rules anyway. Still, they all had a purpose here, and Alden Mercer was the key to making it happen.

Tilley had already mapped out their plan:

1. Observe first. They needed to get a feel for Mr. Mercer's mood—was he open to conversation? Deep in discussion with museum donors? Or on his way out the door?
2. Find common ground. They couldn't just walk up and ask him to sell Hammock House to the museum. They had to ease into the conversation, bring up his interest in historic preservation, and make him feel like part of something important.
3. Deliver the pitch—casually. This wasn't a formal business proposal. It was about making him want to be part of the project.

Peter had even suggested a backup plan: "If all else fails," he had said with a grin, "I'll just impress him with my irresistible charm."

Sarah rolled her eyes. "You do realize this man deals with multimillion-dollar properties, right?"

Peter had shrugged. "Exactly. Which means he appreciates a good deal. We just have to make him see that this is one."

By this time, the gala was bustling with excited patrons. They began scanning the room for Alden Mercer. They found him near the veranda doors, engaged in polite conversation with a small group of museum board members. Mr. Mercer was a distinguished older man, dressed in a well-tailored suit, his silver hair neatly combed back. He had the calm, calculated air of someone who had spent decades making important financial decisions, but there was a warmth in his expression that hinted at a genuine appreciation for the event.

"That's our guy," Peter murmured. "So what's the play?"

Tilley straightened, smoothing her dress. "We let the conversation flow naturally. I'll introduce us, and we'll see if we can steer things toward Hammock House."

Sarah took a deep breath. "Alright. Let's do this."

With quiet confidence, they made their way across the room toward the man who held the fate of Hammock House in his hands. Unlike the other guests, who mingled with glasses of champagne, Mercer stood with a scotch in hand, observing the room with the practiced ease of someone used to assessing investments, risks, and opportunities. His expression was neutral, but the moment his gaze landed on Peter, his lips curved into a knowing smile.

"Well, if it isn't Beaufort's most famous pirate!" he greeted, extending his hand toward Peter.

Peter smirked as he shook it. "Where! Show me!" he exclaimed with a wink.

Mercer chuckled. "I was just telling the board about you. Took my grandkids on your ghost tour last summer —best part of their trip. My grandson swears he saw a ghost in the burial ground. I told him it was probably just your storytelling."

Peter grinned. "Hey, I can't take credit for everything. Some ghosts just don't like to stay quiet."

Mercer laughed, shaking his head before turning toward Tilley and Sarah. "I take it you three aren't just here for the hors d'oeuvres."

Tilley, ever poised, lifted her chin. "No, sir. We know the museum's goal tonight—to raise money to purchase Hammock House. We wanted to introduce ourselves and talk about how important this is, not just to the museum but to Beaufort as a whole."

Mercer studied them, his sharp, assessing gaze shifting between the three. "I admire your enthusiasm, but you realize this is a massive undertaking. The house has been left to decay for years. It's not exactly in habitable condition."

Sarah nodded. "That's exactly why it needs to be saved. Right now, it's just… sitting there, falling apart. If we wait too long, there won't be anything left to restore."

Mercer took a slow sip of his scotch, considering. "Tilley, my dear, you sound personally invested."

Peter smirked. "Well, she has been inside the house, so—"

Sarah shot him a quick look, silently warning him to keep that part out of the conversation. Tilley turned back to Mercer. "I just think it would be a mistake to let it slip away. Hammock House isn't just another old home—it's part of this town's identity. Blackbeard, the colonial era, the British naval history… it all ties together there."

Mercer nodded slowly. "The board members have been pushing this initiative for years. But the truth is, the bank won't let go of it unless they see it as a worthwhile investment."

Tilley took a step forward. "Then that's exactly what we need to prove."

Mercer's brow lifted, clearly intrigued by their determination. "And how do you propose to do that?"

Sarah, Tilley, and Peter exchanged a knowing look before turning back to Mercer. "We have a plan," Tilley said, voice steady.

Mercer swirled his drink in his hand, then gave them a measured smile. "Then let's hear it." Sarah, Tilley, and Peter stood their ground, facing Alden Mercer with a newfound confidence. This was their moment. Tilley, always prepared, took the lead. She opened the leather portfolio in her arms, revealing historic photographs, old property deeds, and carefully drafted plans for restoration. She placed the first document on the nearby table—a map of Beaufort from the 1700s, with Hammock House marked prominently. "Mr. Mercer," Tilley began, "Hammock House isn't just an old property. It's one of the oldest surviving structures in Beaufort, dating back to the early 1700s. If it's lost, we lose a part of our town's living history."

Sarah picked up where Tilley left off, pointing to a photograph of the house in its better days. "Right now, the house is abandoned and decaying, but it's still salvageable. The foundation is solid, the original framework is intact, and with the right funding, we can restore it to its historical original condition—just like the preservation projects at the Maritime Museum. We only need the bank's investment long enough to secure the property for the museum. The rest of the financials for restoration will come from crowdfunding."

Mercer's gaze traveled over the materials, his interest clear, but his expression unreadable. "And what exactly will the museum do with it? Turn it into an exhibit?"

Peter leaned in slightly, his voice casual but confident. "Exactly. The museum already draws thousands of visitors every year for the Queen Anne's Revenge exhibit. Imagine if they could actually walk through a place Blackbeard himself may have owned."

Tilley nodded. "We want to preserve it as a living museum, complete with guided tours, educational programs, and even small community events. It could be part of the museum's maritime heritage collection—a physical space that tells the real history of Beaufort."

Sarah placed a final piece of paper in front of Mercer—a fundraising plan detailing how they intended to raise money for the purchase and restoration. "We know that funding a project like this isn't easy," she admitted. "But the interest is there. People have been talking about Hammock House for decades—historians, tourists, and even international ghost hunters. If we launch a national campaign, we can bring in support from history enthusiasts and preservation groups across the country."

Peter smirked. "And you know how many people would love to say they helped save THE most notorious pirate's house?"

Mercer let out a small chuckle, but his eyes remained sharp as he studied the documents. "This is an ambitious plan," he admitted. "And it's clear you've put real thought into it."

Tilley nodded. "The museum is ready to take on the responsibility. But we need the bank to be willing to sell it to us. If we can prove we have the funding and public interest, will you consider making it happen?"

Mercer was silent for a long moment. He set down his glass, resting his hands on the table as he examined their work. Finally, he looked at them and smiled thoughtfully.

"You've certainly made a strong case," he said. "I'll admit, I expected this to be a simple donation drive tonight—but you three have made a much larger case than I would have expected."

Sarah held her breath. "Does that mean you'll support it?"

Mercer exhaled, his gaze flicking over the materials once more. "If you can prove there's real backing for this project, I'll take it to the bank's board of directors. If they agree, I'll personally ensure that Hammock House is sold to the museum for restoration—not to another private investor."

Tilley grinned, barely holding back her excitement. "We can do that."

Peter smirked. "No doubt about it."

Sarah felt a weight lift from her chest. They had their chance. Now, all they had to do was make it happen. Mercer straightened, nodding toward them. "Then I suggest you get to work." And with that, the future of Hammock House was in their hands.

As dessert plates were cleared and the quartet shifted to a slow, ambient melody, a spotlight warmed the small stage at the center of the gala woodshop-turned-ballroom. Conversation quieted as Dr. David

Tillman stepped into view, the microphone catching just enough feedback to hush the crowd to silence. He stood tall, his suit crisp, a modest maritime pin on his lapel. Years of preserving coastal history had earned him respect from every corner of the region—from scholars and sailors to museum patrons and lawmakers alike. But tonight, his voice carried more than authority. It carried urgency.

"Ladies and gentlemen," he began, "thank you all for being here tonight—for believing, as I do, that the past is not something to be paved over and forgotten, but something to be remembered, studied, and honored." A ripple of agreement moved through the crowd. "As you know, the purpose of this gala is to raise funds to support the acquisition and restoration of Hammock House, a colonial-era home perched on the edge of town—older than nearly every building in Beaufort. It has stood for over three centuries, witnessing the birth of our town, the passing of storms, of wars, of legends…"

He paused.

"And now, it stands on the brink of ruin. If it is not preserved, it risks becoming yet another forgotten foundation beneath the high-rises and condominiums already creeping in from our southern coastline. Beaufort's charm—its history—is under threat. What makes our town unique is not just its beauty, but the stories etched into every clapboard, every shutter, every floorboard that creaks beneath our feet."

A murmur of acknowledgment passed through the room. Even the servers had paused.

Dr. Tillman smiled. "But tonight, I want to step aside and introduce someone with a deeper connection to this house than anyone I know. She's smart, driven, and just as stubborn as her mother. She's my daughter—and one of the fiercest preservationists I've ever met. Please welcome Abigail Tillman to the stage."

The crowd applauded warmly as Tilley stood from her seat. Sarah squeezed her hand, and Peter offered a wink. With her head high and notes in hand, Tilley crossed to the stage and stepped into the spotlight.

"Good evening, everyone," she said, voice clear but touched with emotion. "If you know me, you know I grew up with a deep love for Beaufort's history. It was passed down to me like an heirloom—from my mom's work with the Queen Anne's Revenge project to my dad's passion for preserving our maritime legacy. But tonight isn't just about history in a general sense. It's personal." She glanced toward the back of the room, where the portrait of Sarah Thatch—newly restored and dramatically lit—stood on an easel as part of the evening's presentation. "This project began as a summer research assignment. But it's turned into something more—a mystery unraveled, a story rediscovered. And now it's become a mission shared between three young people who want to make a difference: me, Sarah Whitaker, and our town's beloved Peter vanPelt, also known as Peter Pirate."

She looked out at the room, her voice steady.

"Hammock House is more than an old house. It is living history. It has ties to Blackbeard, to the British Navy, to early Beaufort families. We've uncovered evidence of lost portraits, deeds written in gold, and connections to people whose stories have been silenced by time—until now."

The crowd was leaning in.

"Our goal is to raise one million dollars to acquire and restore the house, transforming it into an extension of the Maritime Museum's Queen Anne's Revenge Legacy project—an educational space where students, historians, and visitors can experience the layered, complicated, and beautiful stories of Beaufort's past."

She took a breath. "We're asking you to help us reach half of that goal tonight. With so many influential business leaders, philanthropists, and preservation supporters gathered here, this is our chance to do something lasting. Something real."

She let the silence linger.

"Because once it's gone, it's gone. We can't let Beaufort's heart get chipped away by dollar signs, bulldozers, and another Pina-coladaville Hotel, not when we have the chance to save it."

Applause broke out—soft at first, then louder, swelling with the energy of conviction and shared purpose.

As clapping from Tilley's impassioned speech slowly quieted, she took one final look around the crowd, her voice softening with heartfelt gratitude. "Thank you all for being here tonight," she said, her eyes glinting under the lights. "Thank you for listening, for believing, and for finding space in your hearts to help us preserve not just a building—but a legacy."

A second wave of applause rippled across the room as Tilley stepped back from the microphone. Dr. Tillman rose from his seat at the head table and gave her a proud nod as she returned to join Sarah and Peter. Above the stage, a large projector screen cast a glowing image of their online fundraising platform, set in real time to show donations flooding in from gala attendees, patrons across the country, and museum supporters following the campaign online.

A counter in bold white numbers ticked upward.

$50,000... $200,000... $447,200…

Tables buzzed as phones came out and fingers danced across screens, pledging support in real-time. Volunteers moved between tables with tablets and pledge cards, helping those who weren't tech-savvy submit their donations. The energy in the building had shifted—electric, hopeful, united. The room watched together as the number climbed closer and closer to the halfway point of their million-dollar goal.

$486,900... $487,000... $488,500... $490,000...

Then it stalled. Guests looked around, murmuring, watching the number hold just $10,000 short of their target. Peter leaned toward Sarah and whispered, "So close I can taste it." Tilley's hands were clasped in front of her face, her fingers crossed tightly.

Then, just as the murmur of uncertainty began to grow, there was a new entry on the screen. *Donation received: $10,000 – From the Law Office of Spruill Carlisle & Whitaker.* The counter rolled forward with a satisfying chime: *$500,000*!

The watercraft center erupted in cheers. Applause burst from every corner of the space, rising like a wave beneath the sails of hope. People rose from their chairs, whistling, clapping, raising glasses. The quartet launched into a joyful tune, and servers popped corks on bottles of champagne. Sarah's eyes went wide as she turned to find her dad across the table, casually slipping his phone back into his blazer pocket. "Dad!" she exclaimed.

Pierce Whitaker gave her a modest shrug, but the corners of his mouth curled into a proud smile. "Someone had to push it over the line. Might as well be us."

Sarah threw her arms around him, and her mother joined in the embrace, holding both of them tight. "I can't believe you did that," Sarah exclaimed.

Her mom smiled through glassy eyes. "We've always believed in you. Now it seems the rest of the world does, too."

Ethan, standing a few steps away with a celebratory glass of sparkling cider, leaned in and smirked. "So… Dad just dropped your college fund to save a haunted house? Hope it's worth it."

Sarah laughed, turning toward him. "It's not haunted anymore."

Peter stepped up beside her and added with a wink, "Nope. Just historically occupied."

Everyone laughed. And beneath the laughter, the glow of lanterns, and the buzz of celebration, Sarah felt something else: a calm joy, a deep sense of purpose, and the love of people who had become her summer family. They were saving the house, and in doing so, they would be saving a story—one that might've otherwise been lost. Peter looked over at Sarah, pride unmistakable in his eyes. Sarah exhaled slowly, her own heart brimming with something bigger than herself.

The celebration inside the Watercraft Center was in full swing—glasses clinked, laughter spilled into the rafters, and the music lifted like a tide over the joyful chatter. But amid the energy and excitement, Sarah found herself pulled away, her gaze drawn toward the wide sliding doors left partially open to let the sea breeze drift through the massive boat house. Beyond the open threshold, Taylor Creek shimmered in the light of a sliver of moon, calm and smooth as glass. Anchor lights high atop the masts of sailboats bobbed in the distance, their reflections dancing on the surface. The barrier island lay quiet on the far shore, a ribbon of pale sand stretching out beneath the stars.

That's when she saw them. A pair—a man and a woman—walking hand in hand along the moonlit beach. The woman's long gown drifted around her ankles like mist, and the man's tall frame moved with the elegant precision of someone born to command. Their silhouettes glowed faintly, not illuminated by the moon, but made of it—ethereal and distant, yet heartbreakingly familiar. Sarah was taken aback.

She stepped outside onto the deck quietly, careful not to disturb the moment. The cool boards beneath her heels were damp with dew, and the soft hum of the music followed her as she approached the railing, but just as she reached the edge, the figures slipped out of sight, vanishing into the trees like mist scattered by wind. Still, Sarah remained. She closed her eyes and breathed in the salt air, her fingers curling around the railing. The music swelled inside—an old jazz standard. The breeze lifted her hair, and the sound of the water lapping at the pilings below soothed the last remnants of adrenaline in her veins. Then—a hand touched hers. Warm. Familiar. Gentle. She opened her eyes. Peter stood beside her, his expression soft and full of unspoken understanding. He didn't ask what she'd seen. He didn't need to. "Hey," he said quietly.

Sarah smiled. "Hi." The music shifted into a slow, romantic tune. From inside, couples began to sway beneath the twinkling lights.

Peter tilted his head, a boyish grin curling at the corner of his mouth. "Would you… like to dance?"

She hesitated, suddenly aware of her heartbeat, but then nodded. "Yeah. I'd like that."

He offered his hand, and she placed hers in it, letting him pull her gently into his arms. His other hand settled respectfully at her waist, and she let her head come to rest on his shoulder, the rhythm of the music guiding them into a quiet, wordless sway. It was like time folded inward. The crashing centuries, the ghostly legacies, the mysteries, the griefs—they all softened into this one moment. Peter's hand traced slow, reassuring circles on her back. Sarah listened to the beat of his heart beneath her cheek and smiled without opening her eyes. When the music ended, they lingered in the hush that followed. Then, a voice chirped brightly behind them.

"Oh my gosh!" Tilley burst through the doors, stopping abruptly at the sight of the two of them still wrapped in each other's arms. "Okay, I knew it! You two are totally like Sarah Thatch and Captain Thorne all over again." Peter and Sarah both chuckled, stepping apart slightly, cheeks flushed, caught somewhere between dream and reality. Tilley threw her arms around both of them. "Come on—everyone's asking for you inside. We've got people trying to donate extra just to have their names engraved on the Hammock House plaque!"

Peter glanced at Sarah, his fingers brushing hers as they turned back toward the glow of the gala. "You ready?" he asked.

Sarah gave one last glance out at the quiet creek, where nothing stirred now but moonlight. "Yeah," she said softly. "I'm ready."

And together, they stepped back into the light.

Chapter 37

The days following the gala were a whirlwind. With Mr. Mercer's conditional approval, Sarah, Tilley, and Peter threw themselves into launching a national fundraising campaign. They needed to prove that people cared about Hammock House, that it was more than just a forgotten relic—it was a piece of living history worth saving.

Tilley, with her museum connections, was able to secure partnerships with historical societies, maritime preservation groups, and even ghost-hunting communities who had long been fascinated with the house. Peter took charge of media outreach, using his charisma and storytelling skills to pitch their campaign to travel blogs, local news, and even a few well-known history podcasts. Sarah, drawing from her artistic background, created stunning visuals—watercolor renderings of Hammock House restored to its former glory, social media graphics, and a video tour of the property that captured both its haunting beauty and its historical significance.

Within days, their crowd-funding campaign and social media pages were flooded with engagement. People from all over the country—historians, educators, and everyday lovers of yesteryear—began donating, sharing, and commenting. Then, something big happened. A well-known history influencer with over two million followers on social media shared their campaign, calling it "one of the most exciting historical preservation efforts of the year." Within hours, donations skyrocketed. News outlets picked up the story. A documentary filmmaker reached out, wanting to follow their journey. And just like that, Hammock House wasn't just a local project anymore—it was a national movement.

Late one evening, Sarah, Tilley, and Peter sat together at their favorite table at the coffee shop, refreshing the donation page over and over as the numbers climbed higher. Tilley covered her mouth in shock. "We just passed $850,000!"

Peter leaned back in his chair, shaking his head with a stunned grin. "I can't believe this is actually working."

Sarah, watching the screen in awe, felt a great, unshakable pride. They were doing it. Hammock House was going to be saved. And for the first time since setting foot in that house, she knew—this was exactly where she was meant to be and what she was meant to do—making a difference.

The campaign had grown beyond their wildest expectations. What had started as a passionate idea between three young people had now become a full-scale historical preservation movement with widespread national attention. With donations pouring in, press coverage growing, and historians across the country taking an interest, the dream of saving Hammock House was no longer just a possibility—it was within reach. To celebrate how far they had come—and to give one last push toward their goal—the Maritime Museum decided to host a special event: A public fundraiser in the Maritime Museum, bringing together the town, donors, and supporters for a night of history, storytelling, and community.

Peter, dressed in his finest historic regalia, had revamped his ghost tour, making Hammock House the centerpiece of the evening, retelling its true history alongside its ghostly lore. Tilley helped organize museum exhibits on the property's past, showcasing original deeds, artifacts, and even Theresa Davis Guthrie's donated portrait of Sarah Thatch, displayed for all to see in a staged vignette of the parlor in Hammock House, the portrait hung above an ornate mantle above a faux flickering fireplace. Sarah, using her artistic talent, created a live painting demonstration, where she worked on a watercolor of Hammock House as it would look restored, selling prints to raise additional funds.

As the sun began setting on Taylor Creek, the museum filled with locals, tourists, and donors, all gathered in support of the cause. Sarah stood beside Tilley and Peter, taking in the scene—primitive iron chandeliers reflecting off the glass museum cases, the laughter and conversation, the sense of something major falling into place. Then came the moment everyone had been waiting for:

Dr. David Tillman, in his signature museum button-down, stepped onto the stage in the museum's auditorium, clearing his throat as he addressed the crowd. "I think it's safe to say," he began, voice carrying over the audience, "that what started as a dream has become something unstoppable." A ripple of cheers and applause filled the air. "I've spoken with the board," he continued, his gaze settling on Tilley, Sarah, and Peter. "And it is my great pleasure and honor to announce that with your fundraising efforts and overwhelming public support, the Maritime Museum has secured funding to purchase Hammock House!" The crowd erupted into cheers.

Tilley let out a breathless laugh, gripping Sarah's arm. Peter grinned wildly, pumping his fist in the air. Sarah felt her heart swell, emotion catching in her chest. They had done it. Hammock House was saved. It wasn't just another forgotten relic; it would become history restored, and they had made it happen.

As the celebration continued, Sarah stepped out onto the museum's front terrace, gazing out toward the waterfront, letting the sea breeze wash over her. Somewhere, in the distant echoes of the past, she imagined James and Sarah Thatch finally at peace, watching over the house they would have once called home.

The next morning, the museum phones rang off the hook. News of the campaign's success spread like fire through the local papers and across social media. History bloggers, regional news outlets, and even coastal heritage publications picked up the story of the three teenagers who saved Hammock House, and suddenly, the quaint seaside town of Beaufort was abuzz with energy and purpose.

Sarah and Tilley, now local celebrities in their own right, were formally invited to assist with the early stages of the Hammock House renovation project. The structure had long stood silent and guarded by vines and shadows, but now, it was bustling with life. The girls were permitted to work alongside museum staff and historic preservationists, helping to catalog the old materials, inventory every creaking door and weather-worn shutter, and carefully document their findings in both sketches and notes.

Sarah, ever the artist, carried her sketchbook like a field journal—illustrating original moldings, fireplace mantels, and the pattern of hand-cut nails along the floors. Her renderings became an essential part of the renovation archive. There was even talk of featuring her artwork in a special exhibit. Meanwhile, Tilley, who lived for this kind of detail, took charge of cross-referencing everything against the historical records her mother had preserved through the museum. She bounced between the Hammock House and the Maritime Museum with uncontainable energy, loving every second of this real-world experience that already felt like her future.

But Peter, bless him, was slammed. His ghost tours sold out nightly, guests practically begging for extra tickets to the one hosted by "the real-life pirate who helped solve the Hammock House mystery." Even kids who had never cared about Beaufort's storied past were suddenly lining up to hear his tales of Sarah Thatch and Captain Thorne under moonlit skies. And if that wasn't enough, his sailing lessons had doubled in bookings after Ethan's enthusiastic storytelling at the gala. Every parent in Beaufort wanted their child to learn from the charismatic sailor who sailed the Cape and knew every stretch of the Crystal Coast.

He loved it—but he was exhausted. Still, no matter how full his calendar became, Peter always found time to steal away a moment or two with Sarah. Sometimes it was a late-night walk on the docks, quiet and unhurried, as the stars blinked gently above Taylor Creek. Other times, it was a spontaneous coffee delivery to the museum's back garden, where Sarah sat cross-legged with her sketchpad, trying to capture the intricate details of a rusted door hinge. And once, he brought her a bouquet of wildflowers wrapped in a scrap of old sailcloth and left it at the steps of Hammock House with a note: "In case I don't get to see you today.—P." Sarah kept the note tucked inside the back of her sketchbook. Though they didn't say it aloud, they both knew summer wouldn't last forever, but that only made each moment feel richer, deeper; however, it didn't stop making Sarah's heart drop when she thought about it.

For Sarah, it felt like she had stepped into her own history—one where she wasn't just a visitor, but a part of something that transcended time, a sense of belonging in not only the present, but also the past. Beaufort had changed her, and it was now nearing the end of summer— leaving would be hard.

Chapter 38

The morning Sarah had to leave arrived with a stillness that felt unnatural. The early-August sky was a perfect Carolina blue, and the humid summer air carried the scent of magnolia blossoms and distant marshes. It was a beautiful day—one that made it even harder to say goodbye. As she looked around her room, making sure she didn't miss anything that needed to be packed, she noticed the watercolor she painted of Hammock House at the very beginning of her time in this enchanted town. She carefully untaped it from the wall and held it in her hand as she took the image in, allowing it to settle deep within her conscience. She carefully placed it in her portfolio, which she packed in her suitcase.

Her bags were already loaded into the car, her family inside doing a little tidying, and one last check of the cottage before their drive home. But Sarah had unfinished business…she walked through the quiet streets of downtown, past the charming colonial homes and fragrant gardens, toward a shop that had become an unexpected sanctuary for her that summer—the Olde

Towne Chandler. The brass bell above the door jingled as Sarah stepped inside, inhaling the familiar mix of beeswax, dried herbs, and parchment. India Reed stood behind the counter, absently twisting a sprig of lavender between her fingers, as if she'd been expecting Sarah. She pulled the worn leather-bound book from her bag, placing it gently on the counter. "I wanted to bring this back before I left," she said.

India ran her fingers along the gold-embossed spine, giving Sarah a knowing look. "And? Did it help?"

Sarah exhaled. "More than I expected."

India's lips curved into a small smile, but her gaze was full of meaning. "Then it served its purpose."

Sarah hesitated. "I just… I wanted to say thank you. For everything."

India nodded, brushing her fingertips over the book one last time before placing it on a shelf behind her. "Some books find their way into the right hands at the right time. If you ever need another, you know where to find me." Sarah smiled, knowing she'd be back.

Tilley met her in front of the museum, arms crossed, a mix of emotions in her eyes. "You have to visit," Tilley said firmly. "Every month. No excuses."

Sarah smiled, though her throat felt tight. "Every month. I promise."

Tilley studied her for a moment before pulling her into a tight hug. “You better mean it,” she murmured.

Sarah hugged her back, feeling the weight of everything they had been through together—the ghost stories, the mystery, the history they had helped rewrite. “Take care of Hammock House for me, and try to keep Peter out of trouble,” Sarah whispered with a playful smile.

Tilley pulled back with a smirk. “You know I will.”

When she returned to the cottage, she found Peter sitting on the porch steps, looking completely at ease as he tossed a small piece of rope between his hands. Her dad stood at the railing chatting easily with him, while Ethan leaned against the post, clearly pleased that Peter had come to see him off. “You didn’t think I was gonna let you leave without saying goodbye, did you?” Peter smiled, but his eyes held something deeper—an ache he couldn’t quite hide.

Sarah shook her head with a laugh. “I was hoping I’d get to see you before I left.”

Peter turned to her parents. “I was actually hoping I could steal Sarah for just a bit before she leaves. Won’t take long—I promise to have her back in one piece.”

Sarah’s mom chuckled, waving them off. “Go ahead, just don’t make us late.”

Peter shot her a mock salute before motioning for Sarah to follow.

The moment Sarah saw where they were headed, her heart skipped a beat. Hammock House stood before them, alive with movement—restoration crews working on the roof, fresh paint brightening the once-faded shutters, scaffolding along the sides as repairs were being made. Peter led her inside, stepping over the threshold into what had once been a dark, forgotten place. Now, the front parlor was completely restored—the walls painted in warm, period-accurate tones, the mantel polished, the air no longer thick with dust and decay. But Sarah barely noticed any of that because above the grand fireplace, in its rightful place, hung the portrait of Sarah Thatch. Sarah let out a breath, stepping closer. She swallowed past the sudden lump in her throat, staring at the portrait that looked so much like her. "Oh wow—she looks beautiful here," she said, her voice soft.

Peter shrugged, stuffing his hands in his pockets. "She is beautiful here," looking at Sarah instead of the portrait.

Sarah turned to him, eyes full of gratitude. He didn't say anything more, just gave her one last lingering look before leading her back out the door. They walked slowly back toward the cottage, saying only a few words here and there about Sarah heading back to the real world. When they reached the gate, Peter turned to her, an unreadable expression flickering across his face. Then, without a word, he pulled the leather cord over his head, the silver Spanish coin catching the sunlight as he slipped it over hers.

She touched the coin, she felt the weight of centuries pressing against her neck—the stories it held, the hands it had passed through, the sea it had once rested in, its uneven edges, the worn markings. It was a piece of history, a piece of him. "It's too much," she whispered. It wasn't just a token. It was a promise. A reminder that some treasures are never truly lost—they just wait to be found again. Sarah's breath hitched as the cool weight of the coin rested against her skin. "Peter—"

"I want you to keep it," he said, his voice quieter than usual.

She reached into her bag and pulled out a flat parcel, wrapped in brown paper and tied with a sprig of sage in a loose bow, placing it in his hands.

"What's this?" He asked, surprised.

"It's yours," she said. "I wasn't sure when I'd give it to you, but…now seems right."

Peter untied the twine carefully and peeled the paper back. His breath caught when he realized what it was—it was him, the sketch Sarah painted when they sailed to the lighthouse together, captured in Sarah's signature loose, expressive strokes. He was sitting on the beach, the Cape Lookout Light rising behind him, his gaze soft and steady.

“I thought maybe…you could keep it…until I come back,” she said quietly, “so you don’t forget me.” She said with a flirtatious grin.

Peter looked up from the portrait and met her eyes, the full weight of her words sinking in. He nodded once, then stepped forward and pulled her into a tight embrace. One hand rested gently at the back of her neck, the other still holding the portrait. He whispered in her ear, “I couldn’t forget you in a thousand lifetimes.” He pulled her back slightly and reached out, his fingers brushing her cheek, his touch gentle, lingering. With a small, almost mischievous smile, he looked deep into her eyes and murmured, “I’ll be waiting for you, Sarah Thatch.”

The feeling of his touch, the sound of the boats rocking in the harbor, the call of the seagulls overhead, the weight of the coin against her chest—It all felt like a moment she would carry with her forever. His words settled deep in her chest, warm and unshakable. She couldn’t find the right response, so instead, she did something she hadn’t done before. She reached up on her toes and pressed a kiss to his lips, just a brief moment, before stepping back.

Peter looked at her in a way that made her feel like she’d never really be leaving Beaufort at all—like a piece of her heart would remain there with him—with Tilley—and with Hammock House. With one last smile, she turned toward the house. She didn’t need to look back to know he was still standing there, watching her go.

I'll be waiting for you, Sarah Thatch echoed in her soul.

The car pulled away from the cottage, the familiar streets of Beaufort slipping past as Sarah stared out the window, her fingers absentmindedly tracing the coin resting against her skin. The summer was over, but some part of her had never belonged anywhere more, and as she watched the town fade into the distance, she knew one thing for certain: this wasn't the end; it was only until next summer.

About the Author

Dolly Rever is a North Carolina-based writer and artist with a passion for storytelling in both words and watercolors. Her young adult fiction is filled with fantasy, mystery, the supernatural, and a touch of romance, often inspired by the rich history of the Outer Banks. Dolly's fine art expresses her love for nature and coastal life through her watercolor paintings—capturing wildlife, marine architecture, and heartfelt portraits of beloved pets with delicate precision and touching emotion.

When she's not writing or painting, Dolly loves spending time in the salt marshes with her husband, Matt, their son, Colt, and their loyal and hilariously funny yellow Labrador Retriever, Patch. Whether they're fishing, exploring hidden creeks, or discovering the stories buried in the sands of North Carolina's shores, Dolly draws endless inspiration from the natural beauty and deep heritage of the state she calls home.